How the West Was Wed

by
Margaret Brownley

Let us not try to comprehend women or eternity;
but if we are determined to ponder on one or the other,
and still retain our reason, then let us give eternity our preference.

San Antonio Light, February 26, 1883

Chapter 1

If what some say is true and the average length of an editor's life is but twenty-five years, then prompt payment for your newspaper will be greatly appreciated. —Two-Time Gazette

Two-Time, Texas
1884

Josie Johnson stared out the window overlooking Main Street and tried not to worry. But how could she not?

All morning long merchants, housewives, ranchers, farmers, and train workers had stopped at the *Lone Star Press* office across the street to purchase her competitor's newspaper. Meanwhile, her own stack of newspapers languished out in front of her office—untouched.   When Brandon Wade had arrived in town and announced his plans to launch a second newspaper, Josie welcomed the competition. As publisher of the *Two-Time Gazette*, she was convinced her readers would remain faithful to her and the newspaper she'd purchased a year earlier.

"Oh, they remained faithful, all right," she muttered to herself. "Faithful as a two-timing husband!" Last week she'd sold no more than a few dozen copies off the racks, and this week didn't look any more promising. Worse, new subscriptions and renewals had dwindled to zero. And just that morning the last of her paper boys had announced he'd jumped ship and now worked for Mr. Wade.

She was still glaring at the turncoat readers across the street when Mr. Wade himself emerged from the building. "Speak of the devil!" she harrumphed.

Dressed in tan trousers and brown frock coat, he looked his usual tall and self-assured self. He doffed his Stetson at a passerby and flashed a smile at Mrs. Kingman waiting to cross the street. The poor woman was so flustered she almost stepped in front of a passing horse and wagon.

Josie scoffed. Mrs. Kingman wasn't the only one taken in by his good looks and charms. The general female population had talked of little else since his arrival in town less than two months ago. All the women talked about was "Mr. Wade this" and "Mr. Wade that" until Josie thought she would scream.

Staring at him now, she was sorely tempted to walk out the door and give him a piece of her mind. How dare he steal away her newsboys!

He stepped off the boardwalk and started across the street toward her building. Not wanting to be caught spying, Josie quickly moved away from the window and to her desk.

Seated, she had a full view of Main Street and the fast-approaching figure. It looked as though . . .

"Oh, dear heaven!"

It appeared Mr. Wade was about to pay her a visit. Now why would he go and do a thing like that, she wondered. Her eyes narrowed. Perhaps to brag about the overnight success of his newspaper?

Reaching for her fountain pen, she dipped the nib into the bottle of ink and busied herself with writing in an attempt to look occupied as the door flung open and the jingling bells all but drowned out her seething breath. Rather than accord him the satisfaction of knowing how his underhanded methods had affected her, she gripped the pen until her knuckles turned white.

"Mr. Wade," she managed, looking up at his tall form. It felt as if his presence had sucked up all the oxygen in the room.

She hated how her eyes seemed to have a mind of their own whenever he came into view. Today was no different. With a quick visual sweep, she noted his wide shoulders, square jaw, and strong cleft chin. His full, sensuous mouth was curved upward, and his brown hair appeared shorter than the last time she'd seen him. Now it fell to just above his collar, making him look younger than his thirty-some years. Today, as always, his eyes drew her in, locking her in their velvet-brown depths.

He touched the brim of his hat with the tip of a finger. "Good morning, Mrs. Johnson," he said in his smooth baritone. "You look hard at work." He closed the door behind him with a backward thrust of his foot. "Writing your next editorial, no doubt."

"As a matter of fact, I am." She returned the pen to the penholder and forced herself to breathe. "What can I do for you?" she asked, more out of habit than politeness. She had no intention of giving him so much as the time of day.

"I'm here because of what *I* can do for you." He flashed a crooked smile, and much to her annoyance her pulse quickened. Heat rose up her neck, and her cheeks flared. Hoping he wouldn't notice, she tucked a strand of brown hair behind her ear and patted her bun.

"And what might that be, Mr. Wade?"

He glanced at the unsold newspapers stacked neatly against the wall. "My experience as a publisher has taught me that nothing whet's the public's curiosity more than scandal. And scandal translates into sales. *Newspaper* sales. But that would mean that you and I would have to engage in a torrid love affair, and I doubt that would meet with your approval."

He gave her an appraising look, and she stiffened as her heart took a perilous leap. "I should say not!"

The very idea. She was a respectable Christian woman still in widow's weeds. To suggest she would dishonor her husband's memory in such a way went beyond the pale. The man clearly had no scruples.

"Putting scandal aside," he continued innocently, as if no shocking suggestion had crossed his lips, "the next best thing that sells papers is controversy."

Glaring at him, she fought to find her voice. "I have no idea what you're talking about."

"What I'm talking about goes to the very heart and soul of this town. As you know, there's been discussion about changing the name from Two-Time to Corrigan City after the founder. How do you stand on the issue?"

"I believe that was your idea, Mr. Wade, and as I clearly stated in last week's editorial, I do not approve. First of all, the town hardly qualifies as a city." Although if the population continued to increase, as it had in recent years, that was likely to change. "Second, the man who founded the town sold fraudulent land grants for his own gain. Why should we honor such a man by renaming the town after him?"

"Excellent points." Tossing his hat on a nearby chair, Wade sat himself down at the small corner table in front of her Remington type-writing machine. He rubbed his hands together like a man on the verge of a lucrative business deal.

She shot to her feet. "What do you think you're doing?"

Ignoring her for a moment, he rolled a clean sheet of paper onto the carriage and began pecking away with two fingers. "I'm writing your next editorial for you." He flashed a smile over his shoulder. "No need to thank me. It's the least I can do for stealing the last of your newsboys."

Josie's mouth dropped open. Of all the nerve . . . "I don't need help with my editorials. And I certainly—"

"Ah, but you do," he interrupted. At the *ding*, he slapped the typewriter lever, sending the carriage flying back and advancing the paper. "That insipid piece you wrote opposing the name change hardly did the subject justice."

Insipid? He'd called her writing *insipid?* "I got my point across," she said, her deceptive calm hiding how much his criticism stung. "Now, if you don't mind, I must ask you to leave. I have work to do."

"Give me a minute. This won't take long. Let's see." Peck, peck, peck. "How does this sound?" He read as he typed. "'That ignoble, despicable, contemptible, employee-stealing scoundrel who pretends to edit that worthless rag known as the *Lone Star Press* has once again shared his lunacies regarding the renaming of this fine town.'"

Had she not been so incensed she might have burst out laughing. She couldn't imagine anyone writing such loathsome things about himself or his paper. Either the man had a strange sense of humor or was woefully deranged.

She folded her arms across her chest. "While I agree completely with what you wrote and couldn't have stated it better myself, I will not subject my readers to such low-flung language." Why, her poor husband would turn over in his grave if he knew his widow had resorted to such tactics.

"Oh, but you will, Mrs. Johnson," Wade said as he continued typing. "That is if you wish your newspaper to survive. Lacking a juicy scandal, nothing sells papers like editorial combat between two newspaper adversaries. That's the controversy I mentioned earlier."

She narrowed her eyes. "Why do you care if my newspaper survives? It would be to your advantage if it doesn't."

"Yes, but what fun would that be? Anyone can be successful without competition."

His fingers paused. "How do you spell *abominable*?"

She glared at his back. "W-A-D-E."

At that, he glanced over his shoulder, his face lit with approval. "That's the way. I knew you had it in you." He turned back to the type-writing machine and continued punching keys, his fingers pecking away like two chickens digging for worms.

"Readers will have to purchase both our papers to see how the battle plays out," he continued with obvious relish. "Better yet, those who normally don't purchase newspapers will do so out of curiosity. What better way to increase circulation? The more readers, the more demand for advertisements. You must admit it's a brilliant plan."

Josie's hands curled into balls by her side. She had always dreamed of owning her own newspaper and wasn't about to let this egotistical man or his large-city ways influence her *or* her newspaper. The integrity of journalism was at stake, not to mention her reputation as a serious businesswoman.

"I refuse to play your games," she sputtered. "So don't expect to see your name in my paper."

Fingers paused, he gave her a wounded look. "It grieves me to hear you say that," he said. "If something happens to me, are you saying you won't even run my obituary?"

"Oh, yes, that I would gladly print," she said with a toss of her head. "Under 'Town Improvements'!"

He surprised her by laughing. A warm, merry sound that almost made her forget they were at loggerheads.

Pressing her hands together, she added, "I will not resort to sensationalism to sell newspapers, and that's final."

He glanced at her again. "My dear lady, you must know that a new day has dawned. People no longer wish to read bland facts with their morning cup of Arbuckle's. They want the news to be served in a fun and entertaining way."

She frowned. What right did he should come into her office and tell her what her readers might or might not want? The fact that there might be some truth to what he said irritated her all the more. "My job is to report the news honestly and fairly. I also print important reader milestones and will continue doing so."

He held his hands over the lettered keys. "And what will happen on the weeks you have no misfortunes such as deaths and marriages to report?"

She glared at him. "My job as editor is also to educate and inform," she said, her voice dripping frost. "In the latest edition, you'll find an article on why Texas needs barbed wire."

The *devil's headband*, as it was called, had led to violence and bloodshed in some parts of the state. She hoped her editorial would help prevent similar occurrences from happening locally.

Wade ripped his paper from the carriage and placed it on the table with a pat of his hand. "A noble endeavor, indeed. But if you don't get papers into readers' hands, no one will ever read it." He rose and reached for his hat. "Run that in next week's issue and you'll sell more papers than you ever dreamed of."

Settling his Stetson on his head, he headed for the door, pausing with his hand on the doorknob. "Oh, by the way, I hope you don't take offense at what I wrote about you in this week's edition." He flashed a smile that set her senses spinning and left.

Josie fingered the gold locket at her chest containing her dear departed husband's photograph and forced herself to breathe. She watched Wade's retreating back through the window until he was out of sight. Never in all her born days had she known such an arrogant man. She hated the uncharitable thoughts that raced through her mind, but if looks could kill . . .

Write about her, had he? Ha! See if she cared.

She eyed the piles of unsold newspapers stacked around the office. Much as she hated to admit it, Wade was right about one thing: she would have to do something to gain back her readers. That is, if she intended to stay in business. The question was what?

She swung her gaze to the window. People were still stopping to purchase Wade's paper. Traitors, all of them!

Tapping her fingers on her desk, she frowned. So what *had* he written about her? Not that she cared. What was the worst he could say? That she was a serious-minded journalist?

If he thought she would run out and purchase one of his papers just to read what he'd written, he had another think coming. Oh, yes, indeed he did!

Chapter 2

Following a riot at the Cranston General Store, Sheriff Hobson marched seven women to jail clutching newly purchased dishpans. They were charged with disorderly conduct and assault with deadly dishpans. One woman said the dishpans were worth fighting for, since they were on sale for only twenty-five cents—a fourth of the normal cost. Bail was set at three dollars each. —Two-Time Gazette

Brandon Wade was still grinning when he returned to his office. How long would it take Mrs. Johnson to break down and purchase a copy of his newspaper? An hour? Two?

He could practically sense her indignation from clear across the street. He'd almost laughed out loud at the curiosity smoldering in the depths of those intriguing eyes of hers upon learning she was mentioned in his newspaper.

Ah, yes. Despite the stubborn look on her face, he'd wager that before day's end she would have read his editorial. He just wished he could see her expression when she did. Just thinking about it made him chuckle. He couldn't recall the last time he'd had so much fun.

Nor could he remember ever having to work so hard to keep his gaze off the intriguing peaks and valleys of a woman's feminine form. As a grieving widow, Mrs. Johnson deserved the utmost respect. Still, he'd have to be a saint to ignore her tiny waist and softly rounded hips.

It surprised him—shocked him, really—that he found the lady's considerable charms so intriguing. Since his wife's death, he'd not looked at another woman in such a way. Hadn't wanted to. Still didn't want to. The last thing he needed in his life was a romantic complication. He had enough on his plate. More than enough.

His decision to move to Two-Time and start a newspaper had not been by chance. He'd investigated several towns before making the commitment. Two-Time had the kind of growing population that any newspaper man would envy. It lagged behind Galveston, Dallas, and Houston in regard to electricity and the telephone, but what it lacked in modern amenities was made up for in other ways. For one thing, at least eighty percent of the population was literate, and that was no small miracle. He recalled one editor telling him that it had been necessary to teach the people in his town to read before he could start a newspaper. Even then, he had to hold public readings in the town square, charging admission.

Two-Time was also a family town, and that satisfied a personal need as well as a professional one. Families needed goods and services—a boon to advertisers, the lifeline of any newspaper.

He'd never meant to put the young widow out of business. No, never that. Some towns smaller than this one had two and even three thriving newspapers. The *Gazette*, with all its faults, served a different purpose than his and appealed to a different readership—or so he'd thought.

No one was more surprised than he at the way things turned out. People of all ages clamored for his paper, even little old ladies. When he'd heard his customers say they'd given up reading the *Gazette* altogether, he'd felt bad for his rival.

Still, as far as his newspaper was concerned, he was first and foremost a businessman. He'd offered Mrs. Johnson a way to salvage the situation. His plan would benefit them both, while at the same time appeasing his conscience. There was nothing more to be done. It was up to the lady to make the next move. When she did, he would be ready.

***

It was dark by the time Josie left her office. She stood in the shadows and looked up and down Main Street. The night air was cool and the full moon half hidden behind lacy clouds. It was almost April, and Texas was in the middle of a drought. Still her neighbor, Mr. McKenzie, insisted that his sacroiliac forecasted rain.

The light was shining in Sheriff Hobson's office, but otherwise the businesses along Main were closed, including her father's clock and watch shop and her sister Amanda's hat emporium.

It was too early for the rowdies, but already fiddle music wafted from the string of saloons anchoring the town on both ends, along with a glow of shimmering lanterns.

Feeling like a thief, she left the safety of the building and stepped off the boardwalk, pulling her woolen shawl tight around her shoulders. The last thing she wanted was to be seen sneaking up to her competitor's office.

Normally she wouldn't hesitate to purchase a rival's newspaper. It was part of an editor's job to keep track of the competition. But the way Mr. Wade had taken over the town—had tried taking over the *Gazette*—made her want to stay as far away as possible from him *and* his newspaper. If only her curiosity hadn't gotten the best of her.

Movement made her freeze in her tracks. A man emerged from the shadows and mounted a horse. It appeared that the bank clerk, Mr. Gilbert, had been working late again. She waited until he rode away before continuing across the street. Two steps led up to the wooden walkway in front of the *Lone Star Press.*

Like her, Mr. Wade left a stack of newspapers in front of his office. Customers could help themselves and leave a nickel in the honor can. It said much about the town that in the year she'd owned the newspaper only once had someone taken a paper without paying.

She pulled a coin from her pocket and froze. The rack was empty except for a sign. She stepped closer. Light spilling from the gas streetlight illuminated the bold handwriting.

My apologies, Mrs. Johnson, but I'm plain out of newspapers. I'd be happy to deliver a paper to you tomorrow after going back to press.

Sincerely, Brandon Wade

"Ohh . . . The nerve of that man!" She stepped back as if confronted by a coiled snake. He's set a trap, and she'd fallen for it, lock, stock, and barrel. "Of all the underhanded tricks!"

Was he watching? She wouldn't put it past him. The sound of a horse's hooves sent her ducking behind a post.

She waited until the horseman had ridden out of sight but. even then, an uneasy feeling washed over her. Suddenly, it seemed as if every shadow hid a knowing pair of eyes directed at her. Clamping her mouth shut, she hurried away as fast as her feet could carry her.

***

The following morning, Josie knew something was wrong the moment she set foot in the general store. The buzz of customer voices stopped, and all eyes turned to her.

Storeowner Mr. Cranston was the first to recover. An older man with white hair and mustache, his two missing teeth caused him to speak with a lisp.

"Howdy, Jo-thie," he said. Was it only her imagination that he avoided meeting her gaze? "What can I do for you today?"

Josie eyed the pile of last week's *Gazettes* still stacked on the counter, and her heart sank. She didn't get paid for unsold papers.

She forced a smile. "I came to pick up the copy for next week's ad."

Mr. Cranston cleared his throat, and his face turned beet red. "Well, here'th the thing, Jo-thie . . ." The lisp grew more pronounced. He rubbed his whiskered chin. "I dethided to run next week'th ad in the *Lone Thar- Thar-* The other newthpaper."

She stared at him, momentarily speechless. Not Mr. Cranston too. He was her most loyal advertiser and had been placing weekly ads in the *Gazette* since long before she took over the paper.

Somehow, she managed to keep her dismay hidden behind a businesslike demeanor. "If you agree to advertise in the *Gazette*, I'll double the size of your ad for the same price."

"That'th mighty generouth of you, but . . ." He glanced at the unsold copies of her newspaper. "Thought I'd give the new fella in town a t-try. Couldn't hurt, right?"

"Guess not," she managed to squeak out. Under the circumstances, she couldn't blame him. In his shoes, she might have done the same thing. "If you change your mind, my offer still stands."

She turned to leave, only to find her way blocked by Mrs. Mooney. Wrapped in a Mother Hubbard dress, the bank president's wife looked like a large balloon about to take flight. The dress was all skirt and no waist, causing some critics to dub it a calico rag bag. No craze had caused as much flack since the dreadful Dolly Varden rage of the seventies, which made women look like upholstered chairs.

"I just wanted to tell you that my sister is traveling from South Carolina for a visit," Mrs. Mooney said, clutching her purse with both ring-laden hands. "Thought your readers might like to know."

Josie reached in her pocket for her ever-present notebook and scribbled down Mrs. Mooney's news. "I'm sure they would love reading about your sister's visit."

"That insipid piece . . ."

The memory of Mr. Wade's mocking words was so vivid she almost imagined him right there in the store.

Mrs. Mooney leaned forward until the feathers on her enormous boat-shaped hat were practically in Josie's face. "Don't worry, dearie. As the bank president's wife, I don't think you're too much of a lady, no matter what Mr. Wade says."

A toss of her head indicated that her social position gave her the final word on the matter. Waving, she toddled off to join her friend, her ample hips swaying from side to side.

Josie stared after her. *"Too much of a lady."* Is that what Wade had written? Hmm. Maybe it was time to show Mr. Wade just how much of a lady she was not!

Josie left the general store, the heels of her high button shoes hammering the wooden sidewalk like two angry woodpeckers. Her black skirt swished against her legs.

"Just you wait, Mr. Wade," she muttered beneath her breath.

The general store owner was only the latest in a long list of clients to pull his advertisement. T-Bone, the butcher, had canceled his two weeks earlier, followed by the blacksmith, the cobbler, and the bakery owner. But the worse blow of all had been the county refusing to renew its contract. Legal notices would now run exclusively in the *Lone Star Press*.

Just thinking how that scalawag Wade had stolen advertisers right from under her nose made her blood boil. If he wanted a fight, she would give it to him. Oh, yes, indeed she would!

Catching a glimpse of herself reflected from a shop window, she sucked in her breath. She hardly recognized herself. Shoulders back, head held high, she looked like a force to be reckoned with, even dressed head to toe in black.

The oldest of the three Lockwood girls, Josie had always been the "sensible" one. The quiet one. The one who never did anything wrong or uttered a misspoken word. Not like her younger sister Amanda, whose advocacy work had constantly landed her in hot water.

Whenever Papa had one of his tirades, it was Josie's calming influence that settled him down. Hers was the shoulder everyone cried on, the voice of reason during every imaginable crisis.

But that was before. Even she didn't recognize this fiery new side of her. Never could she imagine herself raising a fist to the heavens, but she had done a lot of that these past couple of years.

It had all started with her move to Arizona—the worst mistake of her life. The hot dry climate had failed to live up to its promise, and the condition of her husband's lungs had continued to deteriorate. He'd died less than a year after they'd moved to Tucson, leaving her alone in what seemed like a foreign country away from family and friends. Although she'd tried to make it on her own, in the end, moving back to Two-Time had seemed like the sensible thing to do.

Now she wasn't so certain. Mama and Papa were glad to have her back, of course. So were her two sisters, though both were busy with growing families and had little time to spare. The same was true of her old friends.

The worst part was the way Two-Time had changed in her absence. Ralph's leather-goods store was currently owned by someone else. The house that she and Ralph had lived in following their marriage now belonged to her sister Meg and her husband.

The town where she and Ralph had met and fallen in love was but a distant memory. In the two short years she'd been gone, the population had nearly doubled. And that wasn't the only change. It now had a courthouse and secondary school, and a new lending library was in the works. There was even talk about building an opera house and another church.

When she'd heard the *Gazette*'s publisher was retiring because of ill health, she jumped at the chance at making him an offer. It cost her every penny she had and she still had to take out a mortgage, but it seemed like a wise investment of time and money. It also allowed her to return to her love of writing—something she'd neglected while caring for her ailing husband.

She hadn't known at the time she moved back that it wasn't only the town that had changed; she had changed, too, in ways she couldn't imagine. She'd once accepted without complaint whatever life dealt her. But those days were long gone. Even her family didn't seem to know what to make of her.

What had brought on the change she couldn't rightly say. Maybe it was the night she drove like a mad woman to the doctor in torrential rains only to have Ralph die in the wagon by her side. Or maybe the change occurred the day she singlehandedly held off a party of marauding Apaches trying to steal her horse and wagon. Her transformation might have even occurred the night she and her neighbors fought that awful Arizona brush fire and were almost trampled to death by stampeding cattle. Whatever it was, the Josie Lockwood Johnson who'd left town was not the same woman who returned. Not by a long shot.

At one time, she would have gone to any lengths to avoid conflict. Now she was ready to do battle to save her newspaper, even if that meant fighting Mr. Wade tooth and nail. If only she could figure out how to do so without damaging her reputation.

Such were her thoughts that it took a moment for the angry male voice to register. Thinking the voice was directed at her, she whirled about. Mr. Gardner, owner of the produce shop, stood in the doorway of his establishment yelling at a little girl who couldn't be more than seven or eight. Nine at the most.

Holding the child by the arm, he gave her a good shake. "If I ever see you again, I'll tan your hide good and hard."

Alarmed, Josie stepped up to him. "Unhand her at once."

Mr. Gardner's horseshoe mustache failed to hide his quivering jaw. "This is none of your dang business."

"I'm making it my business. Now take your hands off her."

Angry steel-gray eyes lit into hers, but he nonetheless released the child. With a huff, he pointed a stubby finger in the little girl's face. "Don't ever step foot in my shop again. You hear?" Without waiting for an answer, he turned and stomped inside, slamming the door shut behind him.

Josie studied the child and tried to think if she'd seen her before. Time was when she had known practically everyone in town. But those days were long gone.

She was a pretty girl with a round face and long blond hair. Most children would be in tears after facing such adult wrath, but not this one. Her brown eyes were clear and bright. Only the quiver of her lips suggested she was more upset than she let on.

At first her torn dress and scuffed shoes had Josie thinking she was an orphan or belonged to one of the poorer farm families out of town. But a closer inspection revealed otherwise. The fabric of the dress was of good quality, and the blond hair shone, indicating it had been recently washed and brushed.

Much to Josie's surprise, she realized the girl was shaking from indignation rather than fear.

"What's your name?" she asked.

"My name is Haley, and I'm nine years old."

"Nine, hmm? Do you mind telling me what you did to make Mr. Gardner so upset?"

Huffing like an old woman, the girl's eyes blazed, and her hands flew to her waist. "I let that man's chickens out of their cages."

Josie frowned. "Why would you do such a thing?"

"They could hardly move and had nothing to eat." Haley wrinkled her nose. "And the cages smelled awful."

Josie burst out laughing.

Haley frowned, and her hands dropped to her sides. "It's not nice to laugh at people."

"I wasn't laughing at you. Honest. It's just that you remind me of someone I know. My sister Amanda. Letting chickens out of dirty cages is something she would do."

Haley's expression turned hopeful. "You won't tell my pa, will you? I'm not supposed to be here."

"Let me guess. You're supposed to be in school, right?"

Haley kicked an apple core someone had dropped on the boardwalk. "I hate school."

Josie thought of a dozen arguments she could present in favor of school and education but suspected they would only fall on deaf ears. But it did give her an idea for a future editorial. Many people, especially farming families who needed all the hands they could get, put too little stock in formal education.

"I'll make a deal with you. I won't say a word to your pa, but you have to do something in return: you have to go back to school."

Haley didn't look happy about it, but she gave a solemn nod. "All right, it's a deal."

The bell in front of the Lockwood Watch and Clockwork shop announced the noon hour with carefully spaced chimes. Out of habit Josie reached for her pocket watch to check the time. Papa never failed to ring the bell on the precise hour.

"Good. You have a full half hour before afternoon classes begin."

"Today?" Haley's eyes widened. "You want me to go back today?"

Josie stuffed her watch back into her pocket. "Yes. That is, if you don't want your pa to know what you did." It was a bluff, of course. She didn't even know who the child's father was.

Haley looked about to argue, but then gasped and backed away, a look of panic on her face. "I gotta go." Turning, she jumped off the boardwalk and ran into the street without looking.

Josie held her breath until the girl had safely crossed to the other side. Hand on her chest to still her pounding heart, she shook her head. What kind of father did the poor child have that the mere mention of him would create that kind of reaction?

Loud voices caught her ear, and she turned. The dogcatcher had blocked the road with his wagon, and traffic had come to a standstill. Tempers flared, and curses rent the air.

The commotion hadn't stopped Mr. Wade. Looking more commanding than ever, he rode his fine black horse around the ruckus like a general riding through a battlefield. Glaring at him with reproachful eyes, Josie continued on her way. With a quick glance over her shoulder, she stomped into her office, slamming the door good and hard behind her.

Chapter 3

Sheriff Stevens of Kerr County has no use for handcuffs. During an arrest, he simply cuts the buttons off the fellow's pants. While the prisoner is kept busy holding up his breeches, the sheriff then calmly escorts him to jail. — Two-Time Gazette

Brandon Wade stared at his daughter's teacher. "I'm sorry. Did you say truant?"

Miss Langley had recently been hired to take over the class after the last teacher broke school rules by getting married. Scowling over the wire frame of her spectacles, her gray eyes pierced him like a scientist studying a newly discovered species. She stood rigid as a lamppost, her gray skirt and shirtwaist as plain as her tightly wound hair. Though she was probably still in her thirties, she looked and acted much older.

She remained standing during their conversation and seemed to expect him to do likewise. Not that Brandon thought the child-sized desks could accommodate his six-feet-two height, but he was curious to know if the straight-laced women in front of him could bend.

"That's exactly what I said. Your daughter has hardly been to class this whole week. And when she's here, her mind is on everything but her schoolwork."

Brandon's breath caught. It wasn't the first time Haley had been in trouble at school, but never before had she been truant. At least not that he knew of.

"I'll see that it doesn't happen again," he said and meant business. No daughter of his would run wild and grow up an ignoramus.

He'd promised his wife on her deathbed to raise Haley right, but never had he imagined that a promise so easily made would be so hard to keep. He'd hoped moving away from San Antonio and its bad influences would solve some of the problems of raising her without benefit of a mother. Haley wasn't a bad kid. She was smart as a whip. But she was also wild as the wind and would rather run than sit at a desk all day. In that regard, she took after him.

"As for her schoolwork," Miss Langley continued, and Brandon clamped his jaw. There was more?

Rustling through a stack of papers, Miss Langley pulled out a sheet and laid it on her desk.

Brandon gazed down at the drawing with a start. He couldn't believe his eyes. He'd always known his daughter had a talent for art; she took after her mother in that regard. But this far exceeded anything Haley had previously attempted.

Haley had drawn an amazing likeness of the owner of the *Two-Time Gazette*, Mrs. Johnson. Or at least it sure did look like her, down to the heart-shaped face and soft, curving mouth. Haley had captured the shape of the widow's eyes, but not their lively depths. He doubted that even a professional artist could do the lady's sparklers justice.

The sketch was done in pencil, but he mentally filled in the exact shade of Mrs. Johnson's turquoise eyes from memory, could easily visualize the color of her hair that reminded him of polished mahogany. And was it only his imagination that the faint scent of lilacs rose from the penciled sketch?

It took him a full minute to pull himself together enough to focus on what Miss Langley was saying. Her critical tone told him it wasn't good. Irritated that she seemed oblivious to his daughter's artistic talent, he listened with narrowed eyes.

"My instructions were quite specific," Miss Langley said. "But instead of doing what I asked, your daughter drew a picture of her mother."

Brandon felt his back stiffen. "That's not her mother," he said, gruffly. "Her mother is dead."

Miss Langley's mouth rounded. "Oh. I apologize. I just assumed . . ." She cleared her throat. When he offered no hint as to the identity of the woman in the drawing, she reached for a pile of papers stacked neatly on her desk.

"My pupils were supposed to draw a picture of the human body." She held up a drawing to illustrate.

Brandon stared at the sketch with raised eyebrows. "Excuse me, ma'am, but that appears to be a house."

"Of course it's a house. That's what the human body is. The stomach is the kitchen, the dining room the small intestine. The laundry represents the lungs, and—"

Miss Langley was interrupted by the appearance of a pupil, thus sparing Brandon what he supposed would be a tour of the reproductive system.

"What is it, Anthony?"

The boy looked like he was about to be sick. Apparently, Haley wasn't the only one in trouble. "My pa's here like you said."

"Oh, yes, tell him to come in." She dismissed Brandon with a wave of her hand. "I trust that I can expect Haley will change her ways."

"I'll talk to her," Brandon said brusquely.

He'd talk to her all right. Before day's end he would make sure she never thought about skipping school again.

With another glance at his daughter's artwork, he turned and stalked away, pausing to cast a sympathetic look at the dark-haired man who had just walked into the classroom with his son. If a girl was this hard to raise, he shuddered to think of the difficulty in raising a boy.

Stepping outside and into the hot Texas sun, he couldn't decide what bothered him more: Haley's truancy or how the likeness of Mrs. Johnson had appealed to his masculine senses.

***

Late that afternoon, jingling bells made Josie look up from her desk. Her visitor was her sister Meg. Cradling month-old baby Carolyn in one arm, Meg held two-year old Davey by the hand.

Carolyn was a poor sleeper, and Meg looked exhausted. Dark shadows skirted her blue eyes, and even the fashionable hat couldn't hide her hastily pinned-up hair, which lacked its usual shine. She also looked flushed.

"Whew!" Meg said with a sigh. "If it's this hot in March, I dread to think what it will be like in July."

"What a nice surprise," Josie said, rising out of her chair and walking around her desk.

Dressed in knee pants, the boy's chubby face lit up upon spotting Josie, and his eyes sparkled with mischief. "Aun' Cozy," he squealed with delight.

Stooping, Josie held her arms wide and afforded her young nephew a big smile. "How about giving your Aunt *Cozy* a big hug?"

Davey pulled from his mother's grasp and ran to Josie. He had his mother's blond hair and blue-green eyes and had inherited his father's dimpled smile. Josie picked him up and hugged him close before whirling him about. He smelled of peppermint candy.

They were both giggling by the time she set him down. Releasing him, she smiled at the sleeping infant in Meg's arms.

"She's beautiful," she whispered. The baby's skin looked as pink and soft as a rose petal.

Josie's nephews and niece warmed the cockles of her heart, but the love she felt for them wasn't without pain. Six years of marriage had failed to produce a child of her own, and the empty feeling never went away. She'd hope that the newspaper would be enough to fill the hole inside, but whenever she saw her sisters' children, the maternal need returned, knocking her off balance with its intensity.

"Where's Hank?" Meg asked. Hank Chambers was Josie's only employee. He set the type, ran the press, and acted as her sounding board.

"Picking up supplies," Josie said. "So, what brings you to town?" This wasn't Meg's normal shopping day.

Meg glanced at her son, whose attention was riveted upon the large orange tomcat snoozing in a yellow ribbon of sunlight. "Don't bother Mr. Whiskers," she cautioned before turning back to Josie. "I just wanted to make sure you're . . . okay?"

Surprised by the question, Josie frowned. "Yes, of course. Why do you ask?"

"It's just that . . . there's been talk." Meg glanced at the stacks of unsold newspapers. "You're not upset about what Mr. Wade wrote about you in the *Lone Star Press*, are you?"

Josie gaped at her. "You read Mr. Wade's newspaper?"

Meg blinked. "Why, yes. I mean . . . Everyone reads it."

Sighing, Josie pressed her hand against her forehead. "Don't remind me."

"Oh, Josie, I'm so sorry. I didn't mean—"

"I know, I know. It doesn't matter." Josie looked away. She would not ask what the article said about her. Absolutely not. Not after Wade had tricked her into trying to purchase a copy. Not after— "So, what did he say about me?"

"I have the paper right here." Jostling the baby in her arms, Meg reached with her free hand into the rucksack hanging from her shoulder and pulled out a newspaper. "Page two," she said.

Josie took the paper from her and unfolded it. The four-page newspaper was well organized and printed on good-quality paper. Like the *Gazette*, the pages were eight by eighteen inches, five columns to a page. The number of former clients now advertising in the *Lone Star Press* was even higher than Josie had thought and took up nearly two-thirds of the paper.

Stomach clenched, she turned to the second page. It didn't take long to find what she was looking for.

"'Mrs. Johnson, editor of the petticoat journal known as the *Two-Time Gazette* . . .'" Her mouth tightened. *"Petticoat journal,"* indeed! She continued reading. "'. . . took issue with the arrest of Mr. Harper for loading his wagon on a Sunday, and I'm in full accord. He was trying to feed his family by fulfilling a rush order and deserves reprieve. What a pity that Mrs. Johnson is too much of a lady to express the appropriate outrage such unfair justice deserves. Her bland use of the English language is more suitable for Sunday school than news and hardly did the story justice. But since she raised a valid point, I'm sure she will have no objection to my taking up the cause.'"

And take it up he did. In lingo strong enough to raise the dead.

Gritting her teeth, she flung the offending newspaper into the wastepaper basket. It wasn't bad enough that he stole her employees, advertisers, and readers. Now he was stealing her editorial ideas.

Meg watched her with a worried expression. "He didn't really say anything bad. I mean he did agree with you. And there are worst things to be called than a lady."

Her sister's defense of the man didn't help matters. "If I were a man, he wouldn't dare call my writing bland," Josie said with a toss of her head.

"I'm sure no one else thinks your writing is lacking in any way," Meg said.

Meg was wrong about that. Josie had dealt with more than her share of criticism since taking over the paper. Women were considered too "delicate" to write about politics and national affairs. Some critics even expressed concern about her setting foot in such unsavory places as the mayor's office and barbershop in search of news.

"It's obvious Mr. Wade disapproves of women editors," Josie said.

Baby Caroline stirred, and Meg gently rocked her. "He's not the only one. You know Papa was against your buying the business. He said it was unseemly for a woman to delve into men's affairs."

Josie scoffed. Anything that happened in the community was of equal importance to men and women alike, and that included politics.

"Papa's against women working period," Josie said. No one knew that better than Meg, who still handled the clock shop's bookkeeping chores even though she was now the mother of two. Papa let her get away with it only because he loathed paperwork. Fortunately, she could do most of the work at home.

Meg's gaze fell on the stack of last week's *Gazettes*. Josie could well imagine what was going through her sister's mind. The newspaper she'd worked so hard to produce was good for nothing at this late date but wrapping fish and lining bird cages.

"What are you going to do?" Meg asked, eyes rounded with concern.

Elbow on her crossed arm, Josie tapped her chin with her forefinger. For some reason, the memory of fighting off that band of hostile Indians with little more than a shotgun and a prayer came to mind.

"I don't know, but I'll think of something." She wasn't about to lose everything she'd worked so hard to achieve to that thieving newcomer across the street. Not in this lifetime!

***

Following his meeting with Haley's teacher, Brandon rode his horse to the boardinghouse with a heavy heart. Nothing made a man feel worse than failing as a father. And fail he had.

Guilt surged through him like a tidal wave. He'd been so busy getting his newspaper up and running, he'd hardly spent any time lately with Haley. For days, he'd said little more to her than a few words. By the time he arrived at the boarding house at night, she was usually sound asleep.

He told himself it was only for a short time and what he was doing would benefit Haley in the long run. The way things were going, he would soon be able to hire more employees to take the work load off him and free up his time.

Meanwhile he paid Mrs. Greer, owner of the boardinghouse, extra to watch Haley in his absence. The proprietress saw that his daughter had proper meals and went to bed at a reasonable hour, but tended to be flighty and forgetful. More than once Brandon had smelled alcohol and tobacco on the woman's breath. She was hardly the kind of caretaker he wanted for his daughter.

Maybe it was selfish of him not to have made more of an effort in finding a wife. Haley needed a mother. At nine, she was already curious about things that a woman would be better able to handle.

The truth was he didn't think it fair to ask someone to marry him just to mother his child. He was a product of a loveless marriage and knew from experience the negative impact that had on a childhood. He wasn't even sure if he could love another woman. Just thinking about remarriage made him feel disloyal to his deceased wife.

The boardinghouse reeked of cooked cabbage when Brandon walked in. The proprietress was British, which meant everything got boiled to death.

Altogether there were five boarders, including him and Haley. The two-story house was located two blocks away from his work. Haley could walk the short distance through the alley and pop in to see him whenever she wanted. The boardinghouse was also conveniently located to the one-room schoolhouse.

He found Haley upstairs in her room, which was little more than an alcove off his, separated by a freestanding wooden screen. She lay face down on her bed, peering at an open book. Angry voices from the house next door drifted through the open window.

She turned her head when he walked in, and a worried frown creased her forehead. He was so incensed he'd forgotten to knock as was his usual habit.

"We need to talk," he said without apology.

Haley sat up and swung her legs over the side of the bed. "What about?"

Battling the windblown curtains, he closed the window against the raging argument outside. By the sound of things, Mr. Bennett's goat had once again eaten the wash from Mrs. Campbell's clothesline.

He faced his daughter. "I spoke to your teacher. She said you've been skipping school."

Haley folded her arms and pushed out her bottom lip. "I hate school. It's dumb."

He pulled a chair away from the desk and sat. "Not going to school is dumb."

"I don't need school. I know how to read and write and do numbers."

"Those are just the basic skills. Now you must learn how to put them to use. There's also much to learn about history and science."

Haley scrunched up her nose. "Miss Langley makes us do stupid stuff. Like drawing human bodies that look like houses."

He couldn't argue with her there. Leaning forward, he placed his elbows on his lap and folded his hands between his knees. "We all have to do things we don't want to do."

She narrowed her eyes. "Even you?"

"Yeah, even me." He'd never wanted to bury a wife or raise a child alone. Nor had he wanted to start over in a whole new town. But it was either that or continue working for a paper he no longer believed in. A paper that had become too political for his blood. The last straw came when the editor announced his paper would support a candidate for president accused of accepting a bribe from Union Pacific. The charges had never been proven, but they were too serious to dismiss without proper investigation.

Now Brandon sat back in his chair. "Sometimes you just have to make the best of things and do what you have to do."

"But Pa . . ."

He toughened his stance, though he was loathe to do so. If he didn't stand his ground, she would wrap him around her finger, as she was prone to do, and he couldn't let that happen. Not this time. Her education was too important to mess around with.

"There'll be no more skipping school, and that's final. Do I make myself clear?"

She clamped her mouth shut and nodded.

He frowned. It wasn't like her to capitulate so quickly. "I mean it, Haley."

"I heard you."

He sucked in his breath. How could dealing with one nine-year-old make him feel so inept? Slapping his lap with both hands, he rose. "Okay, then."

He replaced the chair and noticed her sketch book laying open on the desk. She had drawn a picture of him.

The likeness wasn't bad. Not bad at all. His face was a little long. And did his ears really stick out that far? But she had captured the indention in his chin just right. The hair, parted at the side and dipping across his forehead as it tended to do, wasn't bad either. His daughter had artistic talent, and she sure in heck didn't get it from him.

She joined him at the desk as he flipped through the sketchbook. The entire book was filled with drawings of him. That was him on his horse, Thunder. One image caught him behind his printing press. Yet another showed him in profile gazing out the window. She'd even captured him sitting in the boarding-house dining room, drinking coffee and scribbling notes to himself as was his daily habit.

"Why did you draw all these pictures of me? Hmm? I'm sure you could find something more interesting to draw."

"I don't have a photograph of you, Papa."

He raised an eyebrow. "A photograph?"

"I don't have one of Mama either."

"Your mother was a very modest person. She didn't like having her picture taken."

The brown eyes staring back at him appeared close to tears. "But I don't know what she looked like."

Something tugged at his insides, and he struggled for words. "I told you what she looked like. She had blond hair, just like you. And a beautiful smile and—"

"But I can't see her in my head. That's why I drew all those pictures of you. If you go away, I want to see you in my head."

A feeling like a rock settled in his chest. By *"go away,"* she meant if he died.

Turning to face her, he rested his hands on her shoulders. "I'm not going anywhere, muffin," he said, his voice thick with emotion. "I'm staying right here with you."

Tears filled her eyes. "Billy Watkins's pa—"

"So that's what this is about." They hadn't been in Two-Time a month before the father of one of her classmates died. Brandon had had no idea it affected her so deeply. "Mr. Watkins had a bad heart. And mine is strong as an ox's." Or at least it had been before they started this conversation. Now it felt like mush. He drew her close. Wrapping his arms around her, he closed his eyes and held her tight. She was the best thing that had ever happened to him, and he intended to do right by her. "Nothing's gonna take me away from you. Nothing."

For several moments neither spoke, until from downstairs came the sound of the supper bell and he released her. "We better go and eat," he said. He sure did hope that the meal tasted better than it smelled.

Arm around her shoulder, he guided her across the room, stopping at the door.

"One more thing: why did you draw a picture of Mrs. Johnson?"

Haley gazed up at him, her forehead creased. "Who's Mrs. Johnson?"

"The lady who owns the other newspaper in town. Your teacher showed me the drawing you drew of her."

"Oh. I didn't know her name. I think she's pretty."

A vision of the widow's face came to mind, and he shook it away. "Is that why you drew her picture. Because you think she's pretty?"

Haley nodded. "Don't you, Papa?"

"Well, I . . . um . . . I think that's the bell again. Let's go and eat."

Chapter 4

That night, Josie waited for Hank to finish setting type and leave the office before scooping the *Lone Star Press* out of the wastepaper basket. Spreading the paper across her desk, she adjusted the oil lamp and read it word for word.

After suffering through the Arizona newspapers with their misspellings, poor grammar, and what her husband, Ralph, had called creative punctuation, she prided herself on putting out a weekly that was, except for rare occasions, error free. How irritating that Mr. Wade's newspaper was equally void of grammatical blunders.

Even more irksome, the articles were well written and appeared accurate. That is, once she got through the hyperbole and boldly worded headlines.

The print was bright and clear and without smudges, which made her ache with envy. Her small Army press could not compete with the perfecting press used by Mr. Wade. Her old printer was on its last legs and required much in the way of coaxing and well-aimed strikes of a hammer to get it going. In contrast, Wade's press printed both sides of the paper with one pass through the machine. Not only did this save time but prevented the possibility of paper wrinkling during initial print runs and creating dreaded logjams.

Her plan of purchasing a new press would now have to wait until she could figure out how to lure back her readers. Replacing the leaky roof over her office was also out of the question. As for the single window . . . It was so warped that it would no longer close all the way and had to be boarded up during blue northers.

Putting off necessary repairs was the least of it; she would also have to cut expenses. But where?

Some newspapers used *patent* pages, which cost five dollars a week. They were cheaper, since most of the work was already done, eliminating the need for employees. The ready pages were already printed with the national and international news on pages one and three. Pages two and four were left blank for editors to add advertisements and local news.

Josie would rather die than resort to such generic journalism, but if things didn't change soon, she might not have a choice. If she had to run the paper by herself, she wouldn't have time to do much in the way of news gathering. Writing, editing, selling advertisements, handling subscriptions, and distribution took up most of the time. Without Hank setting type, she would be lost.

Sighing, she tossed her competitor's paper aside.

Mr. Whiskers jumped up on the desk and batted at her gold locket with his paw. The cat couldn't resist shiny objects. She lifted him by his middle and set him down on the floor. The tom stalked away with an indignant meow, tail in the air like a flagpole.

"Yes, I quite agree," she called after him. "Something's got to be done about that annoying Mr. Wade."

***

During the next three weeks, things went from bad to worse.

Josie offered deep discounts on advertisements and ran specials on subscriptions. The few advertisers and subscribers she landed were nowhere near enough to pay the mortgage, let alone any other expenses. She lowered the print run and used cheaper paper, but with so little money coming in, cutting costs hardly made a dent.

There was only more thing left to do. It was the thing she most dreaded, but it had to be done.

She arrived at the office that Friday morning in April to find Hank busy typesetting a handbill for the women's suffrage march. Josie had agreed not to charge for the handbills as a favor to her sister Amanda.

Already people were lined up across the street to purchase her competitor's newspaper, while the stack outside her building remained untouched.

Bracing herself, she closed the door and removed her straw bonnet. She had twisted and turned all night thinking about this moment, but there was no other way.

Like the cat, Mr. Whiskers, Hank had come with the paper, and that had been a very good thing. A veteran of that awful war, he'd suffered injuries during the second battle of Sabine Pass, including a head wound that left him with a speech impediment. After the war, he fell on hard times.

Before the railroad came to town, goods were transported by way of prairie schooners drawn by twelve or more Mexican mules. A teamster had spotted Hank going through trash and taken pity on him. He brought him to Two-Time and introduced him to his brother-in-law, who at that time owned the *Gazette*. Hank was put to work hawking newspapers and soon advanced to compositor. He was a hard worker, and Josie valued him both as a friend and employee.

"Hank, we need to talk."

He looked up from beneath the green celluloid visor of his cap. He was only in his early forties but looked older, and it wasn't because of his spotted gray beard. War and a hard-scrabble life had aged him beyond his years, giving him a hollow-cheeked look that stayed with him even during better times.

"Let me sinish this fentence" he said in his slow way. He reached into the lower case for a metal letter and placed it into the composing stick.

His war injuries sometimes caused him to swap the consonants of words, usually when he was tired or under pressure. The fact that he was scrambling words now indicated he sensed something afoot.

As a typesetter, his grammar and spelling skills were impeccable—an oddity considering his verbal skills were less than stellar. With her smaller hands, she could set the type faster, but never more accurately. She hated having to let him go, but it wasn't fair to keep him when she wasn't sure how long she could afford his salary.

She also dreaded the thought of having to run the paper without him.

While she waited, she checked the mail. The invitation to subscribe to the *Lone Star Press* set her teeth on edge, and she promptly tossed it into the wastebasket. The announcement of a new photographer in town she kept.

After a few minutes, Hank pushed his chair away from his workbench and spun around to face her. Hazel eyes gazed at her through wire-rim spectacles. The war injuries had left him deaf in his left ear, which is why he approached conversations with his head slightly turned so that his good ear faced the speaker.

"Looks like you're in a tull-bossing mood," he said.

She sat on the edge of her desk and folded her arms across her chest. There was only one thing she would like to toss, and it wasn't a bull. It was that annoying publisher across the street!

Taking a deep breath, she forced herself to concentrate on the task at hand. "As you know, we've had some unexpected problems of late. I'm afraid I underestimated the impact of the competition."

"It's not just the competition," he said. "The town has become as dull as tarnished silver." The eyes behind his spectacles gazed past her as if looking back in time. "I remember the good ol' days when your father carried on that feud with the Farrell fellow. Boy, did we ever get some great headlines out of that!"

Josie sighed. "Don't remind me." The battling jewelers had each insisted they alone had the right time. The feud divided the town into two time zones, which is how the name *Two-Time* originated.

"Then there was the time your sister Meg was left at the altar and sued her wayward groom for breach of promise." Hank slapped his thigh and chuckled, his earlier nervousness forgotten. "'Course, that happened before you took over the paper. But there was no topping those headlines. And just when things started getting dull again, your other sister, Amanda, became sheriff." This time he gave a hearty laugh before continuing. "Hardly a day went by when somebody didn't rush in the office yelling, 'Stop the presses.' We couldn't fit all her shenanigans into a single edition and had to keep bringing out extras."

He frowned with a shake of his head. "It was a sad day when your sister finally settled down and got married. Things just haven't been the same since. Now we have no crime to speak of. No lady sheriff to criticize. No raging feuds to report. If you ask me, the town has sunk into morbid quietude, and that's death to us daily chroniclers."

Knowing that her family had provided most of the journalistic fodder contributing to the paper's prior success didn't make Josie feel any better. "'Morbid quietude,' as you call it, doesn't seem to be hurting Mr. Wade."

Hank rolled his eyes. "Wade could turn growing grass into a provocative headline."

"That insipid piece . . ." She sighed.

Recalling why she'd initiated this talk—which wasn't to discuss Mr. Wade—she moistened her lips. The words forming in her mouth felt like acid.

"Hank, your friendship means the world to me. I just want you to know that. I couldn't have done any of this without your help.

He pushed his spectacles up his nose. "Oh, boy, this sure don't gound sood."

She clutched her locket and swallowed hard. "I'm afraid I have to let you go at the end of the month." Her voice broke, forcing her to clear her throat before continuing. "I wanted you to know in advance so you could make other arrangements."

His eyebrows inched upward. "You're firing me?"

"No, no, I'm not firing you. I'm . . ." She searched for a better way of saying it, but nothing came to mind. "It's a financial decision and has nothing to do with your work. You're an excellent employee, and I hope we can still be friends." She regretted not being able to pay him his true worth. "But unless things change . . ."

He sighed in resignation, and his shoulders slumped. "You're firing me."

She grimaced. She'd known doing business in a man's world wouldn't be easy, but never had she imagined anything as difficult as this.

"I can pay you till the end of the month, but after that . . ." She didn't want to give him false hope. "The last of our long-time clients has abandoned—um—left. Without advertisers . . ." She swallowed hard and forced herself to continue. "I'm sorry, Hank. I don't know what else to do. Maybe . . . Maybe Mr. Wade will hire you."

The thought of Hank working for her competitor cut her to the quick, but realistically, that might be his only chance for employment. "I'll write you a letter of recommendation." That was the least she could do.

Hank clamped his lips together in a tight line and didn't say a word. Turning back to his desk, he continued setting type as if no conversation had taken place. He pulled capital letters from the upper-type case and smaller letters from the lower as smoothly as a pianist playing a scale.

Josie didn't think she could feel any worse. She plopped down on her chair and, elbows on the desk, held her head in her hands. Papa had warned her against sinking all her savings into the newspaper, but at the time it seemed like the right thing to do. The town had been growing in leaps and bounds, and the possibilities seemed endless. By now subscriptions should have increased ten-fold, if not more. Never had it occurred to her that someone could come to town and take away everything she had worked so hard to achieve.

From a distance came the sound of the bell at Papa's clock shop. At one time the bell had been used to announce not only the time but milestones in peoples' lives. Through the years, the bell had rung out news of marriages, births, and deaths. It rang out the arrival of soldiers returning from war. It rang for those who didn't.

Once the town gained its own newspaper, it had no longer been necessary to ring the bell except to announce the time. And since the adoption of standard time, almost everyone had a watch or accurate timepiece anyway. There was now no need to ring the bell at all, but Papa persisted. He said his hourly chimes were the glue that held the town together.

Josie felt the same about her newspaper. The birth of every child, the union of every couple, the loss of every family member, was announced in print with loving care. When little Johnny Shaver died of smallpox, the article she'd written had moved the community to rally around his grief-stricken parents. After Mrs. Murray's husband passed away unexpectedly, leaving her with six children to feed, Josie had used the *Gazette* to ask for donations. Money had poured in, along with offers of housing.

Under her management, she had continued the long and noble tradition of making the *Two-Time Gazette* the very heart and soul of the town. The thought of losing it nearly crushed her.

The thought of losing Hank was almost worse.

Chapter 5

Reverend Wellmaker asked ushers to pass apples out to the congregation as he preached about Adam and Eve. He said the fruit was not to be eaten. Instead, it was to be kept as a reminder to obey God's orders. The service was interrupted when Mrs. Brubaker complained that she couldn't hear the sermon for all the munching. —Two-Time Gazette

The following Wednesday morning Josie caught a whiff of sickly strong perfume even before she entered the office. Surprised to find the madam of the house of ill repute, Miss Bubbles, waiting for her, Josie glanced at Hank, who shrugged and went back to setting type.

Nodding politely, Josie took her seat and folded her hands upon her desk. "Miss Bubbles, what can I do for you?"

Seated upon a ladder-back chair, Miss Bubbles picked an imaginary piece of lint off her purple satin skirt and fixed Josie with a studied look. Her purple eyelids and stained red cheeks emphasized rather than hid her forty-plus years. Hair the color of carrots was swept beneath a tall, feathered hat. With slow, measured movements she peeled off a purple glove and laid it across her lap, her gaze never leaving Josie's face.

"I wish to place an advertisement."

Josie hesitated. As desperate as she was for income, she drew the line at promoting certain endeavors. She cleared her throat and carefully chose her words. "I would like to accommodate you but . . . this is a family paper." At the moment, it wasn't anyone's newspaper, but that was a different story. "Perhaps the *Lone Star Press* . . . ?"

Miss Bubbles wrinkled her nose. "Mr. Wade informed me he has no more advertising space left, and I refuse to be put on a waiting list."

Josie gritted her teeth. A waiting list for advertisers? Whoever'd heard of such a thing? She was just about to cite her policy regarding family-appropriate material when the woman's painted face seemed to crumble like crushed paper.

"Please." Inhaling loudly, Miss Bubbles dabbed at the corner of her watery eyes with a lace handkerchief. "I hoped that a woman would be more . . . sympathetic and understanding. I need your help."

Josie didn't know what to say. This sounded more serious than the simple placement of an ad. "My help how?"

"As you may have heard, one of our girls met with foul play. She went by the name of Miss Ruby."

The crime had occurred just before Josie returned from Arizona, but she vaguely remembered hearing that the prostitute had been found strangled in her bed. Obviously, the young woman's death had deeply affected Miss Bubbles. And who could blame her?

"That must have been a very difficult time for you," Josie said.

"Yes, it was. Some people said it was no more than she deserved."

Josie drew in her breath. How could people be so cruel? "No one deserves to die like that."

Miss Bubbles dabbed at the black streaks running down her cheeks. "I talked to Sheriff Hobson, and he didn't offer much hope of finding the killer." She pursed her painted lips. "He said he'd followed every lead, but since the crime occurred a year ago, the trail is now cold."

"He's very good at what he does."

Josie wasn't just saying that because Scooter was a friend. Since taking over as sheriff, he'd done an excellent job of keeping crime down. Some said too good. In his early twenties, he was one of the youngest and most successful sheriffs Two-Time had ever had. Enthusiastic to a fault, he kept crime down, but some felt the cost was too high. Scooter saw nothing wrong in jailing some of the town's most distinguished citizens, including the pastor and mayor, for minor offenses. Just as annoying, shops and saloons were often forced to stay closed while their owners cooled their heels behind bars.

Things had gotten so bad at one point that the town council passed a law that no more than three businessmen or council members could be arrested on any given day. It was the only way to keep the town running smoothly.

"I'm sure he's doing everything he can."

"Perhaps." Miss Bubbles reached into her purse and drew out a photograph. She laid it on the desk.

Josie picked up the photograph and studied it. Miss Ruby looked about eighteen or nineteen at the time the picture had been taken. She had a pretty, round face, large expressive eyes, and light-colored hair that fell to her shoulders in a cascade of ringlets. She wore pearl earbobs, and a cameo necklace adorned her pale, swanlike neck.

"She was beautiful," Josie said.

"Yes, she was." Miss Bubbles sniffed and her blue-lidded gaze sharpened. "Next week will be a year since—" She swallowed hard. "To mark the occasion, I'm offering an award for any information leading to the identity and arrest of the killer." The madam's chest heaved. "The reward is for a thousand dollars."

Josie laid the photograph carefully on her desk and took a breath. The average wanted poster offered only fifty to five hundred dollars for criminals, with Jesse James being the exception. The reward for his capture, dead or alive, had been set at an astounding five grand, though only a small portion of the money went to Jesse's killer.

"That's quite generous of you," she said after a pause.

Miss Bubbles looked hopeful. "So, then, you'll run it in the newspaper?"

Josie nodded. "Yes, of course." No doubt some people would object and might even drop their subscriptions, if they hadn't already. But it seemed like the right thing to do.

Miss Bubbles looked dubious, or at least as dubious as she could look beneath her thick face paint. "I sense your hesitation."

Not wanting the woman to think she was being judgmental, Josie hastened to explain, "I was just trying to decide how best to position the advertisement. I don't generally place ads above the fold, but I'll make an exception in your case."

"Above the fold?"

"Yes, like this." Josie held up a newspaper folded to reveal the headline. "This is the first part a reader sees."

Her real concern was not placement but distribution and readership. She owed it to her advertisers to give them as much exposure as possible.

"Yes, I believe above the fold will do quite nicely." Miss Bubbles slid a sheet of floral stationery across the desk. She'd written out what she wanted the advertisement to say in ornate Spencerian script and had included all pertinent information.

After Miss Bubbles had signed an agreement, paid, and left, Josie considered ways to get the paper into as many hands as possible. But how? She hated the thought of having to give away the paper for free, but if there was no other way . . .

Outside, a man carrying a bucket of paste caught her attention. She watched as he glued a handbill on a post announcing that a traveling circus was coming to town. A slow smile curved her mouth. Maybe there was more than one way to beat Mr. Wade at his game.

***

Josie had just finished slapping the last of the handbills on a post in front of the office of the *Lone Star Press* when the door swung open and out stepped the paper's publisher, Mr. Wade.

As usual, his presence caused an inner turmoil, which she hid behind an outer calm.

Dressed more casually than usual, he was hatless, and a strand of brown hair fell across his forehead. His rolled-up sleeves were captured by red garters, and a pencil stuck out of his shirt pocket. He looked nothing like the other newspaper publishers she'd known, whose flabby jowls and pasty complexions had reflected long hours spent in saloons or behind desks. Many were hard drinkers and were hardly seen without cigarettes or cigars dangling from their mouths.

In contrast Wade emulated power and strength, his bronze skin suggesting many hours spent outside, the wind and the sun in his face.

"Ah, Mrs. Johnson, I thought that was you." He read the circular on the post out loud. "'A thousand-dollar reward awaits someone with certain information. To find out if that person is you, read Friday's *Gazette*.'"

Arching his eyebrows, he leaned against the post, arms folded. "I must say, that's a brilliant piece of marketing."

"I'm glad you approve," she said. Irritated that the mere sight of him made her heart do acrobats, she reached for the pail of paste.

"I didn't say I approved. I simply said it was brilliant. So, what kind of information are you looking for?"

She straightened, pail in hand. "You'll have to purchase my paper to find out."

"Wouldn't miss it." A look of humor glimmered from the depths of his eyes. "By the way, I saw that you gave our naked friend full coverage in last week's editorial."

The "friend" he referred to was an elderly man with the disconcerting habit of strolling down Main without benefit of clothing. All he wore for his daily jaunts was shoes and socks.

So, Wade read her column, did he? For some reason that gave her perverse pleasure, though she couldn't imagine why. "Something should be done about Mr. Pendergrass. The poor man needs care and should not be living alone."

"I couldn't agree more."

She drew back. "You mean we actually agree upon something?"

Lines furrowed Wade's brow as if the question surprised him. "I believe there's a lot we agree upon. Our differences lie in the presentation."

Josie clenched her jaw. There he went again, criticizing her writing. "How's this for presentation, Mr. Wade?" she said tersely. "I don't believe Mr. Pendergrass is a lunatic, as some say." The conviction in her voice came from the heart. It infuriated her when people called him such names. "He's just old and confused. Unfortunately, the only place for people like him is the insane asylum, and the poor man doesn't belong there."

Wade's head dipped as if in agreement. "It'll take strong words before the problem is taken seriously. Your—"

"'Insipid use of words'?" she managed to say through stiff lips.

He quirked a dark brow. "I was going to say that your editorial was a good start."

"Which you of course will finish!" she snapped.

His penetrating gaze brought a flush to her cheeks. "If only you wrote with as much passion as you spoke."

His criticism stung, but she wasn't about to let on how much. "I wouldn't want to deprive you the satisfaction of stealing my editorial ideas," she retorted.

His crooked grin threatened to puncture a hole in her vexed state of mind. "All's fair in love and journalism."

"Not all, Mr. Wade. Not all."

***

After posting the last of her handbills, Josie stomped inside her office and was surprised to see her sister Amanda waiting for her.

"Oh, there you are," Amanda said. "I was just about to leave a note." She stared at Josie from beneath a hat as gaily and extravagantly decorated as a Christmas tree. The red-white-and blue silk flowers matched the multicolored ribbon beneath her chin. "Are you all right?"

"Of course I'm all right," Josie said, setting the pail of paste in a corner. "Why do you ask?"

"It's just that you look . . . flushed."

Josie fanned her face with her hand. "Must be the sun."

Amanda pulled off a glove. Today she wore a blue frock with a draped panier and braided red trim. "If only you would wear a proper hat."

Amanda abhorred the straw bonnets that Josie preferred. But Amanda's designs—with their wide, circular brims and extravagant use of lace, ribbons, and feathers—never felt right, though Josie admired her sister's handiwork. She simply didn't like calling attention to herself through dress or headgear. It was bad enough that etiquette required her to wear black. Widow's weeds made her stand out like a grim cloud amid the floral spring dresses favored by the other women in town.

"I heard that wearing a hat weighing more than five ounces causes mental afflictions in women," she said, removing her own lightweight headgear.

Amanda scoffed. "Why does no one worry about mental afflictions in men? I can assure you that Stetsons weigh a lot more than any woman's hat in my shop."

"Perhaps that explains why jails are mostly filled with males," Josie said and changed the subject. "And where's my adorable little nephew today?" Amanda's son, Jerrod, was nearly six months old.

"Mama's watching him. Now that he's starting to crawl, it's harder to take him to work with me."

Josie nodded. "I can imagine."

Amanda pulled off a second glove and stuffed both in her purse. "Mama said you were traveling to Austin on Saturday."

"Yes, I'm meeting with a publisher friend. I'm hoping he can give me some ideas on how to increase circulation."

Amanda glanced at the stack of last week's paper, and her forehead furrowed. "I was thinking about enlarging the size of this week's advertisement."

"You don't have to do that." The last thing Josie wanted was her family's charity.

"I know, but I need to lessen the spring inventory to make room for my summer hats."

Before Josie could object a second time, her sister changed the subject. "Mama said you agreed to take the hope chest to Cousin Brenda."

Josie nodded. "Yes, she's engaged to a doctor."

It was no surprise that Cousin Brenda had requested the family heirloom that had been hand crafted by their grandfather in Ireland. The lid was etched with a sailing ship like the one that brought her grandparents to America. Grandmama had carved her initials into the side of the chest, starting what was now a three-generation family tradition. The initials of four more brides, including Mama, Josie, and her two sisters, had since been etched into the wood. It was now time for Cousin Brenda to add hers.

Amanda smiled. "I'm glad Brenda finally found someone to marry."

Josie laughed.

Amanda lifted her eyebrows. "What's so funny."

"You, my dear sister. It wasn't that long ago that you scoffed at love and marriage. And now look at you." Time was when Amanda wouldn't think of missing a women's rights meeting. But now that she was a wife and mother, she stayed home writing speeches for her suffragist friends to deliver. She seemed perfectly content to let others get the credit for her work.

A flush crept over Amanda's face. "People change."

"Yes, they do." Josie tweaked her sister's pretty pink cheek. "And sometimes in the most delightful way. So why are you really here? And don't tell me it's to place an ad."

"I came to ask a favor. Next week also happens to be the quarterly suffrage meeting. The mail is so undependable, and I'm afraid the speech I wrote for Miss Collins won't get to Austin in time. I wondered if you'd deliver it for me?"

"I'd be happy to."

"You're a dear." Amanda reached into her knapsack and pulled out a large brown envelope, which she handed to Josie. "After hearing what I've written about democratic principles, I don't know how anyone can deny us the vote."

Josie didn't share her sister's passion for suffrage. She was far more interested in women's education and employment opportunities than voting rights. Once college and work opportunities were fully available to women, she was convinced the rest would follow.

She fingered the thick packet. Where women's rights were concerned, Amanda didn't skimp on words. "Do you think my writing lacks . . . passion?"

"If you're asking if your writing is as bold as Mr. Wade's, then I'd have to say no. But it's very sweet."

"Sweet?"

"You know what I mean."

No, she did not. "By 'sweet' do you mean boring?"

"No, not at all!" Amanda's eyes widened in alarm. "My goodness, where is this coming from? Are you sure everything's all right? The paper?"

"Everything is fine," Josie said in a tone meant to discourage further discussion.

"If you say so," Amanda said with a doubtful look. "Now about that ad . . ."

Chapter 6

Several well-known criminals vowed to go straight after learning that some prisons are charging fifteen dollars a week for room and board. Mack Peters, in prison for helping himself to the loot on a Wells Fargo stagecoach, declared the practice nothing more than "highway robbery." He should know.—Two-Time Gazette

Josie dreaded attending the annual May dance—and for good reason, as it turned out. Stepping into the open barn with its festive decorations and toe-tapping music was like being slapped in the face with the past. Memories of walking into this very barn on her husband's arm were so vivid they took her breath away. She and Ralph had attended the dance every year during their courtship and early years of marriage. As Ralph whirled her around the dance floor, they'd had eyes only for each other.

Pushing the memories away, she let out a sigh and gave herself a stern warning. *Do not think about Ralph or the past.*

It took sheer willpower, but somehow she managed to clear her head of all but the present. As a newspaper editor, she could hardly avoid the social event of the season, no matter how much she might want to. An endless number of newsworthy gems could be gathered from the gossip that flowed as freely as water from a pump at such functions.

She glanced around for familiar faces. It was early, and people were still arriving. From the back of the barn Mrs. Posey, the designated head chaperone for the night's dance, waved her over.

"There you are," Mrs. Posey said as Josie joined her. "I was beginning to think you weren't coming." She patted the empty chair by her side. "Here, sit by me."

With a sigh, Josie took her place next to the dowager and suddenly felt very old. The line of matronly chaperones looked like a flock of scavenger birds sitting on a telegraph wire. In her black dress, Josie feared she resembled a raven.

Mrs. Posey handed her the rules of conduct that all chaperones were expected to follow or enforce. "Men must remove their weapons and spurs," she said. "And couples are not allowed to stay together for more than two dances."

Josie nodded, and since Mrs. Posey was staring at her, she made a show of reading the remaining rules. She was expected to conduct herself prudently and in a manner befitting a chaperone. There would be no dancing or flirting. Nor were she and the other dance minders allowed to sing or hum along with the music.

By agreeing to keep a watchful eye on young couples, Josie had hoped to make herself feel useful and less conspicuous. Instead, she felt very much out of place. Not only were the other chaperones older, but some were even grandmothers. They did, however, provide plenty of editorial material. That is, if she wanted to fill her newspaper with the adorable sayings of grandchildren or the relentless body aches that seemed to plague women of a certain age. Which she did not.

Mrs. Spencer started to say something about one of her neighbors, but was immediately hushed by the others, who drew her attention to Josie with worried looks. Josie was used to people falling silent or changing the topic of conversation when she walked into a room for fear of being quoted in her newspaper. It was an occupational hazard. Some people worried about being judged biased, rude, or immoral. Fortunately, Mrs. Spencer was not one of them.

"I hate to repeat gossip," Mrs. Spencer declared with a sniff. "But what else can you do with it?" She then shamelessly told them about her next-door neighbor's latest marital infidelity.

Mrs. Simon took advantage of the sudden silence that followed to again remind everyone that in her day she'd been the belle of the ball and had danced with Crockett and Bowie. Though now in her seventies, her mind was still sharp as a pin.

"Did you know that Davy could play a fiddle like nobody's business?" She pointed a hooked arthritic finger at Josie. "You should put that in your newspaper."

Josie thanked her politely for the information, and the conversation turned back to grandchildren and aching body parts.

Feeling at loose ends and trying not to look bored, Josie sat with feet together to keep from tapping her toes to the rousing fiddle music. Hands knotted on her lap, she gazed at the whirling couples and tried not to envy the women—some older than her—dancing with reckless abandon in their bright dresses.

In some ways, widowhood was treated like a contagious disease. Singles avoided her; married friends had simply vanished from her life. If only her sisters were there, they would know how to make her feel less out of place. But both were tied down with small children.

The night wore on, and talk turned from the latest issues with sacroiliacs, dyspepsia, and rheumatism to other things. This was when Josie learned that Sue Anderson had miraculously delivered a bouncing ten-pound baby boy less than six months after her wedding, that Priscilla Landry had broken off her engagement to the mayor's son, and that Mr. and Mrs. Peterson had left for Europe.

She stifled a yawn and looked at her pocket watch for the eighth or ninth time in so many minutes.

Seated to the right of Josie, Mrs. Cambridge fanned herself as she kept up a running commentary on fashions. She had something to say about every dress in the place. The way she carried on, one would think the dowdily dressed woman an expert on fashion. Her floral print made her look like a potted plant.

"I don't know how she does it," Mrs. Cambridge said with a nod at Anna-May Gilbert, a small, shapely woman with honey-blond hair. "If I didn't know better, I'd think her gown was from Paris."

The gown in question was an exquisite raspberry satin dress draped from the waist down and gathered into a ruffled bustle in back. The bodice was embroidered with faux jewels and the puffed sleeves edged in lace.

Mrs. Cambridge continued. "But, of course, it can't be the real thing. She wouldn't be able to afford such a dress on her husband's salary."

Josie didn't know how much bank clerks made—or even how much a Parisian gown cost—but Mrs. Cambridge did seem to be knowledgeable about such things.

"I don't know what she sees in that mousey husband of her," Mrs. Cambridge said to no one in particular.

While the other women expressed shock at Mrs. Cambridge's comment, Josie looked down at her own plain black dress. How she longed for the day she could return to her usual wardrobe, though nothing she owned was as elaborate as Anna-May Gilbert's.

She was still staring at the raspberry dress when Mrs. Getty appeared in front of her. The women's ample bosom heaved with righteous indignation.

"I wish to end my subscription to your newspaper," she said without preamble, her eyes ablaze.

"I'm sorry to hear that," Josie said. She spoke in a low voice, hoping Mrs. Getty would take the hint and do likewise. "If you would kindly stop by my office Monday—"

"I'll do no such thing," Mrs. Getty said, her voice even louder than before. "I refuse to step into a place that supports a house of ill repute."

Mrs. Spencer stopped talking mid-sentence and Mrs. Posey gasped. The other two chaperones simply dropped their jaws and stared

Feeling the weight of their shock and disapproval, Josie's cheeks flared.

"I'm sorry—"

That terrible woman—" Mrs. Getty sniffed. "Miss Bubbles has no business advertising in a family newspaper."

Josie tried to maintain a businesslike demeanor, but the small-minded woman was making it hard. "Al she's doing is asking for help so that justice—"

"Whatever she's doing, I will not be a party to it!"

Josie drew back, hands folded firmly on the lap. "Very well, Mrs. Getty. Consider your subscription canceled. I'm sure the *Lone Star Press* would be more suited to your—" She wanted to say "narrow-minded ways." "—*sensitive* nature."

"Yes, yes, the *Lone Star Press*. That is a very good idea!" The woman stomped off.

Tutting, Mrs. Posey pulled the rules of conduct from her tote and practically thrust the paper into Josie's face. "Rule number eleven says there's no conducting personal business while chaperoning."

"I wasn't conducting business, I was ending it."

Josie was still glaring after Mrs. Getty when Mr. Brandon Wade stepped into her line of vision. She stiffened with a soft gasp. Speak of the devil.

As usual, his mere presence seemed to deplete the room of air. The music, the laughter, the dancing couples all faded into the background, and for one disturbing moment in time it was as if he was the only one in the barn with her.

Acknowledging her with a tip of his hat, he headed her way. Her pulse quickened. He seemed oblivious to the female sighs and gazes that followed him across the floor.

Tonight, he was dressed in denim pants, a plaid shirt, and his ever-present Stetson. Looking more like a cowpuncher fresh off the trail than a newspaperman, he appeared as equally at ease dressed in casual attire as he did in his more formal frock coat.

"Ah, Mrs. Johnson," he said.

Before she could answer, Mrs. Simon clasped her hands together and cooed. "How nice to see you again, Mr. Wade."

He tipped his hat and bowed. "You, too, Mrs. Simon."

Mrs. Simon's face turned florid. Next to her, Mrs. Spencer giggled.

Mrs. Cambridge was the only one of the four who maintained her composure. "I enjoyed your last editorial immensely," she said in a honey-sweet voice

"Why, thank you, Mrs. Cambridge."

On some level, it irritated Josie that he'd only been in town for a few short months but already knew everyone by name.

Mrs. Posey tried to act like she was unaffected by his presence, but when he greeted her with a smile, her red cheeks gave her away.

Mr. Wade turned his attention back to Josie. "I must say, you look like you're in a horn-tossin' mood."

Josie rested her hands on her lap. "I just had an unpleasant encounter with a *former* subscriber."

He raised an eyebrow and stroked his upper lip. "I hope you put the person in his or her place."

"Oh, yes, indeed I did. I sent her over to *your* newspaper."

He laughed. "That'll teach her to mess with you." He glanced at the other chaperones before looking down at her foot keeping time to the music. Blushing, she pulled her feet back, letting the hem of her skirt hide her high button shoes from his probing eyes.

An altercation between two young men sent Mrs. Posey and the other three chaperones scurrying across the room. Since Mr. Wade blocked her way, Josie had no choice but to remain seated.

He lifted his gaze. "You don't look like you belong here, Mrs. Johnson," he said, indicating the row of empty chaperone chairs.

"Oh? And where do you think I belong?"

"On the dance floor with me."

Her hearted fluttered, and she shot a quick glance at Mrs. Posey, who thankfully had her back toward them. "I hardly think that would be proper, Mr. Wade."

His gaze dipped to the gold locket on her chest. "I meant your departed husband no disrespect."

"I was thinking about *your* reputation. Your new subscriber might take issue with you dancing with someone who dares to accept advertisements from a bawdy house."

"I'm willing to risk it if you are."

The challenge in his eyes was too good to ignore. As much as she loathed the idea of dancing with him, she was bored out of her wits. Anything had to be better than sitting on the sidelines all night, even dancing with a man she disdained. She lifted her hand to his just as Mrs. Nosey—she mentally chided herself—Mrs. *Posey* returned, disapproval pouring out of her like smoke from a fire. She stared at Josie's hand clasped in his.

"You do know it's against the rules for chaperones to dance, don't you? To say nothing about women in mourning."

"Yes, of course, Mrs. No— Posey," Josie said, pulling her hand away. Blast the woman and her meddlesome ways. She gazed up at Wade. "I wouldn't think of doing anything improper."

It was hard to know if Mr. Wade's look of disappointment was feigned or sincere. "What a pity. I was hoping we could show these youngsters how it's done."

"How it's done?" she asked. "Oh, you mean how two adversaries can dance without killing each other."

He chuckled, and warm humor filled his eyes. "Since I'm here strictly for pleasure, you can hardly call me an adversary."

"Oh? Then what should I call you, Mr. Wade?"

"Brandon. You can call me Brandon. What can I call you?"

"Your business opponent," Josie said, refusing to succumb to his charms no matter how tempted she was.

A smile ruffled his mouth. "As you wish." He glanced at Mrs. Posey, who had left her seat again to scold a young couple daring to stay together for an alarming *three* dances. "Will your duties as chaperone last till midnight?"

She hesitated. "No, only till ten." The dance ended at midnight, but couples started leaving much sooner, so fewer chaperones were needed after ten.

"Ah." He leaned over to whisper in Josie's ear, his breath sending surprisingly pleasing ripples of warmth down her neck. "Since you are currently indisposed, would you at least consider giving me a raincheck for when you've completed your duties?"

As he straightened, Mrs. Posey returned, her glare suggesting she suspected something awry. The woman missed nothing. Josie flicked her fan, but the slight breeze did little to cool her heated face.

"Sorry, Mr. Wade, but I see only sunny skies ahead," she said firmly, putting him in his place not just for her sake, but Mrs. Posey's as well.

He accepted her decision with a gentlemanly bow. "It's always a pleasure, Mrs. Johnson."

He took his leave and was soon caught up in a ring of young ladies all vying for his attention. Josie glared at the fawning women and forced herself to breathe. It surprised her—

indeed, horrified her—that the idea of being in another man's arms—in Brandon Wade's arms—was suddenly not all that unthinkable.

Chapter 7

A large reward has been offered for the capture of cattle rustler Jack Patterson, who escaped an Austin jailhouse. He left a note saying that he feared a lynching would ruin his reputation.

—Two-Time Gazette

No sooner had Brandon settled at his desk that morning than his compositor, Stan Booker, handed him the proofs for that week's paper.

"Looks good, Chief," Booker said, his white teeth flashing against his dark skin. Booker was a former slave who had originally insisted upon calling Brandon *boss*, the Dutch term for "master." When Brandon objected, Booker took to calling him *chief*.

"You say that every week," Brandon said.

Booker shrugged. "When you work for the best . . ." He headed for the door. "Need anything? I'm on my way to the post office."

"No, nothing," Brandon said. Pen in hand, he set to work proofing.

Though he'd allocated only two inches for last week's May dance, his practiced eye lingered over each obligatory sentence. It wasn't the punctuation, spelling, or even syntax that commanded his attention. It was the vision of Mrs. Johnson seeming to float up from the printed page. How could a woman dressed in stark black—a grim reminder of her sad status—appear so utterly fetching? Though cloaked in the respectable mantle of grief, her strong spirit had been clear in the rigid set of her shoulders and almost defiant lift of her chin.

She'd turned down his invitation to dance, but she'd wanted to accept. He'd bet his life on it. He'd read it in the depth of her turquoise eyes, seen it in the wistful look on her face. Sensed it in the way her body leaned ever so slightly forward to place her hand in his. Had it not been for Mrs. Posey, the lady would have been in his arms, no question.

Surprised to find Mrs. Johnson occupying his thoughts yet again, he initialed the page proof in front of him and moved on to the next. If he had his druthers, he'd yank the boring dance piece altogether. But it was news. No doubt the *Gazette* would give the dance full play, with every dress described down to the smallest detail. He could almost picture Mrs. Johnson at her type-writing machine, graceful hands posed over the keys, lush lips pursed as she considered her choice of words.

The door to his office swung open, offering a welcome distraction from his disturbing thoughts, though he wasn't especially happy that his savior was the land developer Mr. Troop.

"Hope I'm not too late for Friday's paper," Troop said, extending his hand. A round-bellied man with a doorknocker mustache, he was as oily in his appearance as he was in his business practices. The only thing in his favor was his generous advertising budget.

Brandon stood and shook the man's hand. "You missed the deadline. We're just about to go to press."

"I've got something I need you to run in this week's paper." When Brandon failed to respond, Troop added, "I'll make it worth your while."

Hesitating, Brandon lowered himself into his chair. Having to make changes at this late date meant extra work. Something would have to be cut or edited down to make room. On the other hand, Troop was the paper's most lucrative advertiser.

"Get any results from the last ad we ran?" Brandon asked.

"Not exactly." Troop sat on the chair in front of the desk and crossed his legs.

His answer didn't surprise Brandon. Troop was a speculator of the worst kind. He grabbed land at the cheapest price possible and held on just long enough to sell it at great profit to himself. He'd purchase hundreds of acres of prime property outside of town during the last economic downturn and split it into two-acre lots. Now that the economy had picked up momentum, he was ready to make his move.

Brandon had had his eye on one of the lots bordering the river, but the price was too steep for his blood. It was too steep for anyone else, as well, which is why the prime property sat empty.

Troop balanced his derby on his knee. "That's why I'm here. I thought you could help me with a new venture. I'm giving away lot number eleven free."

Brandon's ears perked up. Lot eleven was the one he wanted. The property faced the part of the river where he liked to fish and Haley enjoyed swimming. "Did you say 'free'?"

"Yes, indeed. Give a little, gain a lot." The waxen smile spreading across Troop's face failed to reach his eyes, suggesting that the giving part was done with great reluctance. "As you know, the properties are a distance from town. I've not had much luck convincing people to travel out there to inspect them. I'm convinced that once people see the improvements made to the land, the lots will sell like hotcakes. Of course, that's only gonna happen if I can persuade prospective buyers to travel out there and have a look."

Brandon nodded. "Yes, I can see where that might pose a problem. Living in town is more convenient."

"Yes, but this is Texas, and we Texans like our wide-open spaces. The town is getting too crowded. You can't even tether your horse without risking a black eye. And the sidewalk is so crowded you practically have to walk sideways. That's why I believe the time is right to strike."

Troop rubbed his hands together in anticipation, and the ends of his mustache twitched.

"I believe I've come up with the perfect solution," he continued. "I'm holding a race. The starting line will be located just outside town limits. The first one to reach the property will be declared the winner. Once everyone sees what fine land is out there, the offers will start pouring in."

Interested, Brandon sat forward. "A race, huh? That should get attention." Already, ideas for headlines popped into his head. "When will the race take place?"

"Saturday. Which is why I need it in this Friday's edition." Troop pulled a folded sheet of paper out of his pocket and tossed it onto Brandon's desk. "That has all the information you'll need. The race will start promptly at ten in the morning at the sound of a pistol."

Brandon unfolded the paper and quickly scanned the hand-written copy. "This should get you a good turnout, but since you missed the deadline, I'll have to charge more."

"No problem," Troop said. He pulled a wad of money from his pocket and peeled off a generous-sized banknote. After paying for the ad, he then placed his bowler on his head and rose.

"Is the race open to everyone?" Brandon asked.

"If you're wondering if you can enter, the answer is yes. In fact, I insist. The more the merrier."

Brandon pulled away from his desk and shook the man's hand. Already he pictured a house facing the river and a front porch where he and Haley could sit at day's end to watch the sunset.

With a satisfied nod, Troop turned to the door. "See you Saturday."

***

Josie sat at the type-writing machine working on her next editorial—or at least trying to. She knew what she wanted to write but was unable to think up a fresh slant. She needed a bold headline or compelling opening sentence—something that would catch readers' eyes. Hoping for inspiration, she searched through the stack of papers in the "ideas" basket and came across the column Mr. Wade had written. What was that doing here? She could have sworn she'd discarded it.

Everything he'd written about himself was true and then some. It would serve him right if she did, indeed, publish that awful editorial of his. But of course she wouldn't. There had to be a way of saving the *Gazette* without stooping to such tactics. She ran a fine newspaper and once the initial novelty of Mr. Wade's sensational type of journalism wore off, her readers were bound to return. Or at least she hoped so.

Stooping to his level was not an option, but the thought annoyed her enough to break through her writer's block. Swallowing her irritation, she rolled a fresh piece of paper into the typewriter and began striking keys. Something needed to be done about the traffic problem in town—the subject of that week's column. During business hours, horses and wagons were parked helter-skelter, blocking the road. Flaring tempers and daily fistfights between frustrated drivers were now the norm.

She typed away for a few minutes, then paused. Rereading what she had written, her heart sank.

"That insipid piece you wrote . . ."

"It's not insipid." She sighed. Nor was it sweet. Yes, the article was the result of good reporting. She'd quoted several prominent citizens including the mayor and her friend the sheriff. The facts were accurate, and she'd offered possible solutions. Okay, maybe it wasn't the most exciting piece ever to grace the pages of her newspaper, but did everything have to be fun and entertaining?

For answer she tore the sheet of paper out of the roller and ripped it into a dozen little pieces.

Just as the scraps of paper fluttered to the floor, Hank's voice floated across the room. "I'm lot neaving."

Josie pushed herself away from the type-writing machine and stood. "What?"

"I said I'm . . ." He hesitated as if struggling to get the words right. "Not leaving."

She knitted her brow. "I'm not sure what you mean."

"I said I'm lot neaving." His voice grew more insistent, the look on his face more stubborn. "I belong here, and this is where I intend to stay!"

"Hank, you know I can't afford to keep you. And . . . and you could work for . . . that other newspaper."

"Maybe. Maybe not. But this is not just a job. It's my home. If you want me to leave, you'll have to carry me out feet first."

Sighing, she picked up the balls of paper that had failed to reach the wastepaper basket. Trust Hank to offer the one line of reasoning that allowed no room for argument. Humble as it was, she, too, loved the old place. Loved the smell of paste and ink ingrained in the rough wooden walls. Loved the way the sun seeping through the holes in the roof cast glimmers of light onto the dark wood floor.

The *Gazette* was housed in one of the few wooden structures left. Built long before the town existed, it had once been the cabin of a buffalo hunter. All the newer buildings in town were built from the more fire-resistant adobe but didn't have the same homey feel as her office.

Her fondness for the old place had a long history. She'd been only ten when she first walked into the office of the *Gazette* and handed the editor a poem she'd written about a beloved pony who had passed away. Having poured heart and soul into that poem, she'd been certain that the editor would hate it. Or worse, even laugh. Much to her surprise, he'd agreed to print it and had invited her back to watch it roll off the press.

She'd taken him up on his offer and had watched in wide-eyed amazement as the printing press spread her words of loving grief onto sheet after sheet of paper. It was magic. Still seemed like magic all these years later. The thought of the *Gazette* folding under her management nearly broke her heart.

Oh, good heavens, now she was going to cry. She pulled a handkerchief from her sleeve. "I hate the thought of you working without pay."

Hank swung his chair around to face her. "I didn't say I'd work without pay. I said I'm lot neaving." After a pause, he added, "Maybe, as part of next week's pay, you'll let me place an advertisement in the paper."

She dabbed at the corner of her eyes. "You want to advertise for a job?"

He shook his head. "Nope. For a wife."

***

On that Saturday morning in mid-May, dawn broke bright and sunny—the perfect day for traveling. Josie had every intention of getting an early start for Austin, but everything conspired against her.

It all started with Papa, who cornered her in the kitchen to inquire as to how things were going at the newspaper. She couldn't lie to him, but neither could she bring herself to admit the full extent of her problems.

"I've hit a little bump in the road," she said.

Papa's eyebrows practically rose to his receding hairline. "Word around town is that your paper is in trouble. Don't sound like no little bump to me."

She ran her hands up and down her crossed arms. "I'm sure there are people who wish that was true."

He narrowed his eyes. "I told you buying that newspaper was a mistake." Papa was a tall, broad-chested man with definite ideas on how a woman should conduct herself. As far as he was concerned, his three daughters had soundly failed on all accounts. "How can anyone consider you respectable when you dabble in politics and crime?"

"I write about them, Papa. I don't dabble."

"You know what I mean."

Fortunately, she was saved from his "the trouble with women today" lecture by Mama, who made it her business to step in whenever things grew too tense between Papa and his daughters. Grateful for the reprieve, Josie quickly made her escape. But it was already nine thirty by the time she reached Meg's house to pick up the hope chest promised to her cousin in Austin.

While Meg's husband, Grant, lifted the heavy wooden trunk into the back of her wagon, Josie stood in the shade of a tall magnolia tree fanning herself.

"Are you all right?" Meg asked.

"No, I'm not. I'm hot. I don't know why I have to wear these awful widow's weeds for a full two years!"

She still had five months of public mourning left—a thought that did nothing for her spirits. She could hardly wait to return to her normal wardrobe. Not only did the dark fabric absorb the heat, but Ralph had hated seeing her in drab colors. He would no doubt consider her black dress more of an affront to his memory than the sign of respect it was meant to be.

Meg's eyes filled with sympathy. "It won't be long, dear sister."

"Long enough." Josie dabbed her damp forehead with a handkerchief. "The whole idea is ridiculous. Just because Queen Victoria chooses to make widowhood a full-time occupation gives her no right to force her mourning etiquette on the rest of us." The queen's influence on America was a great source of puzzlement to Josie. Despite the War of Independence, America still hadn't completely broken its ties with the motherland.

"If the queen lived in a hotter climate, like Texas, she'd be far less inclined to wear black. She would probably choose something more sensible to mourn in. Like white." Josie fanned herself with her hand. "Or run around naked."

Meg's eyes widened, but she said nothing.

Josie continued. "Grief is not something that can be worn. Even dressed in scarlet or polka dots, I would still mourn my loss."

Meg's eyes filled with compassion. "I know it was hard losing Ralph."

"Hard doesn't even begin to describe it," Josie said. "Did you know that it's possible to cry for six straight months?" Had she stayed in Arizona Territory, she might still be crying.

"Oh, Josie, I wish I could have been there for you."

"I was a thousand miles away. Your place was here with Grant."

"But you're my sister and I hate seeing you hurt." Meg sighed. "I miss Ralph too. And as far as wearing black is concerned, you're right."

"'Course I'm right," Josie said. "Men aren't required to follow such ridiculous rules. Did you know that Mr. Cotter remarried within three months of his wife's death and no one said a word?" Not that she ever planned on remarrying. Ralph had been the love of her life, and no man could ever fill his shoes. "It's not fair to place such restrictions on women and not men."

Once started on the subject, Josie couldn't seem to stop as she cited other examples of how widowers could go about their business as they saw fit. Words flowed out of her like a never-ending freight train. She only got off her soapbox when she noticed Meg's eyes had glazed over and now looked like two frozen pools.

"My goodness, Josie. What's gotten into you? It's not like you to—"

Josie's gaze sharpened. "Not like me to what?"

Meg looked like she was struggling for words. "Voice such strong opinions. Now you sound like Mr. Wade."

Josie's mouth dropped open. "What a thing to say."

"I didn't mean it in a bad way," Meg said in a placating voice. "It's just . . . You don't sound like yourself. You've always been so—"

"Insipid?"

Meg shook her head with an audible sigh. "I didn't say that."

Josie tucked her handkerchief into her sleeve with a sigh of her own. "You didn't have to."

***

The streets were crowded by the time Josie left Meg's house. Traffic was always a problem, but today it seemed even worse than usual. The number of vehicles parked in front of the *Lone Star Press* while the owners purchased newspapers only made matters worse. It took twice as long as expected to work her way down Main.

Much to her surprise, traffic grew even worse as she neared town limits.

Even though it was still early, tempers flared. T-Bone and saloon owner Ken Kerrigan raised their fists and yelled at each other as they jockeyed their vehicles for whatever advantage could be found on that crowded street. Kerrigan's hot temper had earned him the moniker Pepper.

Mr. Wade rode by on his horse. He lifted his hat to her and flashed a smile. "Ah, Mrs. Johnson. So glad you could join us."

Before she had a chance to respond, he pulled away and vanished in the crowded street ahead. Josie frowned after him. Glad she could join them? The man definitely had a strange sense of humor.

Josie spotted an empty alley. It was narrow, with a sign that read "Closed to Traffic," but Josie wasn't about to look a gift horse in the mouth. She turned down the alley, clipping a trash receptacle as she passed. A series of back streets allowed her to bypass the traffic and reach the road to Austin.

Though it was only mid-morning, the sun was hot and shimmered off the ground like strands of wavy hair.

Thinking about her conversation with Meg, Josie puckered her nose. She still couldn't get over her sister comparing her to Mr. Wade. If anything, Josie thought she had sounded more like her sister Amanda. Or that little girl—what was her name? Haley.

Pushing her thoughts aside, she concentrated on the sunbaked road ahead. The azure sky was cloudless and the heat from the sun unrelenting. But bluebonnets lined both sides of the road, scenting the air with sweet fragrance. Leaving town had been a good idea. Despite the warmth, she already felt better—or would once she passed the bend in the river. It had always been Ralph's dream to own riverfront property, but she couldn't think about that. Not now. Not ever.

Her one and only concern at present was getting her newspaper on track, and she hoped her meeting with John Cardman, publisher of the *Austin Statesman,* would help her accomplish that goal. A friend of Ralph's, Cardman had told her that if she ever needed anything, all she had to do was ask. Maybe he would have some ideas how to attract new subscribers.

She had driven only a short distance from town when she heard a gunshot. Tugging on the reins, she guided the wagon to the shade of a tree by the side of the road. After setting the brake she reached for her canteen. It sounded like trouble. Another dispute over parking? She wondered what the details might be. Thankfully, Hank had agreed to keep her informed if anything happened in her absence. He didn't have the nose for news that any good reporter needed, but he was quite capable at collecting on-the-scene facts.

She unscrewed the cap of the metal water bottle and lifted it to her mouth. The water would have to last till she reached Austin, so she allowed herself only a sip.

Just as she hung the flask on the hook behind her, she saw something that startled her. Craning her neck, she anxiously scanned the horizon and prayed that her eyes were playing tricks. But, no. A dust cloud rose from the direction of town. Within seconds the dark haze stretched across the full width of the valley to the hills on either side, turning the air a murky brown.

A distant memory came to mind, and her blood ran cold. Gasping, she covered her mouth. *Oh, dear heaven! Not that. Anything but that!*

Shuddering at the fearful thought, she grabbed the reins and released the brake. Only one thing could explain the mile-wide wall of dust: a cattle stampede.

And it was heading her way!

Chapter 8

A Pullman railroad car has been sidelined outside of Houston with eleven passengers aboard. Mr. Albert Wanamaker came down with small pox and the rest of the passengers will have to be isolated for two weeks. That is, unless they kill each other first. —Two-Time Gazette

Forcing her horse to race over hill and dale, Josie told herself not to panic. She'd been in worse straits. Or almost worse.

The wagon veered wildly from side to side and bounced over ruts and rocks. The hope chest slid back and forth, hitting the slatted wagon sides with worrisome thuds. Worse, she feared the axles would break or wheels fall off. Or she'd be thrown. Or . . .

Her straw hat lifted off her head. Held by the ribbons still tied beneath her chin, it batted against her back.

From behind, the pounding cattle hooves grew louder, and she could almost imagine hearing the angry clash of horns. She cast a glance over her shoulder. The wall of dust was closing in fast. Grit filled her mouth and stung her eyes. Terror gripped her heart, holding her breath in its icy grip. She could hardly see.

She had no chance of outrunning a stampede. Not with her old wagon. Not with her old horse. Already her mare was showing signs of fatigue.

"Don't you dare give up on me now!" she cried with a frantic slap of the reins.

Every horror story she'd ever heard about stampedes ran through her head. Men died in stampedes. Experienced cattlemen had been trampled to death She'd lost an Arizona neighbor to one.

Pushing the gruesome thoughts away, she snapped the whip through the air and yelled, "Gid-up!" Horse and wagon sailed over a hill as if airborne. The wheels hit the ground with a jolt, rattling her bones and nearly knocking her teeth out.

Something appeared alongside her, and she gasped as she turned to look. She expected a steer, but instead found . . . a horseman. Thinking she was seeing things, she blinked. But there was no mistake. What's more, the horseman was Brandon Wade!

Saluting her, he flashed a smile and shouted something before pulling ahead. Her mouth dropped open. It sure sounded like he'd said, "Too bad."

She glared after him in disbelief. She was in a life or death situation and that's all he could offer? "Too bad"?

Her gazed riveted on his retreating back, she failed to notice the horse and buggy now racing alongside her until its wheel clipped her wagon. She recognized the driver at once as Ken Kerrigan.

What in the world was *he* doing there? What's more, why was he was now purposely trying to push her off the road?

"Stop!" she yelled in confusion and fear. "What are you doing?"

For an answer, his buggy sideswiped her.

This time her wagon fishtailed, pulling her across the road as she desperately tried to steer her panicking mare. Before she had time for more than a breath, the wagon's rear wheel smashed against a tree. She heard a crack below her as their momentum slowed.

But now her horse fought her with a vengeance. With a squeal, the frantic animal yanked the traces from her hands and broke free from the hitch. Josie barely had time to note the animal's exit, harness dragging behind it, before the wagon's momentum carried it off the side of the road and down a sharp incline, jolting her. It then sped toward the river.

She screamed just as she clipped a second tree. Everything cartwheeled, then went black.

***

"Mrs. Johnson . . . Mrs. Johnson, can you hear me?"

The male voice seemed far away but eventually cut through the darkness. The persistent tone forced her to open her eyes. At first, she couldn't put a name to the masculine face staring down at her.

The voice sounded again. "Are you all right?"

She tried moving her legs. Feeling gradually returned to her limbs, and the fog cleared from her head. "Mr. Wade?" She was vaguely aware of strong hands on her shoulders. Brandon?

"Don't move," he said.

Ignoring his advice, she tried sitting up, but was only able to do so with his help. Wincing, she reached for the back of her head. Already she could feel a lump.

"What . . . what happened?"

"You had an accident. Your wagon . . ."

His voice faded away as she shook off a dizzy spell. As soon as her head cleared, she followed the line of men and women circling them and her eyes widened. "Where are the cattle?"

Wade sat back on his heels with a worried frown. "Cattle?"

"I saw them." At least she thought she had. Why were all those people staring at her?

She turned back to Wade. "What's everyone doing here?"

For some reason the question only deepened the lines in his forehead. "What year is it?'

She stared at him. "What year?"

"Who's the president of the United States?"

She shook her head. Was he out of his cotton-picking mind? "Why are you asking these questions?" Noting the concern on his face, she frowned. "You don't think that I . . ."

He rose and turned to the crowd of onlookers. "Is anyone here a doctor?" he shouted.

She tugged on the leg of his trousers. "I don't need a doctor. I'm perfectly all right." Or she would be when the ground stopped spinning.

Wade ignored her protests, his attention riveted on the man standing next to a dust-covered wagon advertising Hastings's Miraculous Tonic. His checkered pants, red vest, and top hat were better suited to showmanship than medicine.

"Dr. Hastings at your service," the man said in a voice that defied anyone to contradict the legitimacy of his claim.

While Wade's back was turned, Josie glanced around, trying to make sense of the scene around her. Dust still clung to the air, and she blinked to clear her vision.

The sight of the nearby river filled her with dismay. Glancing around herself, a feeling of desolation swept over her. Unless she was mistaken, this was the exact piece of property Ralph had dreamt of buying.

The cottonwood standing taller than all the others confirmed her suspicions. Ralph had carved their initials in the trunk of that very tree, thus marking the property as theirs even though they had no legal right to ownership.

The realization hit her like a fist. Could fate really be so unkind as to play such an awful trick on her? Of all the places she could have landed, why did it have to be this particular spot? Ralph had had such high regards for this piece of land. During their whirlwind courtship, he'd even brought her here for a picnic before the area had been snatched up by a land developer. On that long-ago day, Ralph had dropped to his knees and proposed marriage. After telling him yes, she would marry him, they took turns scratching the outline of their dream house in the soft soil with a stick. The large house would face the river and have ample bedrooms for all the children they planned on one day having.

Desperate to escape the overwhelming memories, she looked for her wagon. Spotting it, she groaned in dismay. It was tipped on its side, a back wheel spinning lazily in the breeze. But it was the remains of the hope chest that filled her with despair.

Oh, no! She crawled on hands and knees toward the pieces of scattered wood. The treasured family hope chest lay in ruins.

She heard Wade's voice behind her. "What the devil?" Long strides carried him to her side.

Before he could get a word out, she stood and shoved a pile of wood into his arms, then immediately dropped down to gather more broken pieces. "They'll kill me," she mumbled to herself. "They'll kill me."

"Who will kill you?" he asked, sounding mystified.

She gazed up at him. "Why, my family, of course." She reached for a piece of cedar lining. "It's ruined," she cried. "Ruined! Do you know what that means?"

Poor Cousin Brenda would be so disappointed. She wouldn't be the only one. So would Mama. To make matters worse, Amanda's speech wouldn't make it to the suffrage meeting in time.

"Do you know what this will do to democratic principles?" Josie moaned.

Brandon stared at her. "Democratic—" Without finishing his thought, he dropped the wood pieces and grabbed hold of her wrist. "Come on. We need to get you to a doctor. A *real* doctor."

She pulled her arm away. "I told you, I don't need a doctor."

Their gazes clashed. They might have continued glaring at each other had a man she recognized as Mr. Troop not strolled up, clapping his hands. He was smiling at her, for some odd reason. The fool man acted all friendly-like, as if he hadn't recently pulled his ads from her newspaper. The nerve!

Troop lifted a speaking trumpet to his mouth. "It's time to announce the winners," he yelled for the benefit of the waiting crowd.

Brandon's eyebrows shot up. "Did you say 'winners'?"

Mr. Troop lowered the speaking trumpet to his side. "That I did." The developer pushed his hat back with his free hand. "That is, unless you can prove full ownership of that pile of kindling." He indicated the pieces of wood scattered around Brandon's feet.

Brandon frowned. "What's that got to do with anything?"

Troop thumbed the lapel of his jacket with his one free hand. "When that wagon reeled out of control, some sort of wooden chest or trunk shot from it and landed on this here lot at the exact same moment you reached it. That makes the owner of this—" He pointed to the scraps of wood again. "—whatever it is, a winner. Lest my eyes were deceiving me, I'd say this here little lady—" He leveled his glance at Josie. "—won part of this land fair and square."

Kerrigan made a face. "How can you say she won it fair? She didn't stay on the road."

Mr. Troop shrugged. "Nothing in the rules said you had to. Anyone crazy enough to drive a wagon off the road and down a slope like that deserves to win."

Mrs. Mooney folded her arms across her ample chest. "But the rules did say the first one to reach the property won. Josie wasn't the first one to reach the property. Mr. Wade was."

Mrs. Cambridge concurred with a titter. "I saw him with my own eyes." She shot her very best chaperone glare at Josie.

Everyone started speaking at once, but the more people protested, the more Mr. Troop dug in his heels and insisted his decision was final. For her part, Josie had a hard time trying to make sense of it all. Her head was spinning and all she wanted was to go home.

Finally, Mr. Troop had had enough. "Quiet!" he yelled. "Like I said, Mrs. Johnson and Mr. Wade won the property fair and square. End of subject."

His announcement was met with more grumbles before people started moving away, some wandering down to the river's edge.

Josie was still puzzling over the 'fair and square' part when night fell upon her senses once again and the ground came up to meet her.

***

Josie opened her eyes and blinked. She was momentarily lost in a sea of roses before finally recognizing the wallpaper. This was her room. Her bed. The body sprawled upon the covers she wasn't so sure about.

Nor could she put a name to the white-haired man gently thumping on her chest. That was her chest, wasn't it?

The man straightened. "Ah, there you are."

Josie stirred and groaned. It seemed like every bone in her body was on fire. The last of the fog lifted, although the pounding in her head remained. Finally, she recalled the man's name: Dr. Stybeck. How could she have forgotten even for a second the name of the man who was not only the family doctor but had also attended her birth?

She tried sitting up. Someone had removed her shoes, but she was still dressed in her black crepe skirt and shirtwaist.

"Take it easy," the doctor said. Hands on her shoulders, he gently pressed her back against the pillow. "You have a concussion, but it doesn't appear to be too serious."

Mama's worried face hovered over his shoulder. "Is anything broken?"

"Not as far as I can tell," he assured her.

That was good to hear, but Josie would have felt a whole lot better had he not looked and sounded so serious when he said it.

Dr. Stybeck snapped his black leather bag shut. "Keep her comfortable and apply this to her bruises." He handed Mama a brown vial containing tincture of arnica. "With a couple of days of rest, she should be good as new."

Josie sincerely doubted that, but his assurances earned Mama's grateful smile.

After the doctor left, Mama undressed her and helped her into a linen nightgown. It was a slow, torturous ordeal. There wasn't a bone or muscle in her body that didn't hurt. Once back in bed—under the covers this time—Josie spent the rest of the day drifting in and out of sleep, her dreams marred by fragments of sights and sounds that ended up with her being caught beneath the pounding hooves of cattle. Such was the horror that she woke up each time in a cold sweat to a less frightening but still disturbing memory of being held in strong arms, her head cushioned against a firm, masculine chest. The vision seemed too real to be only a dream.

Mama appeared by her bedside throughout the day, regular as clockwork. She plied her with tea and wrapped warm towels around her bruised legs.

"Mama, how did I get here?" Josie asked during one such visit.

Mama straightened the blankets on the bed. "How did you get here?"

"Who brought me to the house?"

Mama thought for a moment. "I believe his name was Dr. Hastings."

"Hastings?" Josie closed her eyes. A vision of red plaid trousers and a tall silk hat flashed through her head. The oddly dressed man conflicted with the memory of strong arms and a bracing masculine fragrance.

"Yes," Mama said with a nod. "He drove you home in the back of his wagon. Mr. Wade carried you inside."

At mention of Wade's name, Josie's eyes popped open. "Mr. Wade did that?"

"Yes, and he waited in the parlor until he knew you were all right."

Josie bit her lip. Was it possible that those strong heavenly arms she couldn't stop thinking about belonged to Brandon Wade? She squeezed her eyes tight.

Oh, please, please, please don't let it be so.

＊＊＊

Amanda stopped by the house later that afternoon. If she was upset that her speech wouldn't make it to the convention, she did her best to hide it.

"The important thing is that you're all right," she said, patting Josie's hand. "My speech will be just as relevant at the next convention."

No sooner had she left than Meg arrived and fussed over her like an old mother hen. "I don't understand." She touched her palm to Josie's forehead as if to check for fever. "I thought you were going to Austin."

"That's exactly where I was heading."

Meg withdrew her hand. "But then what were you doing in that race?"

Josie stared at Meg in confusion. A race? What was her sister thinking? "I wasn't in a race. I was trying to outrun a cattle stampede."

Meg gasped and her hand flew to her chest. "There was a stampede?"

"No, no, I just thought there was." Josie rubbed her forehead. Her head still hurt and her thoughts were disjointed, but it was obvious from Meg's face that Josie owed her an explanation.

"When I lived in Arizona, there was a terrible brush fire and it started a cattle stampede." Her mind drifted back in time for a moment before she could refocus her thoughts. "It was a miracle Ralph and I escaped alive. Unfortunately, one of our neighbors wasn't so lucky."

The poor man had been trampled to death, leaving behind four small children and a heartbroken widow. Josie shuddered at the memory.

"This morning, when I saw the cloud of dust, I was convinced it was cattle, and I tried to get away."

Meg's eyes softened. "Oh, you poor, poor thing."

Josie suddenly thought of her mare. "Oh, no, Maizie!"

"Don't worry." Meg reached for Josie's hand. "T-Bone found her and brought her home. She's fine. And Grant has already checked the wagon. He says repairs shouldn't take him but a day or two."

"He didn't have to do that," Josie said. Her brother-in-law was in much demand as an attorney and had little free time.

"It was Grant's choice to take care of it," Meg said. "So, see? You have nothing to worry about."

"Except for the hope chest," Josie said with a groan. "Mama will have a fit."

Meg squeezed Josie's hand between her own. "We'll worry about that later. Right now, the only thing you need to think about is resting."

Josie grimaced at the thought. Who had time to rest? Certainly not her; she had a newspaper to run. "Don't say a word to Mama. You know how she feels about that chest."

"My lips are sealed," Meg said. "Now stop worrying. Mr. Woodman is an expert. Remember when Amanda accidentally shot it? Not once, but twice. And then there was that fire. He made the hope chest look good as new and will do so again. I know he will."

Josie covered her face with her hands. "Only if he's a magician." She didn't even know the location of the wood pieces.

"Right now, you simply must tell me how you managed to win that riverfront property. Everyone's talking about it."

Josie regarded Meg over her fingertips before dropping her hands away from her face. "What are you talking about? What property?"

Meg gave her a wide-eyed stare. "Why, the property you won with Mr. Wade, of course."

Josie gazed at her sister in dismay. Either the heat had affected Meg's brain, or things had just gotten a whole lot more complicated.

***

After leaving the Lockwood house, Wade had ridden into town. The doctor had assured him that Josie would be good as new with some rest. Still, he'd been reluctant to leave.

He hadn't been able to believe his eyes when he saw her drive the wagon over the side of the road and down that dangerous precipice. The crazy woman. What had she been thinking? She could have been killed.

Reaching his office, he dismounted and tied his horse to the hitching rail. With a glance at the *Gazette* office across the street, he shook his head and stomped up the steps to the boardwalk.

Booker greeted him as he entered the office. "Congratulations, Chief. Heard you won the big prize."

Wade tossed his hat on a wall peg and sat at his desk. "Thanks, Booker. Have you seen my daughter?"

"No, sir." Booker looked uncertain. "You don't seem all that happy. Is it 'cause of the lady editor? Heard you two have to share the prize."

"That's still to be determined. Right now, Mrs. Johnson is recovering from an injury to her head."

The door flew open and his daughter stepped into the office looking all pink cheeked and out of breath.

Brandon nodded. "Ah, there you are. I was wondering where you were."

"Hello, Mr. Booker," Haley said before turning eyes rounded with appeal to her father.
"Papa, can I ride Thunder? Oh, please, please say yes."

Brandon tapped the edge of his desk with a pencil. "Haley, we've gone through this a dozen times."

"You know I'm a good rider."

"That's not the point. I have to keep my horse close. If a news story breaks, I may have to go somewhere in a hurry."

"It's Saturday. Nothing important ever happens on Saturday."

Brandon laughed and tossed his pencil down. "Is that so? Do you agree with that, Booker?"

Booker grinned and held up the palms of his hands. "Don't ask me. I'm just an innocent bystander."

"So, can I? Papa, please."

Brandon felt himself wavering. "What's going on? Why do you need to ride Thunder today?"

"It's hot, and me and the others want to go swimming. My friend Susie is gonna show me where the swimming hole is."

Brandon felt a sense of gratitude that his daughter was starting to fit in and make friends. For that reason, he gave a reluctant nod. "All right." He glanced at his watch. "But I want you back by three o'clock."

"Oh, Papa, thank you." Haley threw her arms around his neck and squeezed him before rushing away. A moment later he watched her mount his horse and ride away. Her slight body looked almost too small to be perched upon such a large animal, but she was a good little rider. He'd worked hours to make sure of that, and his horse was well trained. Still, he couldn't help but worry.

Chapter 9

Upon hearing a drowning man cry for help, Mr. Winkelman handed his coat containing a roll of banknotes to an obliging fisherman. Thanks to Mr. Winkelman's quick action, the drowning man was saved, but the obliging fisherman hasn't been heard from since. —Two-Time Gazette

First thing that Monday morning, Josie headed straight for Mr. Troop's office, her parasol propped open. During the night, it had rain hard enough to muddy the streets, but not hard enough to end the drought. Now the sky was clear. Despite the early morning hour, it was already uncomfortably hot, and the humid air felt heavy as a wet blanket.

Her shoulders were still sore, and her legs bruised, but most of the swelling on the back of her head was gone, and it only hurt if she turned a certain way or moved too quickly. Her brain was now functioning more clearly, and her memory had returned. This was both a good and a bad thing, for she now had to set things right again.

The developer had sent a message asking her to join him and Mr. Wade at his office first thing that morning to sign papers. Of all the crazy things, she'd been named a winner in a contest she hadn't even entered. A terrible misunderstanding had occurred, and she hoped to straighten out the mess before Mr. Wade arrived.

Wherever she went people commented on the race and the thrilling conclusion, which had ended with her concussion. The bank president's wife seemed to speak for everyone when she proclaimed that "Since the winners are the editors of two competitive newspapers, fireworks are bound to follow." Her prediction was the talk of the town.

Any protests on Josie's part fell on deaf ears. She was accused of being too much of a lady to own up to her amazing accomplishment.

Josie hated disappointing everyone, but there would be no fireworks. Mr. Wade had won the race fair and square. She couldn't in good conscience accept property she had no earthly right to.

Admittedly, she was tempted to claim ownership, and *that* she wasn't proud of. If only the prize in question wasn't the piece of land Ralph had loved and dreamed of one day owning.

The last thought almost made her stumble on the boardwalk. Breathing hard, she paused for a moment and tried to swallow the lump in her throat. Such dreams they'd had—none of which had come true.

Refusing the prize was the right thing to do. Still, it pained her more than words could say. How she hated the thought of turning over Ralph's dream lot to the man who had nearly bankrupted her and who might still do exactly that. With this burning thought in mind she snapped her parasol shut. Tucking it under her arm, she burst through the door of the land office with such force Mr. Troop practically jumped out of his skin.

Recovering quickly, he shot up from his desk and greeted her like a long-lost relative. One would never guess that this was the same man who had only a few short weeks ago yanked all his scheduled advertisements from her paper.

"Ah, Mrs. Johnson. Sit down. Sit down. As soon as Mr. Wade arrives, we'll get started. Would you care for some coffee or tea?"

"No, thank you," she said. Retrieving her hand from his strong clasp, she sat and waited for him to do likewise. "I came to tell you that there's been a . . . grave misunderstanding."

Troop's eyebrows rose like hot-air balloons. "A misunderstanding, you say?"

"Yes." She placed her parasol across her lap and pulled off her gloves. "You see, I was on the way to Austin and—"

The door flung open and in stepped Mr. Wade. Meeting his gaze, her heart sank. She had hoped to finish her business and leave before his arrival. The last thing she wanted was to see him gloat upon learning he was the lone winner.

Troop jumped up and enthusiastically greeted him—but not before checking his watch. The man's warmth was as thin as a penny.

Her mind suddenly went blank and she momentarily forgot why she was there. If only she could keep from recalling the memory of Brandon Wade's arms around her, or the feel of her head against his manly chest . . .

Realizing with a start that her gaze had followed her thoughts, her cheeks flared.

Any hope that Wade had failed to notice her wayward glance was dispelled by the look of amusement that flashed across his face. "Mrs. Johnson," he said, pulling off his hat. "I trust you're feelin' better."

"Yes, thank you," she said, forcing a cordial tone. His concern seemed genuine, and he had taken care of her following the accident. For that she was grateful. "I understand you were kind enough to see me safely home."

"I'm sure you would have done the same for me," he said, then frowned. "Or maybe not."

She afforded him her brightest smile. "We'll never know, will we?"

Troop cleared his throat, drawing their attention away from each other. "Now that you're both here, we can take care of business and be done with it." He picked up two legal documents and placed them side by side on the edge of his desk. "The race was a complete success," he gushed. "I've already sold half the properties."

"I'm not surprised," Wade said, seating himself on the chair next to hers. "That's prime land." With a sideways glance at her, he picked up the document closest to him and proceeded to study it.

Playing for time, Josie reached for the second document, forcing herself to breathe. She had intended to explain the situation to Mr. Troop in private. Had she not suffered a concussion and been thinking right, she would have straightened out the confusion at once. At her mother's insistence, she'd been forced to stay in bed for most of the weekend. Unfortunately, this was her first opportunity to set matters straight.

She steeled herself. "You can remove my name from the deed," she said. "The property is yours, Mr. Wade."

Wade dropped the paperwork onto the desk. "You're giving up the land, just like that?" he asked, incredulous.

"I have no need for the lot and splitting it will only ruin it."

He gazed at her a moment before responding. "Mrs. Johnson's right," he finally drawled. He addressed Troop, but his eyes never left hers. "Splitting the lot *will* ruin it."

"I don't agree," Troop said, reaching into a desk drawer for a map. "The lots are long and narrow. That's so that as many lots as possible front the river." He spread the map across the desk and stabbed the center of it with his forefinger. "The most logical way would be to split it width-wise. With some careful planning, the rear lot would still have a view of the river."

Josie stared at the map. The thought of Mr. Wade building a house on the very spot where Ralph had proposed marriage near broke her heart. She felt dizzy, but whether from grief, the heat, or her head injury she couldn't say.

Wade examined the layout, then shook his head. "If we divided it here," he said, pointing with his finger, "it would leave the back lot with no access to the river, except through someone else's property. And the front lot would have no access to the road. The only way to reach the road would be to trespass."

Troop looked at the map. "That's true," he admitted. "I didn't expect the race to end in a tie." His gaze traveled from one to the other and his smile faded. "I'm sure the two of you can work out the details."

Brandon turned to her. "Perhaps you'd be willing to sell your half to me."

Her thoughts having drifted back to Ralph and the day of the picnic, it took a moment to realize that Brandon had directed his comments to her. "T-that won't be necessary," she stammered. "You see, the lot rightfully—"

Troop rudely interrupted. "If you will look at the contract, you'll see that the winner—or, in this case, winners—are not allowed to sell the property for one full year or until all properties are sold. Whichever comes first. I don't want to have to compete with other sales."

Brandon's expression stilled and grew dark. "Are you saying I can't buy Mrs. Johnson's half?" His look suggested that had been his plan all along.

Troop shrugged. "Sorry." His gaze slid between them like a fox measuring the distance to the hen house. "Do you need time to discuss how you wish to divide the land among yourselves?" he asked, though his tapping fingers stated he was impatient to get their business over with. No money could be made here.

"That won't be necessary." She and Wade spoke in unison.

She lifted her chin and tried not to think of the land as Ralph's. Just as she tried not to think of the children, she and Ralph had planned on having. How could a marriage that seemed so perfect leave behind so many broken dreams?

She clenched her hands. "The lot should not be divided, and it won't be!"

"I quite agree." Wade rose and replaced his wide-brimmed hat. "Dividing the property makes it virtually worthless. And since I'm an all or nothing type of guy, I hand over my half to Mrs. Johnson. At least one of us will benefit."

Josie shot to her feet with such force her parasol flew off her lap. "Oh, no! You don't understand. The property is yours. All of it."

Wade bent over to retrieve her parasol. Straightening, he handed it to her. "No, no, that wouldn't be right. Contrary to what you might think, I didn't purposely set out to ruin you or your newspaper. Please accept my half by way of apology." Without another word, he stalked to the door.

"Wait! You don't understand." She started after him, but her skirt snagged on the chair. By the time she'd worked it free and rushed to the door, Mr. Wade had already mounted his horse and started riding away.

Mr. Troop glanced at his watch. "It appears that you are now the sole owner of a prime piece of land. If you would just sign on the line."

"I'm sorry. I can't. Ralph's property— I mean . . . The prize should go to Mr. Wade. Please see that he gets it." She turned to leave.

"Since both you and Mr. Wade have refused to take ownership, in all fairness I will have to contact Pepper— eh, Mr. Kerrigan."

Her hand froze on the doorknob for a split second before she whirled about. "Whatever for?"

"He came in second."

"Pepper came in second?" That despicable man?

He nodded. "Right after you and Wade."

"That man ran me off the road."

Mr. Troop looked startled. "I'm sure it was an accident."

"Accident, my—" She thought for a moment before storming back to his desk. Tossing her parasol to the side, she grabbed the pen. "Never mind. I'll sign."

Pepper would get his dirty hands on Ralph's property over her dead body.

***

Josie stood at the window staring across the street at the office of the *Lone Star Press*.

For three days she'd debated what to do. That particular property would always hold a special place in her heart. And the thought of turning the parcel of land over to her nemesis made her shudder. But she couldn't in good conscience keep a prize she hadn't honestly won. What else could she do but turn the land over to its rightful owner?

That wasn't the only reason for her dilemma. She didn't want anyone feeling sorry for her, and that went double for Brandon Wade. Would he have suggested turning over the deed so willingly had he not pitied her? She doubted it.

She was still debating how to handle the situation when the town carpenter, Mr. Woodman, entered the office, bringing with him the smell of sawdust and cedar.

"'Morning, Josie."

"'Morning, Mr. Woodman," she said, surprised to see him so soon. While she was recovering, Hank had driven horse and wagon out to the river to retrieve the broken pieces of the hope chest and deliver them to the woodshop for her. "Is there a problem?"

He closed the door behind him and pulled off his felt hat. Dressed in overalls, his skin was the color of old oak. "I tried putting your chest back together, but there's a piece missing. The lid."

Her heart sank. "Oh, no." The lid contained the carving of the ship that had brought her grandparents to America.

"I can make up a piece, but it won't have all that fancy engraving."

The idea made her cringe. The hope chest wouldn't be the same without the original lid. The carved ship was a vital part of family history. No substitute would do. "I'll drive out to the river and see if I can find the missing piece."

Nodding, he turned to leave, then paused, his hand on the doorknob as he cast a look over his shoulder. "Never saw a piece of furniture go through so many repairs. I thought your sister was rough with it, but at least she managed to keep the chest in one piece."

Josie sighed. The hope chest that had once harbored her dreams as a young bride now mirrored the pieces of her broken heart.

Chapter 10

Mr. Walters, whose attempted suicides failed when his gun jammed, the rope broke, and the "poison" he drank turned out to be castor oil, announced that he's now in the life insurance business.—Two-Time Gazette

No sooner had Woodman left her office than Hank sat himself down in the chair in front of her desk and handed her a sheet of paper. Never had she seen him look so earnest.

"What do you think?" he asked.

She read what he'd written: *Wanted: a wife. A dull but loyal man, slow of speech but not wit, wishes to share his life with the right woman. If interested, contact the paper.*

Josie raised her eyebrows. She hadn't really thought him serious about advertising for a wife.

"Is this wise? I mean . . . with your job in the air."

He shrugged. "A woman who'll take a chance on an unemployed man would have to be very special."

"Or dumb," she said and laughed. When he didn't share her humor, she grew serious. "For your information, I don't think you're dull."

"Would 'boring' be a wetter bord?"

"'Boring'? No. You need to describe yourself in a more appealing way. Women like men who are intelligent and funny and—" A vision of Brandon popped into her head, rattling her for a moment. "And . . . and . . ."

Hank's brow creased. "I don't want to make myself bound—sound—better than I am."

"But you *are* intelligent," she insisted. "Or were before you decided to advertise for a wife." She couldn't help but tease him and was disappointed when the hoped-for smile failed to materialize.

"Maybe I was before the war, but when I took that bullet, it shot a piece of my thinking cap clear off my noggin'."

Josie sympathized. The things most people took for granted posed a challenge for him. It would indeed take a special woman to see his fine qualities and to look past his speech difficulties.

"You need to focus on your good points. I like that you mentioned loyalty." He was the most loyal person she knew. "I would also describe you as kind, considerate, and dependable."

"I don't know, Josie," he said in that slow way of his. "I don't want to sound like I'm braggin'."

"Telling the truth isn't bragging," she said and then clamped down on her jaw. She was a fine one to talk. She still hadn't told Mr. Wade the truth about lot eleven. What earthly right did she have giving anyone advice on honesty?

***

Josie woke early the next morning intent upon riding to the river and retrieving the missing piece of the hope chest before going to the office. After her morning ablutions, she dressed and ducked out of the house without so much as a cup of coffee and saddled her horse. Less than an hour later she reached lot eleven and dismounted.

It was a perfect day, though it felt more like July or August than May. The blue sky was the same shade as the carpet of bluebells at her feet. The spring-fed river coiled around a grove of spindly cypresses and limestone cliffs. The water sparkled beneath the morning sun like a diamond necklace tossed carelessly upon a lady's dressing table.

It was no wonder that so many people wanted this particular lot. It sickened her to think that by tomorrow it would belong to Mr. Wade. Sometimes she hated the part of her that insisted upon doing the right thing.

After tethering Maizie to a stake, she began the search for the missing lid, checking every tall clump of grass and prickly bush. With the precision of a Navajo weaver she walked back and forth, looking under or behind everything in her path.

Careful to watch for snakes, she turned over a fallen log, then stopped to examine the cold ashes of a campfire. Her heart sank. Hoboes were known to roam the area. It was possible that the chest lid had been used as firewood. Hoping that wasn't the case, she continued the search.

When she reached the sprawling cottonwood of her memories, she stopped and ran her finger over the heart Ralph had carved onto the trunk with their initials. Grief squeezed her chest like a too tight corset. That's when the tears came—a real toad-floating gully gusher. The sound of water rushing over rocks mingled with her sobs as she lowered herself to the ground. The swift current carried away leaves and other debris but not her grief.

It wasn't only her husband that brought her to bended knee, but also the thought of lost dreams and a scary future. What would she do if she lost the newspaper? She was too proud to depend on Papa's generosity and had hoped to be totally independent by now. But what other options did she have?

She allowed herself a good ten-minute, soul-wrenching cry before she rose, wet eyed and emotionally drained. It was time to stop feeling sorry for herself and get back to work. She gave her head an emphatic nod. If there was any way to save her newspaper, she would find it. Yes, indeed she would!

With new resolve, she picked up her pace and forced herself to concentrate on the purpose of her visit. The sooner she accomplished her mission, the sooner she could leave the memory of shattered dreams behind.

She found a piece of wood buried in the tall grass. A black stain covered one corner of the plank, and she wiped the gooey sludge off with a handkerchief. But the wood wasn't part of the hope chest, and her heart sank. She tossed it aside and kept looking but came up empty.

Fearing another deluge of tears, Josie headed down to the river, where she lowered herself to the ground to pull off shoes and stockings. That done, she walked barefooted down the slight incline to the river's edge, hiked up her skirts, and stepped into a pool of cool, clear water. Lifting her gaze to the sky, she let the water whirl around her ankles and carry her sorrows downstream.

She had just bent to lower a cupped hand into the river's depths and splash water onto her heated face when the sound of horse's hooves reached her. A male voice called out. "Hello, there."

Recognizing the horsemen as Pepper, she straightened and lowered the hem of her skirt to just above the water's surface. Her pale white feet were still visible, but nothing could be done about that.

Pepper rode to the water's edge and reined in his horse. His gaze told her he didn't miss a thing, and that included her bare feet. Feeling unduly exposed, she glared at him. A gentleman he was not.

"Congratulations on winning the race," he said.

"An apology would be more in order!" she snapped.

The brim of his wide hat shaded his eyes, but not the grim set of his mouth. "An apology? For what?"

"Don't act so innocent. You ran me off the road. You know you did. I could have been killed."

He discounted her accusations with a wave of his hand. "That was an accident. I would never do anything so . . . unsportsmanlike. I simply lost control of my rig."

She studied him with narrowed eyes. Was it possible he was telling the truth? Everything had happened so fast, and she had been in a frightful state. Maybe she had misread his intent. Even now she had difficulty recalling the full details of that day. According to Dr. Stybeck, loss of memory and confusion wasn't that unusual following a concussion.

Pepper leaned forward in his saddle and rested an arm on the horn. "I planned on stopping by the *Gazette* later today, but you saved me the trouble. Troop told me that you're now the sole owner of this fine piece of land. I'm prepared to make you an offer."

She stared at him; not sure she'd heard right. "Why would you do such a thing?" she asked. "You can purchase other lots."

"Ah, yes, that's true." Sitting upright, he ran a finger across his mustache. "But purchasing from Troop would cost an arm and a leg. Since you won the land, I thought you'd be willing to accept a more, shall we say, reasonable offer? Perhaps even half of what Troop is asking."

At half the price, he would be getting a bargain, but it would still add up to a handsome sum. "What makes you think—" She almost said, "Ralph's lot." "—this property is for sale?"

His goatee twitched. "I imagine it's not easy running a business without a husband. Especially now that Two-Time has *two* papers. I dare say you would benefit from some . . . additional capital. You could probably use some new equipment and maybe even an extra employee or two. Under the circumstances, I would say you'll find my offer quite generous."

Just thinking of what she could do with so much money was tempting. She could finally pay Hank what he deserved and buy a new printer to replace the old one. She could even hire enough staff to go twice weekly. That would give Mr. Wade a run for his money. Now wouldn't that be something?

He lifted his hat and wiped an arm across his forehead. "So, what do you say?"

"I'm forbidden by contract to sell the land for a year."

His smile failed to reach his eyes. "I'm sure we can work around that little detail." He replaced his hat. "Our business arrangement would just be between you and me. No one else need know about it. I'll make no improvements to the land until the year is up."

"There's just one little problem," she said. "The property is not for sale." It wasn't rightfully hers to sell. Even if it were, she wouldn't sell it to the likes of him. She still wasn't convinced he hadn't purposely tried to run her off the road. "Good day, Mr. Kerrigan."

"If you change your mind—"

"I won't."

He looked about to say something more, but instead raked her over with glittering eyes, his mouth a straight, thin line. Finally, tugging on the reins with a click of his tongue, he rode away. She watched him until he vanished beyond the trees, then stepped out of the water, her feet sinking into the soft soil. Despite the heat of the sun, gooseflesh traveled up her arms.

On the way back to her office, she stopped at Mr. Woodman's carpentry shop to tell him she couldn't find the missing part of the hope chest. Unfortunately, the shop was located next to the saddle shop Ralph had once owned. The new owner hadn't bothered to change the window, and the saddle on display had been made by Ralph's own hands.

Fearing another wave of grief to unravel her, she yanked her gaze away and dismounted, tethering her horse to the hitching post. Somehow, she would have to break the news to Mama that the beloved family heirloom was ruined and couldn't be repaired. She groaned at the thought. Poor Mama.

Poor her. The day she'd carved her initials into the side of the hope chest she'd still believed in "happily ever after," just like in those fairy tales she'd read as a child. Little did she know "happily ever after" would last for such a short time.

Oh, Ralph. How she missed him!

Usually a good cry like the one by the river made her feel better, but today the benefits had been short lived. Now depression hung over her like a thunder cloud, and she could hardly catch her breath for the lump in her chest.

"How come you look so sad?"

Josie turned toward the young, thin voice. She'd been so deep in thought she'd failed to notice the little girl Haley on the boardwalk, holding what looked like a paper sack of penny candy.

Irritated at being caught feeling sorry for herself, by a child no less, Josie forced a smile and drew her hands away from her saddle. "I was just . . . thinking of someone I loved very much."

"Was it your ma or pa?"

"No, actually, he was my husband." Josie swallowed the prickle in her throat and, not wishing to upset Haley, blinked back the threatening tears.

"Is he dead?"

Ah, the bluntness of children. Family and friends had all avoided saying the *D* word. Instead, they referred to Ralph's passing as a journey or departure, as if death was only temporary. It was as if they thought that substituting some prettified euphemism would soften the reality. It did not.

"Yes. Yes, he is," Josie said.

"Maybe he knows my mother in heaven."

Josie studied the child. Today she was dressed in a pretty pink gingham dress with a ruffled hemline and sleeves. Her hair fell to her shoulders in soft yellow curls and was tied with a pink satin bow.

"Is . . . is that where your mother is?"

Haley gave a solemn nod. "That's where all good people go when they die."

Josie inhaled, and something caught in her chest. At a loss for words, she felt a strong sense of compassion stir inside. It was hard enough dealing with loss as an adult. How much harder it must be for a child, especially one as young as this.

"I'm so sorry. I'm sure you must miss your mother very much."

Haley didn't look motherless, at least not in the conventional sense. Her clothes were of good quality and her long blond hair well groomed. Her nails were neatly trimmed, and her boots polished to a shine.

"I guess you miss your husband too."

"Yes, yes, I do. Very much."

"Do you have a picture of him?" the girl asked.

"What?"

"A picture?"

Josie nodded. No one had ever before asked to see a picture of Ralph. "I do." She reached for the heart-shaped locket at her neck. "Do you want to see it."

"Uh-huh."

Josie undid the clasp and opened the locket, revealing a miniature photograph. Haley stepped to the edge of the boardwalk for a closer look.

"That picture's really small."

"That's so I can keep it close to my heart." Josie snapped the locket shut. "Do you have a photograph of your mother?"

Haley shook her head. "Mama didn't like having her photograph taken. But I drew a picture of her."

"That's good," Josie said. "I wish I could draw. Maybe one day you'll let me see the picture you drew of your mother."

Haley held out the sack in her hand. "Want a peppermint candy? It'll make you feel better."

This time Josie's smile came unbidden. For some odd reason, she felt better already. Maybe it was because she didn't feel so alone in her loss. "Then in that case, I guess I better take one." She reached into the offered sack and pulled out a red-and-white candy stick. "Thank you."

"I gotta go," Haley said. "My friend Susie is having a party. It's her birthday." With that she waved good-bye and skipped along the boardwalk in a whirl of ribbons and lace.

Josie sighed. Oh, to have the resilience of a child whose moods could shift as quickly as the wind. Saddened to see Haley go, Josie watched her until she was out of sight.

Chapter 11

Cattle rustler Mr. Levingston sent a dispatch from the Huntsville prison, which he says has been greatly improved since his last visit. He contemplates staying ten years, if not longer.

—Two-Time Gazette

Moments later, Josie left the carpentry shop and rode straight home to break the news to her mother. Mr. Woodman had agreed to make a new lid for the hope chest. It would be plain without any carvings, but at least the wooden sides with grandfather's handiwork could still be salvaged.

Mama took the news hard. With a cluck of dismay, her hand flew to her mouth. "Oh, no!"

"I'm so sorry, Mama. Hank and I both searched for the piece. I'm afraid it might have been used as firewood." Josie explained what Mr. Woodman planned to do.

"The ship . . ." Mama whispered.

Josie grimaced. That ship had signified new beginnings. Not only for her grandparents but also for the brides who had carved their initials into the fine-grained wood. "I know, Mama. I know. Will you ever forgive me?"

Her mother inhaled deeply, and her expression softened. "I don't blame you, pet. It was an accident. I'm just grateful that you weren't more seriously injured when your wagon overturned."

Josie left the house with a heavy heart and headed for her office. Mama was being kind, as usual, but it only made Josie feel worse. Papa's rants were less guilt inducing than Mama's serene acceptance. Her mother might not blame her, but Josie blamed herself.

Moments later she reined in her horse and blinked. A long line stretched from the front of the *Gazette* office all the way to the end of the block. It wasn't until she saw people leaving with newspapers tucked beneath their arms that she dared believe her eyes.

The *Two-Time Gazette* was selling like hotcakes!

She'd hoped her handbills announcing Miss Bubbles' reward would solicit interest, but never had she imagined anything like this—especially that Miss Bubbles' advertisement would be an answer to prayer.

Spirits soaring, she quickly dismounted and tied Maizie to the hitching post. Rushing up the steps to the boardwalk, she greeted her customers with a smile. She could hardly contain her excitement as she stepped into the office.

"Good morning, Hank."

He looked up from his desk with a wide smile. "'Morning, Josie."

"I hoped the generous reward would sell papers, but I had no idea it would sell this many."

His grin widened. "Yeah, well your editorial didn't hurt, either. It's got beople puzzing like a bunch of crazed bees."

Josie felt a warm glow inside. "Really?" She was right. People really did appreciate good journalism. It was just a matter of getting the *Gazette* back into readers' hands. Miss Bubbles' reward had done that in spades.

She glanced across the street at her competitor's office. *Take that, Brand*— She corrected herself. *Mr. Wade.*

"It's time we did something about the elderly people who can no longer take care of themselves," she said. "People like Mr. Pendergrass deserve better than being locked up in an insane asylum."

A puzzled frown crossed Hank's face. "Oh, that's not what's got everyone talking. It's the editorial you wrote calling Mr. Wade despicable."

Her breath caught in her lungs. "What are you talking about? I called him no such thing." At least not in print.

Hank looked confused. "Sure, you did. I printed it just exactly as you wrote it." Shuffling the papers on his desk, he pulled one out and showed her. It was the editorial that Mr. Wade had typed himself.

She slapped her forehead with the palm of her hand and groaned. "Oh, no!" She could have sworn she'd tossed that awful piece in the wastebasket where it belonged. "I didn't write that. Mr. Wade did."

Hank's eyes nearly popped out of his head. "Wade called himself those awful names?" He scoffed. "Sounds like I'm not the only one with a hole in my head."

Before she could explain, the door flew open and a male voice called, "Can we have more papers out here?"

Standing, Hank shrugged and picked up a stack tied with twine. "At the rate we're pelling sapers, we're gonna have to go back to press."

Josie's gaze traveled through the open door. Across the street, Mr. Wade leaned against a post, arms crossed, watching the line in front of her office. His face was lost in shadow, but she could pretty much guess at his smug expression.

"I'll be back," she called to Hank.

She stepped outside and, ignoring the line of people still waiting to make a purchase, marched down the boardwalk steps to the street, careful to sidestep a pile of fresh manure. Wade moved away from the post. He waited for traffic to clear before meeting her halfway.

Standing in the middle of Main Street, he doffed his hat. "Mrs. Johnson. I see our little plan worked."

Eyes flashing, she planted her hands at her waist. "*Your* plan. It was never mine."

He shrugged. "I hate taking *all* the credit, but if you insist."

A farmer in a horse and wagon raised his fist. "If you two don't stop holdin' up traffic, I'll—"

Josie cut him off with a raised voice. "I never meant for that awful piece to be printed. It was a mistake."

A look of amusement crossed Wade's face. "If that's true, you have to admit it was a most fortuitous mistake. You're now back in business. Just wait till you see how I plan to respond to the awful things you said about me."

"Awful things you said about yourself, you mean."

"Granted. But you have to admit, you thought them. You were just too much of a lady to put them on paper, so I saved you the trouble."

"I assure you that the words you wrote are mild compared to what is going through my head. But I refuse to be a party to such childish games." She turned and stalked away, dodging the hotel omnibus.

"You'll be sorry," he called after her.

***

On Saturday Josie arrived at the office to find yet another line stretched along the boardwalk. Never had she witnessed such a demand for her paper. She only wished that it was her editorial, and not Mr. Wade's, that had gotten folks abuzz.

Hank had run off so many extra copies that they ran out of paper. She'd telegraphed her distributor for more, but it wouldn't arrive on the train until Tuesday.

Oddly enough, this morning no men stood in line, only women. Odder still, some were dressed in their Sunday-go-to-meeting best.

At the head of the line was Josie's former schoolteacher, Miss Read. She had been forced to retire a few years ago to take care of her ailing father and now tutored. She had never married, but that was only because her fiancé died during the War Between the States.

Josie hugged her. "I'm sorry, I believe we're all out of newspapers."

"Oh, I'm not here for a newspaper," Miss Read said. "I'm here about this." Her hat's white feathers quivered as she dug into her purse and pulled out a newspaper clipping.

Josie blinked. It was Hank's advertisement for a wife. "You're here because of that?"

"That's why I'm here too," the second woman in line said, glaring at her nearest competitor. The stuffed blackbird on her hat quivered with each shake of the woman's head.

"Me too," admitted a third person, the only woman in view sporting a sensible bonnet.

Josie was dumbfounded. Her gaze stretched the length of the line. There had to be at least fifty women there. Times were a-changing, but was this how husbands were found these days?   Was this how the West was wed?

Miss Read lowered her voice. "I figured if he's as dull as he claims, he'll find me interesting." The former schoolmarm then did something totally out of character: she blushed, giving Josie a glimpse of the girl, she must have been before fate changed the course of her life.

Josie squeezed Miss Read's hand. "Any man who takes the time to get to know you would find you interesting."

Miss Read had been a strict teacher, but she'd expected the best from her students and had generally gotten it. Josie owed her own writing skills to Miss Read, and for that she would always be grateful.

"Good luck," she whispered for her former teacher's ears only. The woman deserved to find happiness. Hank did, too, but whether the two were right for each other was anyone's guess.

Josie stepped inside and found Hank interviewing a birdlike woman who looked old enough to be his mother.

"I'm a great cook," the woman was saying without modesty. "You won't find better. Nor would you find a lovelier house than the one I keep."

"Nothing like a hovely louse," Hank said politely, though the look he cast in Josie's direction was an obvious plea for help.

The woman stood. "*Harrumph!* I have you know, there are no louses in my house. Hovely or otherwise!" With that she stormed out of the office.

Covering her mouth to stifle a laugh, Josie sat at her desk. Hank hadn't known what he was getting himself into, that's for sure.

The interviews continued all morning. Some women cast one look at Hank and left without a word. One took offense at him calling her "oppressive" instead of "impressive." At the end, Hank had five prospects who looked promising, one of which was her old schoolteacher.

"Whatever happened to meeting someone at a barn dance?" Josie asked. That was where she'd met Ralph. Interviews were for jobs, not for striking up love relationships.

Hank shrugged. "Did you see anyone here likely to attend a dance, except as a chaperone?" he asked.

He had a point. Even Hank stayed away from any social gatherings that might bring attention to his injured foot.

"I just feel bad for all the women you'll have to turn down."

Hank knitted his eyebrows. "What about me? I got durned town plenty. Some women took one look at me and didn't even bother following through with an interview."

"Maybe you should have been more explicit regarding age," she said. Half the women who had showed up were either too young or too old.

She gazed at him thoughtfully as an idea began to form in her head. What if . . . A thrill of excitement coursed through her. Never before had the *Gazette* acted as a matrimonial service, but if a single advertisement created this much interest, what would several ads do?

"The handbills I distributed through town sold papers, but readers responded to your ad."

Hank nodded in agreement. "Yeah, but they're talking about your editorial."

She sighed. "*Wade's* editorial, you mean." The success of that week's paper would be a tough act to follow, but she was never one to rest on her laurels, and she wasn't about to start now.

"What do you think about selling ads to people wishing to wed?" She'd heard about the many marriage brokers that had sprung up in recent years, but most were based nationally and required long-distance courtships. Hers would be local and would be a boon to people like Hank who didn't feel comfortable in social settings.

She began a mental note of the single people she knew who might be interested. "If we sell enough ads, that will make up for the advertisers we've lost."

Hank pursed his lips. "Do you think it will work?"

She glanced around the office. Not a single copy of that week's newspaper remained. "What I think is that we're back in business."

She then did something that no self-respecting widow would do she picked up the hem of her skirt and before Hank's startled eyes danced a little jig. Brandon Wade had his way of gaining readers and she had hers. Oh, yes, indeed she did!

***

The following Tuesday she walked into her office and found Brandon pecking away on her type-writing machine. Once again, she was reminded of the unfinished business with lot eleven. She'd been so busy forging ahead with her idea of selling matrimonial ads, she'd plumb forgotten about the deed tucked into the drawer of her desk.

"What are you doing?" she demanded.

For answer he ripped a sheet of paper from the carriage and handed it to her. "A rebuttal to my editorial against establishing an old-folks home."

"You're against it?" she asked, more than a little shocked. Surely someone with his intelligence would see the need for such a place. "Why?"

He stood and faced her. "As I wrote for this week's paper, such homes are a disgrace. The residents are called *inmates* and forced to wear uniforms. Old people are often abused and fed food unfit even for hogs. Shall I go on?"

Unfortunately, every word he said was true. "It doesn't have to be that way," she shot back.

He raised an eyebrow. "Oh, no? And who's going to see that it's not? The state?"

"Not the state," she said heatedly. The state couldn't oversee a children's game of checkers. "There are people out there, caring people. People like Mr. and Mrs. Wendell who run the county poor farm."

"Granted. But as I'm sure you know, people like that are rare."

"So, what is your answer?" she asked with a toss of her head. "Let people like Mr. Pendergrass continue to roam the streets?"

"We need to get groups and organizations to accept responsibility. If the suffragists were as concerned about the care of aging folks as they are about voting, we might get somewhere."

"And if women had the vote, they might be able to clean up our state-run institutions," she argued back.

"Ah, good point," he conceded, "and one worth battling out in print at some future date." He reached for his hat. "Don't worry. The rebuttal I wrote for you points to all the reasons you think me wrong."

"I doubt that you thought of everything," she said.

"For the sake of argument, let's say I thought of most."

She tossed the paper back at him, and it fluttered to the floor. "As I told you, running your column was a mistake, and it won't happen again."

"Now, that's a real pity." He walked to the door. "Good day . . ." He turned and his gaze fell upon the locket clutched in her hands. ". . . Mrs. Johnson."

She watched him leave with seething breath. How dare he waltz into her office like he owned the place? Who did he think he was?

Chewing on a nail, she stared at the sheet of paper on the floor, then paced back and forth a moment before finally giving in to her curiosity. Snatching up the page, she read it word for word. Except for the insulting comments directed at himself and the *Lone Star Press*, he'd captured her sentiments exactly. It was as if he'd peered into her head and written down every opinion she had on the subject.

Still, how could he take such liberties with her thoughts?

The idea for a caring facility for the aging was close to her heart. Partly because of Mr. Pendergrass and others like him. But that wasn't the only reason. Her grandfather had suffered from dementia and had to be put in a state-run institution. One night he'd wandered away and died of exposure. The man who had brought his bride to America to start a new life didn't deserve to die like that. No one did. Grandpapa's death had delivered a terrible blow to the family, which had believed he was getting the best of care.

Pushing the painful memories away, she debated what to do. Her impulse was to tear Brandon's editorial into shreds. On the other hand, he did make a strong case for her side. However, running it in the paper would send a message that she approved of his type of journalism, and she most certainly did not!

Then, too, there was Papa, who had voiced strong disapproval regarding last week's editorial. Even her explanation that it had been a mistake didn't appease him.

No, she would not—absolutely, not—run that column.

But no sooner had she made up her mind than the sight of Mr. Pendergrass walking past her office in his usual state of undress give her pause. She was just about to rush outside and cover him with a blanket kept for such an occasion when the sheriff beat her to it.

She shook her head. Something definitely had to be done about the problem. So far, her editorials on the subject had failed to reap results.

She sat at her desk and reached for her pen. As usual, Brandon hadn't minced words, and the fact that his insults were directed only at himself didn't soften the impact.

She crossed off "heartless" and after much thought replaced it with "insensitive." Not for one moment did she believe Brandon Wade was malicious or unkind.

The word "muckraker" made her hesitate, but she decided to keep it. If she played too nicely, both papers would lose readers.

"Vituperative pen," though, had to go, and she finally settled for "misguided pen."

She finished editing just as Hank returned from the train depot. Huffing and puffing, he carted in crates of paper and other supplies.

"Train was late again," he complained with a swipe of his forehead. "And it's botter than hazes."

"It's hot in here too," she said. The wooden building didn't keep out the heat like adobe bricks. Still, that only partially explained the flush of her cheeks. Something about Brandon Wade always made her blood boil, and today was no different. She'd been so rattled that once again she'd forgotten to hand over the deed to lot eleven. Oh, he made her so mad!

While Hank stacked reams of paper neatly on the shelves, she tried to calm down by rereading what she'd written. Satisfied, she wrote the number thirty—the standard journalistic signoff—at the bottom of the page and waited for Hank to finish before handing him the article.

He read it with raised eyebrows, his tongue rolling inside his cheek. "I have to say, things sure are getting interesting around here."

***

"Mrs. Johnson! Mrs. Johnson!"

Josie had just stepped out of the general store when she heard her name. She turned and, shading her eyes against the sun, waited for Haley to catch up to her.

"I wanted to show you the picture I drew of my mother," Haley said, sounding breathless from running. She held up a charcoal likeness.

Josie slipped her reporter's notebook into her purse and took the picture from her. "Oh, Haley, what a wonderful drawing." The face was a bit too pointy and the eyes too large, but otherwise Haley had drawn what looked to be a likeness of herself, albeit older.

"Papa said Mama had blond hair and blue eyes just like me," Haley explained.

"She's beautiful." Josie handed the picture back. "You're beautiful, and I'm sure she'd be very proud of you."

"Do you think your husband would be proud of you?" Haley asked.

The question made Josie laugh. "I hadn't thought about it quite like that. Now that I have, I think he'd be pleased that I'm doing something that I've always wanted to do."

Haley thought about that for a moment. "When I grow up, I'm gonna be a teacher, and I won't make my pupils do dumb things like draw humans that look like houses."

She looked so indignant, Josie had a hard time trying not to laugh, but she didn't want to hurt the girl's feelings. "I'm surprised that you don't want to be an artist," she said. The girl definitely had talent.

A wistful look stole over Haley's expression. "I can't be an artist. Only men can be artists."

Josie drew back. "Whatever gave you that idea?"

"We studied all the great artists in school, and they were all men."

"That might have been true in the past, but today women are doing all sorts of interesting things. "

Haley looked interested. "Are they artists?"

"My sister's an artist of sorts. She makes hats. And I heard that there's a woman photographer in Dallas. I think that qualifies as being an artist too."

"Have you ever heard of a woman who draws pictures?"

"No," Josie admitted. "But I have a feeling that we're going to hear about one in the future."

Haley tilted her head. "Do you think that will be me?"

"I wouldn't be surprised."

Haley glanced at Josie's locket. "Would you like me to draw a larger picture of your husband, so you don't have to squint to look at it?"

Josie laughed. "I would like that a lot," she said. "That way I can frame it and put it on the wall."

Haley looked pleased. "I've gotta go," she said. "See you later." With that she turned and ran along the boardwalk, the ribbons on her bonnet trailing behind her.

Watching her go, Josie felt a warm glow inside. It suddenly occurred to her that she didn't even know Haley's last name. Or who her father was. Whenever they were together, it seemed like there were so many other things to talk about.

Josie started along the boardwalk, smiling to herself. Next time she'd remember to ask all the right questions of her new little friend. She was particularly curious about the child's father. Anyone able to raise such a delightful child without a wife had to be pretty special.

＊＊＊

During the following week, the feud between the town's two newspapers was all anyone talked about.

"This is better than your pa's feud with Farrell," T-Bone said when Josie stopped by the butcher shop to pick up advertisement copy for the next issue. The butcher had decided to run ads in both papers.

Later, when Lily Matthews stopped by the office to place an ad for a husband, she squealed with delight. "I can't wait to see what you and Mr. Wade will fight about this week."

Josie read Lily's handwritten copy with pursed lips. Lily had described her pickle-barrel figure as "dainty."

After she left, Hank shook his head. "A man would be wise to reinforce the floors before he takes her as his bride," he muttered.

No sooner were the words out of his mouth than the door flung open. It was Mrs. Foster, and she looked fit to be tied. Not everyone approved of the editorial flames being tossed back and forth, and Mrs. Foster was among the most vocal.

Parking herself in front of Josie's desk, she shook like a wet dog. "This is a disgrace," she said, stabbing at the newspaper in her hand with a pointed finger. "Calling that nice Mr. Wade such awful names is absolutely scandalous."

"Do you wish to cancel your subscription?" Josie asked.

Mrs. Foster lifted her pointed chin and scowled. "Certainly not!" She left the office in a huff, slamming the door shut behind her.

Mrs. Foster's departure was followed by Josie's father, who minced no words in expressing his disapproval.

"I did not raise you to stoop to such . . . such demagoguery!" he thundered.

"Papa, please. Your heart!" It had been nearly four years since her father's heart scare, but that didn't keep the family from worrying, especially since he expressed any contrary opinions with all the subtleties of a raging bull.

"The only thing hurting my heart is you and your total disregard for what your mother and I taught you. And it certainly wasn't to pollute the town with such garbage!"

Josie sighed. Why couldn't her father see how much good the clash of editorials was doing—had already done to the town? People were reading newspapers like never before. More important, it was making them think about things that mattered.

"Unfortunately, the *garbage*, as you call, it is what people want to read," she said.

"Just because people want to read it is no reason for you to provide it!"

"Papa, I tried it the other way and almost went out of business."

"As far as I'm concerned, what you're doing is no better than what Madam Bubbles does. You just found a different way to prostitute yourself." Papa swung his bulky shape around and stormed out of the office.

Stunned by her father's harsh words, Josie sat frozen at her desk.

Hank limped over and patted her on the shoulder. "Your father didn't mean that."

Elbows on her desk, Josie dropped her head into her hands. "Oh, yes, I'm afraid he did."

Chapter 12

Mrs. Beulah Patterson left instructions in her will that under no circumstances should it be said that she died of old age. She was 101. — Two-Time Gazette

That Monday night in early June, the fire alarm rang at a little after nine. Mama lowered her knitting and Papa placed a bookmarker in his book. Josie dropped the ledger she was working on and rushed to the front parlor window.

In the dim glow of gas streetlights, volunteer firemen could be seen racing toward town, some on foot, others on horseback.

"Can you tell where the fire is?" Mama asked.

Josie craned her neck. "I'm not sure. It could be on Main Street."

"Probably another mattress fire," Papa said. "That chicken coop they call a hotel is nothing but a tinderbox."

Her father was right. The hotel had recently had a rash of fires started by guests smoking in bed. Fortunately, the flames had been put out before much damage was done. But the danger continued, and Josie had decided to do a story on it. Signs should be placed in the lobby warning guests of the danger, but unless the *Gazette* pressed the matter, the problem would continue to exist.

Mama resumed her knitting, and Papa returned to his book.

Josie took her seat again and reached for her ledger. The recent success of her paper didn't take her out of the red, but it was a start. At least now she had enough money to pay Hank's wages. She wasn't sure how Friday's paper would be received when readers discovered the editorial feud had come to an abrupt end. But promising Papa to end the war of words was the only way she could restore peace in the family.

Still, if her matrimonial ads continued to prove successful, she would no longer need to lower the standards of her paper to stay afloat. She would soon be able to go back to using a better grade of paper. The cheap paper kept jamming in the press. Worse, it wasn't as absorbent as the higher quality paper, and the ink tended to smear.

After checking and rechecking her figures, she closed the ledger with a yawn. She was just about to call it a night when someone banged on the door.

Papa set his book aside and rose. "Who could that be at this late hour?"

It turned out to be Sheriff Hobson. Crowding into the doorway next to her father, Josie addressed him. "Scooter, what's the matter? What happened."

Never had he looked so serious. "Sorry, Josie, but I thought you oughta know there's been a fire."

Papa nodded. "We heard the alarm."

Grimacing, Scooter hung his thumbs from his belt. "We tried saving it, but there was nothing we could do."

Fearing the worse, Josie felt a prickle of gooseflesh race down her arms. "What . . . What did you try saving, Scooter?"

His mustache twitched. "The *Gazette.*"

* * *

The fire brigade was still passing buckets and tossing water on the smoldering flames when Josie arrived. Papa's wagon had barely rolled to a stop before she leaped to the ground.

Even knowing that her office and everything in it had gone up in flames, she was still ill prepared for the destruction that awaited her. A gaping hole like a missing tooth stretched between the adobe buildings on either side of her property. Nothing was left of the structure except an acrid smell, a few stubborn sparks, and curling smoke that looked like a pit of snakes. Her printing press rose from the ashes like an enormous black bird about to take flight.

Something occurred to her. "Mr. Whiskers!" she cried, glancing around in a panic. "Did anyone see my cat?"

Scooter looked up from where he was studying a pile of smoldering ashes. "Not that I know of."

Her knees threatened to buckle. "Oh, no!"

She called to the group of spectators talking in hushed whispers. "Please, did anyone see my cat?" The shaking of heads added to her dismay, and she felt like was going to be sick.

Mr. Wade broke away from the crowd and moved to her side. He looked like he'd dressed in a hurry. His shirt was half buttoned, and his hair mussed.

"Mrs. Johnson, I can't tell you how sorry I am. If there's anything I can do . . ."

She shifted her gaze to his. He looked and sounded sincere, shocked even. "There's nothing," she whispered.

He glanced around in uncertainty, and she sensed his frustration. He was obviously a man used to being decisive and in command. "I'll look for your cat," he said.

She drew in her breath. "Thank you."

She felt his reluctance in leaving her, but there really was nothing he could do. Nothing anyone could do. Some onlookers walked over to murmur words of sympathy. Others offered to help. There were also those who didn't seem to know what to say and so left in stoic silence. In some odd way, she felt like she was experiencing Ralph's death all over again.

Gripped with shock and disbelief, she could barely move. Everything she owned, every penny she had, every ounce of energy she'd possessed had gone into that paper.

For once Papa was speechless, his face grim as death. Even though she'd told her father that her mudslinging days were over, their relationship remained strained. Still, it was clear by his stunned expression that he'd never wanted it to end in this way. Normally one to take charge in every situation, his uncharacteristic quietude was almost as alarming as the pile of ashes at her feet.

Mama pulled Josie into her arms, tears streaming down her cheeks. "Oh, my dear child. I am so sorry."

Josie tried to speak, but the words rattled in her throat like gravel. There was no way to release the pain that felt like a brick in her chest. Words failed; tears refused to flow. Josie was at a loss as to what to do.

I don't know what to say," Mama said.

Josie closed her eyes. There was nothing anyone could say. Not one blasted thing.

* * *

Unable to sleep that night, Josie rose long before dawn and hurriedly dressed. She left the house on tiptoe so as not to wake Mama or Papa and drove her horse and wagon to town through the deserted streets. Stars shone brightly in the still dark sky, and cold air nipped at her cheeks.

Surprised to find the area still ablaze with the light of a dozen lanterns, she set the brake and jumped to the ground. Moths hurled themselves against the glass lanterns with flapping wings. From the distance came a dog's mournful howl, reflecting the sorrowful echoes of Josie's heart.

Despite the early hour, Scooter was already on site, setting up his camera. He insisted that the camera often saw things that escaped the human eye and that that made it a valuable crime-solving tool.

He poked the toe of his boot into the still smoking wasteland before choosing a spot for his tripod. His expression was as bleak as the destruction at his feet.

Hank was there also, scattering debris with a long stick, tears rolling down his cheeks. "Oh, Hank." She threw her arms around his slender shoulders. In the yellow light he looked pale, and the scar on his forehead stood out in an angry red slash.

They hugged briefly before she drew away. "How did you know?" One of the things she'd most dreaded was having to tell Hank that his "home" was gone.

"My landlord is a member of the bire frigade," he said. "Thought I'd see if anything could be salvaged." He said more, but his words became so tangled she couldn't understand him.

"I'm afraid Mr. Whiskers . . ." Her voice died away and she shuddered.

Hank drew in his breath and said nothing, but the expression on his face spoke volumes.

They stood side by side in silence, each with their own thoughts, as the sky gradually turned silver, then pink. At last, the sun rose, casting long fingers of yellow light over the blackened area. The bright rays were greeted with the crow of a rooster and a chorus of barking dogs

Hank left to get coffee at the hotel. When he returned, he thrust a tin cup into her hand and handed another one to the sheriff.

Scooter blew on the steaming brew. "Maybe you should go home, Josie. Nothin' you can do here."

Ignoring his suggestion, she sipped her coffee. It was bitter and strong, but she appreciated the warmth. Despite the sun, she couldn't stop shaking. The acrid smell of ashes and smoke filled her nostrils and burned her eyes.

"Do you know how the fire started?" she asked, her prickly throat turning her voice hoarse.

Scooter stooped to indicate the place where the window had been located. "This seems to be where the fire was the hottest. That's a good indication it started here. Did you leave a candle or lantern burning? I'm thinkin' maybe your cat tipped it over or something."

Josie thought back to the day before. "Hank and I left together, and everything
was turned off."

"She's right," Hank said, speaking slowly.

Scooter straightened, the sun glinting off his badge. "Well, then." Holding his coffee cup in one hand, he rubbed his whiskered chin with the other and scraped the toe of his boot into the dirt. "I'm not done with my investigation. But if what you say is true, it sure does look like arson."

"What?" Josie exclaimed, spilling her coffee.

Hank looked equally shocked; his eyebrows arched like crescent moons over rounded eyes.

Gooseflesh ran up her arms. The fire was bad enough, but to think that someone had purposely started it was more than she could bear. "But who?"

Scooter shrugged. "Make any enemies recently?"

"Enemies? No, none." No sooner were the words out of her mouth than a disturbing thought came to mind. Was it only a coincidence that the fire had occurred following the *Gazette*'s latest success? She shot a glance across the street at the office of the *Lone Star Press*, and her stomach knotted.

Almost as soon as the thought occurred to her, Brandon—Mr. Wade—rode up on his horse, sitting tall and straight in his saddle. Unlike last night, today he looked ever so much in command. Josie watched him with mixed feelings. She didn't want to think him capable of such a dastardly deed, but once the idea occurred to her, she couldn't shake it. She knew for a fact that last Friday's *Gazette* had outsold his newspaper by a wide margin, but that was because the matrimonial ads gave her the edge.

Still . . . He was the most annoying man she'd ever met, but that didn't mean he was capable of arson. He was the one who had come up with the feud idea. Why would he do that if he wanted her to fail?

Unless he wanted to hide his real motive, which was to put her out of business for good. Who else had a motivation for burning down her building?

The thought sent cold chills racing down her back. Oh, dear heaven.

After dismounting and wrapping the reins around a post, he crossed the street with long, hurried strides.

Feeling herself tense, she moistened her lips and curled her hands by her side.

"Did you get any sleep?" he asked before reaching her. He looked and sounded genuinely concerned.

She eyed him warily. "Not much."

His probing gaze seemed to pierce through her. "I meant what I said. If there's anything I can do."

She drew in her breath. "Scoot— The sheriff believes it was arson."

He pulled back. "Arson!" As if seeking confirmation, he glanced at Scooter fiddling with his camera before turning back to her. "Who would do such a thing?"

She searched his face. "That's what I want to know."

"Me too," Hank said, examining a piece of charred wood. Josie recognized it as the nameplate she'd given him last Christmas.

Ducking behind his camera, Scooter's head vanished beneath a black cloth. "Whoever it is, I'll find him. Don't you worry none about that."

"I'm sure you will, Sheriff." Wade's gaze locked with hers. "Meanwhile, my offer still holds. If there's anything I can do, just name it.
"

"Thank you," she said.

He apparently heard something in her voice because he repeated his offer. "And feel free to use my printer. Let me know when you need it, and I'll make sure it's available."

Hank tossed his ruined nameplate down, and ashes scattered as it hit the ground. "That's mighty neighborly of you."

"I'm sure it's no more than what Mrs. Johnson would do for me in similar circumstances." He looked straight at her as if expecting her to object.

"That's a very kind offer," she said. "But I don't think I'll be publishing anytime soon." Maybe never again. The thought was followed by what felt like a knife plunging into her heart. Everything she'd worked for was now up in smoke. It seemed that all the things she loved and cared about kept slipping through her fingers, and there wasn't a blasted thing she could do about it.

Wade pushed his hat back and hung his thumbs in his vest pockets. The early morning sun turned his eyes into what looked like melted chocolate. "Well, now, that's a crying shame. You'll be missed."

"I rather doubt that, Mr. Wade."

"It's true. In fact, I'd like you to come and work for me. I'll even give you your own column."

The offer surprised her. "You're offering me a job?" She couldn't help but add, "An insipid writer like me?"

He grinned sheepishly. "Surely you didn't take me seriously."

"Seriously enough to know you would object to my . . . civil style of writing. So, thank you, but I'll pass."

"Then perhaps you wouldn't mind if I hired your typesetter?" He gave Hank a questioning look.

"Not at all," she said. She hated the thought of Hank working for the *Lone Star Press,* but the poor man needed a source of income.

Hank glanced at her before answering. "I'm mighty obliged, but I'm lot nooking for another job."

If Brandon noticed Hank's speech impediment, he showed no sign. "I hate to see you both give up."

"Oh, we're got niving up," Hank said. "Not as long Miz Josie here has a few arrows left in her quiver."

Hank's confidence brought a lump to Josie's throat. She doubted she was deserving of such conviction and loyalty, but it touched her deeply. More than that, it awakened something inside, and she felt a new sense of resolve begin to stir.

Brandon's dark eyes sought hers. "It'll be interesting to see where Mrs. Johnson aims those arrows next. If there's anything I can do, don't hesitate to ask." With a tip of his hat, he turned and jogged down the three steps leading to the dirt street.

She waited until Brandon was out of earshot before turning to Hank. "You really should take him up on his offer. I won't feel bad if you do." Okay, so she'd feel rotten, but she'd feel even worse knowing Hank was out of work.

Hank shrugged. "I told you, this is my home."

She scoffed. "Some home. There's nothing left."

Hank looked surprisingly unfazed. "Nothing but the printer, and I think I can get it going again."

She stared at him; not sure she'd heard right. "Y-you can?"

He nodded. "It'll take more than a bit of heat to ruin that old iron horse. It needs a good gleaning and creasing, is all."

She cast a dubious glance at the machine, the only thing left standing. He made it sound so easy, but it sure did look like it would take more than a good cleaning and greasing to get the thing running again.

"We need more than a printer to run a newspaper." Her desk— everything was gone.

Hank pulled his spectacles off, huffed on the lens, and wiped away the ashes with his handkerchief. "I found some lead typeface that's still usable. That is, if you don't mind printing in circus font."

She laughed. Circus font was generally used for advertisements and was meant to look big and bold. To accommodate the larger type, she would have to use more paper or less wordage.

Hank continued. "I have a little money put away. Enough to buy whatever supplies we need to get started."

His generous offer brought tears to her eyes. "Hank, I appreciate what you're trying to do, but we don't even have a roof over our heads."

Slipping his spectacles back on, he gazed at the cloudless sky. "Won't be the first time I've been rithout a woof."

Josie reached into her pocket for her handkerchief "Are you saying we should open up shop here? With no building? Nothing? Why . . . why that's crazy."

He shrugged. "Blame it on the war. You know how it huddled my mead."

Hands clasped to her chest, she blinked back tears and glanced around, her mind in a whirl. It might work. At least for a while. That is, if it didn't rain.

"You know what?" she said, slipping an arm through Hank's. "I kind of like that muddled head of yours."

He looked at her askew. "Does that mean we're back in business?"

"I don't know. Maybe." She pulled her arm away and tapped her chin.

"I ordered paper and ink last week," she said, thinking out loud. "It should be here on tomorrow's train."

A grin spread across his face. "We have paper, ink, and a printing press. In my book, that adds up to a newspaper. So, what's the problem?"

Her gaze traveled to the ugly black scar where her office had once stood. "There is no problem," she said. Swiping away the last of her tears, she laughed. How ridiculous to think that they could put out a paper under such dire circumstances. It was utterly, utterly insane. And yet....

"What are we standing here yakking for?" she said. "Come on, we have work to do."

Chapter 13

The Spinsters' Club decided to hold meetings jointly with the Bachelors' Club. This paper predicts that the demise of these two fine clubs is not far behind. —Two-Time Gazette

Mayor Troutman stared in utter disbelief at the old army tent now filling the lot once occupied by the *Gazette* office. He shook his head until his jowls wobbled. "Are you out of your cotton-pickin' mind? A tent? In the middle of town?" he railed, pulling his cigar from his mouth.

Josie tried not to laugh at his horrified expression, but it was hard to keep a straight face. "It's only temporary," she said. Hopefully, it wouldn't take her any longer than five years to rebuild—ten at the most.

Her assurances did nothing to soothe the mayor's ruffled feathers. "That . . . that tent is a blight on the community." He knocked the ashes off his cigar and stuck it back into his mouth. "That's what it is. A blight!"

So far, he was the only one taking issue with her new accommodations. She still couldn't believe the number of Two-Time citizens who'd rallied around her and pitched in to help. People had showed up with shovels, rakes, and hoes. They'd set to work scooping ashes from the ground and carting debris away in wagons.

The tent had been donated by a war veteran, and Meg's husband, Grant, had surprised her with a type-writing machine. And people had dropped off casseroles and flowers at the house until her father protested that it looked and smelled like a "danged funeral parlor."

Mr. Woodman had contributed the sign. Since there was nothing to hang it on, he nailed it to a post.

There was no room in the tent for the printing press, so it had to remain outside. One of the church ladies loaned Josie an old quilt to throw over the press when it wasn't in use.

Josie let her thoughts fade away, only to find the mayor still on his soapbox. "I cannot allow such an affliction to tarnish our fine town," he barked, jabbing his cane into the ground for emphasis.

She bit back her irritation. "I told you it's only temporary," she said, barely able to get a word in edgewise. "And if you don't mind, I have a business to run." She walked away.

He'd called her temporary office a blight on the community, but to her eyes it was a sign of love and acceptance. For the first time since returning to Two-Time nearly a year earlier, the town felt like home again.

The mayor stomped after her. "That tent is an eyesore," he sputtered. "And I want it down now!"

Temper flaring, she pivoted, hands at her waist. "So, what do you suggest I do? I don't have the money to rebuild."

"Not my problem," he bellowed, his cigar dangling from the side of his mouth. "But you better do something and fast. I won't have my town looking like . . . like the slums of New York."

With seething breath, she watched him trudge off, muttering to himself. "If you paid more attention to the traffic problem," she shouted after him, "you wouldn't have time to worry about my tent!" As if to underscore her argument, the angry voices of two farmers vying for the same parking space could be heard in the distance.

Nearly as soon as the mayor had stomped away, Miss Bubbles drove up. Her horse-driven wagon was a garish affair decorated with brightly painted flowers. Today the madam was dressed from head to toe in eye-popping red, her skirt draped with enough ruffles to confound the eye.

"Thought you could use a desk," she called, tossing a nod toward the back of her wagon stopped in the middle of the street.

"Sure can," Josie called back.

The madam climbed out of the driver's seat and watched as Hank and the sheriff lifted the desk from the back of the wagon. The piece of furniture had been painted a bright purple, and Josie couldn't help but laugh. What would the mayor say about that?

Josie hugged the madam and got a face full of feathers in return. "Thank you so much. I can't tell you how much I appreciate your generosity."

Madam Bubbles waved a ring-laden hand through the air. "It's the least I could do to repay you for all that you've done. Posting those handbills all over town was a lot of work."

"The sheriff said nothing came of it," Josie said, her voice tinged with disappointment. It was hard to believe no one had responded to the large reward, except for a few cranks who would turn in their own mothers just to claim a thousand dollars. "Did anyone contact you?"

Miss Bubbles shook her head. "No, but that doesn't take away from what you did."

"We're not done yet. We'll keep running the ad at no additional cost to you." Someone must know what had happened to that poor girl.

Miss Bubbles surprised her by tearing up. Two rivers of black charcoal streamed down her ruby-red cheeks. "I'm not used to such kindness." She reached into her sleeve and pulled out a dainty lace handkerchief.

"I'm just as anxious as you to see the perpetrator brought to justice," Josie assured her.

"Where do you want the desk?" Hank called.

"Where else?" Josie said, pointing to the moth-eaten canvas tent. "In my office." *In my beautiful, beautiful office.*

***

A week later, the first copy of the *Gazette* rolled off the press to loud cheers and applause.

Brandon stood in his office doorway watching the startling sight from across the street and shook his head. Who would have thought such a thing possible? Mrs. Josie Johnson certainly did have arrows in her quiver, not to mention starch in her corset.

Darting around a passing horse and wagon, he crossed over to join the crowd watching Hank work the press. A noisy old thing, it sounded more like it was grinding nuts than spitting out paper, but it got the job done. Barely.

Mr. McGinnis played his bagpipes for the occasion, and for once no one complained about the whiny sound. Though Mrs. Mooney did comment unfavorably on the knobby knees displayed beneath the man's green-plaid kilt. The Scotsman's legs received more attention than Mr. Pendergrass, who walked by in his usual state of undress.

But most eyes were fixed on Hank, who made a big production of hanging each newly printed paper on a rope strung across the property to dry.

Mrs. Johnson's two sisters folded the papers as soon as the hot sun dried the ink. Almost at once each copy was snatched up by eager readers tossing coins into tin cans.

Mrs. Johnson herself ducked out of the tent and waved to the crowd. Despite what she'd been through the last week, she appeared remarkably relaxed, her smile as dazzling as the noontime sun.

When her gaze met his, Brandon felt himself sinking into the blue-green depths of her eyes. A shiver of awareness unnerved him, rendering him momentarily at a loss for words.

She acknowledged his presence with a slight nod. "Mr. Wade."

Realizing with a start that he was still staring, he hid his fascination behind a conciliatory smile. "Congratulations," he said with a clap of his hands. "I see my worthy opponent is officially back in business."

An odd expression that he couldn't decipher flashed across her face. The look was both wary and combative, as if she didn't know whether to fight him or trust him.

"I'm sure you would rather that I wasn't," she said.

"On the contrary. Nothing keeps a man on his toes better than a little competition." His gaze traveled through the open tent to the typewriting machine sitting upon a monstrosity of a purple desk. "If you like, I'd be happy to write your next editorial for you," he said with a droll smile as he swung his gaze back to her. "I'm sure you must have other things to do."

Mrs. Johnson abrupt decision to discontinue their war of words had been a disappointment.

"And what has me all fired up this time?" she asked. "Editorial-wise, I mean."

Resting his elbow on his crossed arm, he tapped his chin. "My column demanding the town build a larger jailhouse. Of course, you object."

Her forehead creased. "On what grounds?"

He thought a moment. "You're convinced the money would be better spent on more pressing matters. A larger school and better roads, perhaps. A place for our *au natural* friend."

A smile tugged at the corners of her mouth, but the wariness remained in the depth of her eyes. "How fortunate that I have you to tell me how I feel."

"Oh, I believe you know quite well how you feel, Mrs. Johnson. But newspapers require a more . . ."

Her eyes flashed blue fire. "Vociferous tone?"

He dropped his hands to his side. "I prefer to think of it as a more persuasive use of words."

"Actually, I believe you'll find my way with words in next week's editorial to be quite persuasive."

"In that case, I look forward to reading it." He cocked his head to the side. "Did you mention my name?"

"Is there any reason that I should have, Mr. Wade? Mention your name, that is, in an article about arson?"

Something in her tone of voice made him knit his brow. Surely, she wasn't suggesting that he'd had anything to do with the fire?

"None that I can think of," he said, but she had already turned and walked away.

***

The *Gazette*'s "Love Links" column was only in its fourth week, but already the matrimonial ads had proven to be a resounding success. Josie couldn't be more pleased. The four-line personals filled two pages and more than made up for the loss of county legal notices.

Even more surprising, not everyone placing an ad was single. Mrs. Jeffries had been married to her husband for fifteen years and just wanted to see "What else is out there before I kick the old fool out." Becky-Sue Harris's reason for buying an ad was that she hoped to make Scooter jealous. She and the sheriff had been a couple for two years, and things weren't progressing as quickly as she expected or even wanted.

"If I wait for him to make the first move, I'll die an old maid," Becky-Sue moaned.

"I know he cares for you deeply," Josie said.

Becky-Sue tossed her head, and her blond sausage curls bounced off the back of her neck. "Good. Then maybe when he sees me with someone else, he'll pop the question."

No sooner had she paid for her ad and left than Hank voiced his own complaints. Some of the women under his consideration had grown tired of waiting for him to make up his mind. They'd taken matters into their own hands by placing their own ads in the *Gazette*.

"Dang women don't give a man a chance," he grumbled.

Josie laughed. "Maybe they're just trying to make you jealous." She picked up the mail and rifled through it . . . until a soft mewing sound outside the tent made her drop the stack of envelopes.

"Is that—"

She and Hank exchanged hasty glances before the two of them made a mad dash to the flap of the tent. It was Mr. Whiskers all right, looking a little thinner but otherwise none the worse for wear.

Laughing with delight, Josie scooped the cat into her arms and carried him inside. "Where have you been, eh?" She sighed. "If only you could talk."

Grinning, Hank looked every bit as happy as she to have his old pal back. "You might not like what he has to say."

"Maybe not. But at least we'd know the name of the arsonist." Not knowing had filled her with suspicion and she no longer knew whom to trust. If Mr. Wade was not the arsonist, then somebody else was. But who? And why?

Hank ran a hand the length of Mr. Whiskers' back. "I'll go and fetch him some milk."

Nodding, she worked a thistle out of the tom's matted fur.

Hank lifted the flap of the tent and glanced back. "How do you suppose he escaped the burning building?"

"That's a good question," she said. "A very good question."

She'd been so busy setting up her office she hadn't had time to think beyond getting that weeks' edition out. Now that things had settled down, she couldn't stop thinking about the arsonist. The questions of who had burned down her building, and why, continued to fester the rest of that morning like a burr in her side. Possible suspects and motives streamed through her thoughts, putting her on edge. Unable to think of anything else, she headed for the sheriff's office that afternoon, hoping for answers.

Unfortunately, Scooter had none to give her, only speculation.

"You don't think Mr. Whiskers escaping the fire is significant in some way?" she asked.

Scooter shrugged. His office was hot, and beads of perspiration dotted his forehead. "Maybe the arsonist is an animal lover and let the cat out before he set the place on fire."

"I suppose that's possible." Josie dropped into the chair in front of his desk. Who could explain the criminal mind? "But that means the arsonist knew a cat was in the building."

"That's hardly a secret. Mr. Whiskers suns himself on the windowsill in plain sight," Scooter said, then added, "I've questioned the other business owners. So far nothing."

Josie drew in her breath. "Did you question Mr. Wade?"

"Yes, and all his employees." Scooter's gaze sharpened. "Why do you ask?"

"No reason," she said.

"Come on, Josie. I know you better than that. Do you know something?"

"No, absolutely not."

Scooter narrowed his eyes. "It's no secret that there's bad blood between you two. So far, Wade's the only one who stands to gain by burning down your building. He claims he was home when the fire started, and his landlady confirmed it. Still, he could have sneaked out without her knowledge."

Josie bit her lip. It was hard to imagine a man with such a large presence sneaking around. "I don't think he's the culprit."

Scooter frowned. "How can you be sure?"

Josie clutched at her locket. That was the problem; she couldn't be sure. It was just a feeling she had. "Do all arsonists have motives?"

"Usually. Unless they're crazy. The first one who comes to mind in that category is Mr. Pendergrass."

Josie's back stiffened. "Pendergrass is old and confused. He's not crazy."

Scooter leaned forward. "I know how you feel about him, Josie. But several people reported seeing him in the area the night of the fire."

"That doesn't mean he started it. He has nothing to hide. I'm sure of it."

Scooter scoffed. "Maybe not. But I wish he'd hide it anyway."

Josie chewed on a nail. "You don't think Mr. Pendergrass is really guilty, do you?"

Scooter shrugged. "He's a suspect."

"Did you question him?" she asked.

"Yes, I questioned him. He denied starting the fire. Claims he has no place to keep matches."

"He has a point," she said and laughed.

"Yeah, maybe." Scooter rubbed his chin. "Much as I hate to admit it, Josie, we might never catch the perpetrator. It's been two weeks since the fire, and I'm no closer to solving the crime. Arsonists have an advantage that other criminals don't have. Any clues left behind go up in smoke. It's what they count on."

What Scooter said was true, but Josie had the strangest feeling they were missing something. A vital clue?

As if to guess her thoughts, Scooter added, "I'm not giving up. I'll do everything I can to find the culprit who burned down your building. And I sure as shootin' ain't givin' up on findin' Miss Ruby's killer, neither"

"I know that, Scooter." No one worked harder to maintain law and order than he did. Hesitating, she bit her lip. "There's something else I hope you're not giving up on. Becky-Sue."

He mopped his forehead with a handkerchief. "What makes you think I'm givin' up on her?"

Plucking a piece of lint off her skirt, she debated how to answer. Telling him that Becky-Sue had put an ad in the "Love Links" column might only make him more resistant.

"A girl doesn't think a man's serious unless there's a ring on her finger or wedding bells in the air."

Scooter scoffed. "That's the trouble with women. They spend too much time thinkin'. Grandpappy always said one shouldn't think too much about marrying or taking pills."

"My grandfather was a blacksmith and he believed in striking while the iron was hot."

He sat back in his chair. "Ah, give a man a break, will ya? You know I've been busy cleanin' up this town."

"I do know that, Scooter. And you've done an outstanding job. But maybe it's time you got some help. Have you given any thought to hiring a deputy?"

"Some."

"Maybe you better give it more thought. You know what they say about all work and no play."

Scooter lifted his eyebrows. "You get to die a millionaire?"

She laughed. "On your salary?"

He pocketed his handkerchief and threw up his hands in surrender. "All right, all right. I'll see about hiring a deputy."

"That's a start. Now what are you going to do about Becky-Sue?" I'll talk to her."

"Good." Satisfied, Josie stood and drew on a glove. Her gaze fell upon the manila folders on his desk. One was marked with Miss Ruby's name and the other simply tagged with the word *Arson*. The two side-by-side folders made her think of a possibility not previously considered.

He noticed her eying the folders. "Miss Ruby's ad made me revisit the case."

"Do you think there's a connection?" She tossed a nod at the two files. "Between the fire and Miss Ruby's death?"

His forehead creased. "A connection?" He narrowed his eyes. "What makes you say that?"

Now that she had more time to think about it, it did seem farfetched. Still . . .

"I don't know. The timing, perhaps. The fire happened shortly after I began running Miss Bubble's reward in the paper. Maybe the killer got nervous." She tapped her chin with the tip of her finger. "Of course, it could be just a coincidence."

"Could be," Scooter said, his eyebrows knitted. "Still, that's an angle I hadn't thought of." He tapped his fingers on the desk. "Any chance I can talk you into being my deputy?"

She laughed. "Not on your tintype."

Chapter 14

Wanted: deputy sheriff. Must have a fast horse, be quick on the draw and able to stay awake during the mayor's speeches. —Two-Time Gazette

Brandon sat at his desk that Friday morning reading Mrs. Johnson's editorial with raised eyebrows. She'd minced no words where the arsonist was concerned, for certain and sure. More than just her office had caught fire. So had her pen.

The most scathing wordage was used in describing the firebug's nefarious deed. After calling the scoundrel every name under the sun, she demanded he turn himself in.

He scoffed. Fat chance of that. She'd even hinted at knowing who the rogue was—a bluff that no self-respecting arsonist would fall for.

Still, she had a perfect right to be riled. No one could blame her for that.

He lowered the newspaper and let his gaze wander out the window to the tent across the street. How anyone could put out a paper under such dire circumstances was beyond him. He couldn't imagine doing such a thing. The stubborn woman and her loyal sidekick had turned down all his offers to help. She was one independent woman—no question—and had earned his respect. Or more respect.

Shaking the thought aside, he scanned the rest of the *Gazette*. Mrs. Johnson sure did know how to put together a professional-looking newspaper, even with the unconventional-sized type and low-grade paper. Her piece on page four made him laugh out loud. She had taken the local grocers to task for placing their vegetables outside where dogs could reach them.

When a shopper wishes to serve spinach or carrots to her family, she'd written, *she does not wish to buy pees!*

"Well, what do you know," he murmured out loud. Even when the lady was spitting fire, she had a sense of humor.

The door of his office swung open, and Brandon looked up. He dropped the paper on his desk and sat back in his chair. "'Morning, Sheriff. You're up and about early."

Sheriff Hobson closed the door behind him. His mustache and shaggy hair did little to hide his age, which Brandon guessed was probably in the early to mid-twenties.

"Well, you know what they say. 'Crime never sleeps.'" Without waiting for an invite, he parked himself upon the straight-backed chair next to Brandon's desk.

It was the second time since the fire that the sheriff had stopped by. Today he looked just as serious as he had the first time.

"How can I help you, Sheriff?"

Hobson pulled off his hat and balanced it on his knee. "If you don't mind, I have more questions regardin' the *Gazette* fire."

Brandon raised an eyebrow. Since the sheriff had drilled him thoroughly the first time, he couldn't imagine what other questions remained. "Not sure I can help you much there. Like I told you, I'm an early riser. I was already asleep when the fire started."

"Your office is directly across the street. Thought you might have seen suspicious activity a day or so before the fire. Maybe a stranger hangin' 'round. That kind of thing."

"Can't say that I did."

Hobson shifted in his seat and glanced out the window with narrowed eyes. "Can't believe that Josie's still in business. That's pretty amazin', don't you think?"

"Yes, I have to give the lady a lot of credit."

Hobson's gaze met his, but he said nothing.

Brandon was pretty good at reading between the lines, but it was hard to know what the sheriff had on his mind. "I take it that you still don't have any suspects."

"A couple."

Hobson's piercing eyes had a way of making a man feel guilty even when he wasn't. Feeling slightly uncomfortable, Brandon ran a finger along his shirt collar. Surely, he wasn't a suspect.

"Arsonists are a creative bunch," the sheriff was saying. "Some even figure out ways to leave a building before the fire starts. Thus, creatin' an alibi for themselves."

"I didn't think arsonists were that smart," Brandon said.

"You'd be surprised. I even heard tell of an arsonist who tied a piece of meat over a lantern and left. When the buildin' owner's dog leaped to get the meat, the lantern overturned, creatin' an inferno."

"So, do you think that's what happened here? Someone used Mrs. Johnson's cat to start the fire?"

Hobson's eyes sharpened. "I don't recall my saying anythin' about a cat, but the thought did cross my mind. Fortunately, the cat escaped. It showed up unharmed."

"So, I heard," Brandon said.

Hobson's eyes narrowed. "Then, of course, there's the matter of motivation. Like my Grandpappy always said, chickens don't lay eggs for no reason." The sheriff's gaze dipped to the newspaper on Brandon's desk. "Do you know anyone other than yourself who would benefit from puttin' the *Gazette* out of business?"

Brandon stiffened. Other than himself? "I never wanted to put Jo— To put the *Gazette* out of business. That was never my intent. I welcome the competition."

Hobson looked skeptical. "Been my experience that anyone says he welcomes competition is generally speakin' though his hat."

The sheriff's insinuations were beginning to irritate. "Maybe so, but in my case, it just happens to be true," Brandon said, his voice taut. Had Mrs. Johnson put a bug in the sheriff's ear? He wouldn't put it past her. She'd been acting strange around him ever since the fire.

Hobson stood and took his own sweet time donning his wide-brimmed felt hat. "If you think of anything, you know where to find me."

***

Josie's elation at publishing the paper under such difficult circumstances lasted only till the end of June. Enough time had passed for readers to figure out that the popular "Love Links" column contained more fabrications than fact.

It had all started early that Monday morning when Miss Newberry stormed into the office and slapped a carefully cut square from the newspaper on Josie's desk with such force, she startled Mr. Whiskers. Waking with a start, the poor cat dashed under the desk.

A tall, thin woman built with awkward angles; Miss Newberry looked like she was put together with clay pipes. "He said he was a man of means. A man of mean *spirit* is more like it! He wouldn't even pay for my supper!" She sniffed. "If you can't trust an advertisement, what can you trust?"

Nothing Josie said could calm her. Miss Newberry left the office in the same state of agitation as when she arrived—only a little bit richer. Josie didn't like having to reimburse the woman for the cost of the paper, but it was the only way she could get her to leave.

No sooner had Josie's ears stopped ringing from Miss Newberry's complaints than Chuck Cummings burst through the flap of the tent. A short man with a soup-strainer mustache, he shook that week's edition in Josie's face.

"She says she's matrimonially inclined but can't explain why two husbands absconded!"

Another unhappy man followed on his heels. "She advertised herself as a natural beauty. Padded hips, fake hair, and bolstered bosom ain't natural. The only thing real about her is her nose, and I ain't even sure about that!"

The line of disgruntled readers continued for the remainder of the week, leaving Josie exhausted. One of the many drawbacks of working in a tent was the lack of a door that could be locked.

After an especially trying day dealing with unhappy advertisers, Josie slumped forward and laid her head on crossed arms. "And here I thought I'd come up with the perfect solution to our problem."

Hank's chair squeaked beneath his weight. "Maybe we should include a warning that the paper's not responsible for false advertisements."

She lifted her head. "Everything printed reflects on the paper's integrity." She had no idea how to control what people wrote about themselves. If someone described himself as rich or handsome, who was she to suggest otherwise?

The following week saw another batch of disgruntled readers stream through the flap of the tent. Just when it looked as though she'd seen the last of them, Mayor Troutman walked in and plopped an official-looking document on her desk.

"What is that?" she said, reaching for it.

"*That* is an official notice. You have exactly thirty days to remove this tent from the premises. That gives you till August first."

Her hand froze. "Thirty . . ." She forced herself to breathe. "I told you I don't have the money to rebuild."

"And I told you that wasn't my problem."

Josie clenched her teeth. "Give me ninety days." That might not even be enough time, but it was a start.

"Forty."

She swallowed her dislike of the pompous man and tried appealing to his compassionate side. She did everything but turn on the waterworks. When it appeared he lacked the ability to sympathize, her temper flared.

"I'm trying to run a newspaper here."

"And I'm trying to run a town!" The mayor tucked his cane beneath his arm and leaned over her desk. "Your tent is a blight. There's no other word for it."

Rising, she bent forward, leaving mere inches between her and his bulbous nose. "If you're so worried about blight, why don't you do something about the rutted roads and traffic problems?"

Troutman straightened with an indignant toss of his head. "If you think you can do better—"

"A mule could do better!"

With a *harrumph*, he pointed his finger at her. "Thirty days!" He spun around and left.

Hank pushed his revolving chair away from his desk and spun around to face her. "Ghat are ge donna wo?" he asked in such a mess of muddled words it took Josie a moment to decipher.

"I don't know, Hank." If she were a man, she could take out a loan, but no bank would give one to a woman. She couldn't ask her father to sign for yet a second loan when she didn't even know how to pay for the first.

She fell back in her chair. "I just don't know."

***

Later that day, Josie visited Amanda at her hat shop. In the past, whenever Josie's sisters had had a problem, they'd always come to her for advice. Now the tables were turned, and Josie was the one seeking help.

Josie waited for Amanda to finish with a customer. If the number of hat boxes the woman left with was an indication, Amanda's business was booming.

As soon as they were alone, Josie quickly explained the mayor's ultimatum. "I need to find a place to work until I figure out how to rebuild."

"Oh, Josie. I don't know what to say." Amanda gave her a hug. "Things were going so well for you. The last thing you needed was that awful fire"

"I know."

Amanda brightened and dropped her arms. "You can work here until you figure out something else."

Josie glanced around the tiny shop. Hats of every imaginable size, shape, and design were on display, some on wooden pegs, others on shelves. Ribbons spilled out of drawers, and feathers trailed across Amanda's workbench. Hardly any room was left in which to turn around.

Josie gave her sister a loving smile. "That's very generous of you, but I don't think it would work. Where would I put my printer?"

Amanda chewed on her bottom lip. "I wish there was something I could do. I'll talk to Rick. We don't have much in the way of savings, but—"

"Absolutely not!" Amanda and her husband, Rick, had started a horse farm outside of town, but it wasn't yet profitable, and Josie knew they'd been struggling financially.

Amanda brightened. "Why not ask Papa for a loan?"

Josie shook her head. "The bank insisted on a male signature before I could take out a mortgage. If I default, Papa will be responsible for it. I can't ask him to sign for a second loan."

Amanda frowned. "But your paper has been flying out the door."

"I'm afraid that's about to change. We've been bombarded with complaints about the integrity of the matrimonial ads and have lost subscribers. It's only a matter of time before we'll lose advertisers too. Again."

Amanda's expression softened. "Oh, Josie, I'm so sorry. You've worked so hard. What are you going to do?"

Josie lifted her shoulders with a sigh. "I don't know. I just don't know."

Amanda picked up a white feather and stuck it into the brim of an unfinished hat. "You could resume the editorial wars you started with Mr. Wade."

Oddly enough, the idea didn't seem as objectionable as it had at one time. "I can't do that. You know how much Papa was against it the first time."

"Papa's never going to change, but that doesn't mean we can't," Amanda said with a toss of her head. "Those weeks of feuding between you and Mr. Wade were all that anyone talked about."

Josie couldn't help but smile. "I have to admit it was kind of fun." She blushed at the thought.

Amanda studied her. "At first I was shocked by the awful things you wrote about Mr. Wade—"

"And he about me."

"Actually, he never said anything awful about you, personally."

"He called my writing 'insipid.' I heard it with my own ears."

Amanda shook her head. "I'm talking about what he writes in his columns. In any case, I kind of liked seeing a different side of you."

Josie looked away. Amanda had no way of knowing that the crux of the editorials had been written by Brandon Wade himself with only some slight editing on her part. Still, her sister was right about one thing: Wade did bring out a new side of her—a side she hadn't known existed. The funny thing was she liked the new feistier, more assertive, self.

When Josie remained silent, Amanda continued, "You used to be so . . . I don't know what the word is."

Josie met Amanda's probing gaze. "Unexciting. Boring?"

A look of alarm crossed Amanda's face. "Oh, no! I didn't mean to imply you were boring. But you were always the peacemaker in the family. I can't count the times you kept Meg and me from killing each other. I never thought you had it in you to hold your own against the likes of Mr. Wade."

"He's . . . a very good businessman. I'll grant him that. He knows what the public wants."

Amanda folded her arms. "I think you do too. The question is are you brave enough to give it to them?"

***

Later that day Josie stood peering through the tiny opening of the tent flap. Dusk had fallen, and the lamplighter had already made his rounds. The conversation with Amanda still on her mind, Josie stared at the newspaper office across the street.

The windows were dark. It irritated her that Mr. Wade had already closed up shop and gone home. Due to the numerous interruptions from disgruntled readers, she and Hank were still trying to put Friday's paper to bed.

As much as she hated to admit it, Amanda was right. Her choices were to bury the *Gazette* or do something she was utterly opposed to doing: resume the editorial wars. Was she brave enough to go that route? That question kept her very much on edge.

Poor Papa would have a conniption, but what else could she do?

She called to Hank. "What did Mr. Wade write in his editorial last week?" She knew Hank read the competitors' paper.

Hank looked up from his desk where he was setting type. "School books."

She dropped the flap and returned to her desk. "School books? You're kidding, right?"

Hank shook his head. "Nope, that's what he wrote about. He took issue with pupils having to purchase different textbooks whenever a new teacher takes over. Said it creates a grievous hardship on families. He suggested that the County Commissioner's Court adopt a uniform series of books and stick with it."

Blast it all! How could she disagree with that? Teachers didn't last long on the job. Most got married within a few months. Since that was against school policy, married teachers were forced to resign. Last year, the school had lost three teachers in quick succession, and that meant three textbook changes.

As much as she hated to admit it, Wade's opinion made perfect sense. She drummed her fingers on her desk, her mind in a whirl.

Until a thought occurred to her. Running a newspaper had made her aware of just how quickly things changed. Hardly a week went by when some new medical or scientific discovery didn't make headlines. Just that week a large city paper had printed a story about a Frenchman taking out a patent on artificial silk, stating that it was likely to change the fashion industry forever.

"Wait," she said, her voice rising with excitement. "Keeping the same textbooks over a period of time could result in children learning outdated material."

Hank considered this a moment before nodding. "I suppose."

Elbows on her desk, she folded her hands beneath her chin. "And why should county commissioners decide which books must be used? Why not a convention of public-school teachers? They're the ones who should have the say as to what is taught in the classroom."

Hank shrugged. "Makes sense to me."

Her mind raced. "Textbooks should last at least a year, maybe two." That would certainly cut down on expenses.

With a surge of inspiration, she reached for pen and paper and started writing. Once started, she was surprised how quickly the words flowed.

While the editor of the paper-wasting Lone Star Press *brought up a good point regarding the adoption of uniform schoolbooks,* she wrote, *Mr. Wade was, as usual, short-sighted and . . ."*

Her pen paused as she searched her brain for the perfect words that would get her message across without sending Papa into a frenzy.

Chapter 15

Miss Nancy Hamilton left her corset on the clothesline during last week's surprise storm and the metal ribs were severely demoralized by lightning.
—Two-Time Gazette

Josie spent that Monday morning trying to secure a temporary place for her newspaper office, but had no luck. What few empty buildings were available cost an arm and a leg to rent.

Though she could do the editorial work at home, she still needed a place for the noisy printer. Maybe the blacksmith would let her rent out a corner of his place. No sooner did the idea occur to her than she changed her mind. It wouldn't be fair to make Hank work around all that heat and noise.

A better idea might be to ask Mr. Gardner if she could work behind his shop where he kept the chickens. But after their last unpleasant encounter involving the little girl Haley, she doubted he would comply.

Such were her thoughts that she failed to see Mr. Wade until she plowed straight into him.

"Whoa," he said, steadying her with a hand to her elbow. "Where are you off to in such a hurry?"

She looked up and was once again reminded of his height. Though she stood at five feet eight, he topped her by a good five or six inches. But it wasn't his height that made her heart take a perilous leap, but rather his winning smile.

She struggled to find her voice. "Sorry," she muttered. "I'm due back at work." She pulled her arm away and continued along the boardwalk.

He fell into step by her side and his smile vanished. "'Shortsighted'?"

She slanted a sideways gaze at him, but said nothing.

"'Paper-wasting rag'?"

She tossed her head. "I take it that you read my editorial."

"I read it. Not bad,' he said. "Except for the part where you called me a snollygoster."

"I meant it as a compliment."

His eyebrows shot up. "You think being called unprincipled is a compliment?"

"I said that your concern for our schools proved you weren't a complete snollygoster."

"I don't know which is worse, your compliments or your insults."

She stopped to face him. "If I recall, editorial combat was *your* idea."

"And I seem to recall you decided against it. So, what changed your mind? Ah, don't tell me. Your little foray into the matrimonial business didn't work."

He knew darn well it hadn't worked. Everyone in town knew. "We found it difficult to control the integrity of the advertisers," she admitted. "Some people exaggerated their good qualities."

He burst out laughing. "You mean Two-Time isn't brimming with handsome millionaires and stunning beauties?"

She joined him in laughter. She couldn't help it. "It was a bit much, wasn't it?"

His eyes filled with warm humor. "It did make for entertaining reading. As for your editorial, you're right about teachers choosing textbooks. I should have thought of that myself. Of course, I would never admit that to my readers."

"Of course not," she said, though his unexpected compliment gave her a jolt of pleasure. She started along the boardwalk again, and he walked by her side.

"Two people agreeing with each other is deadly boring," he said. "Especially in print."

"Is that why you never admit that you're wrong?" she asked lightly to downplay his effect on her.

"I always admit when I'm wrong," he said.

"Do you, now?" Upon reaching the *Gazette* tent, they stopped and faced each other. "Would you also admit you're wrong about my writing?" she asked. "About it being insipid, I mean."

"Still dwelling on that, are we?"

She glanced askance at him. "Just want to set the record straight."

"After reading your last two editorials, including the one about the arsonist, I'd say your writing is as sharp as an arrow."

She turned her head away to hide the heat rushing to her face. "Thank you."

"While we're setting the record straight . . . I didn't set your place on fire."

She gave him an arched look. "I never said you did."

His gaze locked with hers, his eyes sparkling with the love of combat. "But you suspected it. Suspected it so much that you even went to the sheriff. Admit it."

She lifted her chin. "I might have given the sheriff that impression," she admitted.

"A-ha, I knew it!" he crowed. After a moment he added, "For your information, I'm perfectly innocent."

"Oh, I sincerely doubt that," she said.

His mouth quirked. "I'm referring to the fire."

She studied him. He certainly sounded sincere. Had she misjudged him? It certainly seemed that way. Or was that just wishful thinking on her part?

Hoping his good looks and charm hadn't blinded her to the truth, she said, "In that case, I apologize for suspecting you."

"Apology accepted," he said with a tip of the hat and slight bow. "And I also apologize for calling your writing insipid. Now that we've cleared the air between us and made nice, do you think we can write despicable things about each other for next week's editions? I'm thinking about taking issue with your stance on barbed wire."

"In that case, I'll take you to task for suggesting that shops should be allowed to open on the Sabbath," she said.

He grinned. "Sounds like war."

"Yes, doesn't it?" she said, surprised to find herself eager to get started. Since his crooked smile was doing strange things to her insides, she turned abruptly and headed for the safety of the tent.

He called after her. "May the best man win!"

"Oh, she will," Josie called back. "Count on it."

***

Becky-Sue Harris was waiting when Josie stepped through the canvas flap.

Hoping her friend had some positive news to share about her relationship with Scooter, Josie sank into the chair behind her desk. "What brings you here?"

Becky-Sue watched her from beneath a poke bonnet. Wisps of blond hair feathered her forehead. "I'm here to apply for a job."

Josie sat forward. "What kind of job?"

"A writing job."

Josie's eyebrows rose. "I didn't know you liked to write." Becky-Sue didn't strike her as the serious type, which was why she made a good match for Scooter. He tended to be too serious at times and needed someone like Becky-Sue to get him to relax and lighten up.

"I've always liked to write," Becky-Sue said. "Mostly letters. But I've also written some stories and would like to do a column on fashion." She gave her head an emphatic nod. "Did you know that the bustle is back in style?"

"God have mercy," Josie murmured. She picked up a sheet of paper and fanned herself. It was hot and getting hotter by the minute

Becky-Sue giggled. "I thought I'd start by interviewing Mrs. Gilbert. Everyone is dying to know how she manages to dress so fashionably on a bank clerk's salary. So, what do you say?"

Josie hated turning the girl down. Especially since Scooter was such a good friend. Did her wanting a job mean she'd given up on the idea of marriage?

"My goal is to report the news and other matters of importance to my readers." Not wanting to hurt Becky-Sue's feelings, Josie tried to be as tactful as possible. "I'm afraid fashion is of interest to only a few. In any case, I would prefer that any such fashion news include health issues."

Becky-Sue looked perplexed. "Health issues?"

"Yes. For example, women should be warned of the dangers of wearing whalebone or metal-rib corsets instead of the healthier cord. They should also be aware that letting skirts drag on the ground is unsanitary."

Becky-Sue looked as deflated as a flat rubber balloon. "I don't have to write about fashion. I can write about other things. I know a lot about the events in town."

By events, Josie guessed she meant gossip. Unfortunately, that was something both men and women were interested in, though no one would admit it.

When Josie remained silent, Becky-Sue continued, "I can even write an advice column. I'm a good writer. You won't be sorry."

Josie wasn't opposed to the idea of hiring a reporter. If only the paper's financial situation wasn't so up in the air. "I'm really not looking to hire anyone right now."

"Please." The girl gave her a beseeching look. "The job means a lot to me."

"I'm sorry, but to be perfectly honest, I can't afford to hire anyone." Right now, she couldn't even afford to stay in business.

"You don't have to pay me."

Josie sat back. "You want to write for free?"

"No significant newspaper will hire me without experience. I'm looking to gain some. That's all."

Ignoring the subtle affront, Josie hesitated as she considered the pros and cons of taking her on. Training the girl would take time, but she did seem eager to learn. Having another pair of eyes and ears around town couldn't hurt.

"Okay, we'll give it a try. Like I said, I can't afford to pay you. But if it's just experience you want, I can give you that." Josie thought a moment and decided to start the girl off with something easy. "You can report on the Independence Day celebration. That's your first assignment." The town was planning a big picnic and fireworks display for that Friday. "Also, next Thursday the circus is coming to town." If Becky-Sue covered those activities, that would give Josie more time to find a place for her office.

"Oh, thank you, thank you, thank you!" Becky-Sue gushed and broke into a wide smile.

"You should be advised that I require good writing with no weasel words," Josie said. Nothing peeved her more than journalists giving their articles more credence than they deserved. Such vague terms as "people say" or "a recent study shows" were meaningless. Good journalism required naming reliable sources.

Josie went through a list of dos and don'ts. "Always be sure to spell the names of your resources correctly. And be sure to end your articles with the numeral '30' to indicate end of story. You should also know that I'm particular about punctuation."

"You don't have to worry. I'm never late," Becky-Sue said and giggled.

Josie sighed. Already she was beginning to regret her decision to hire the girl.

***

The circus train arrived in town early that Thursday morning to a cheering crowd. No circus had ever before traveled to Two-Time, and the air was thick with excitement. Little Davey kept trying to pull away, and it was all Josie could do to hold onto him.

Laughing at her son's exuberance, Meg parked Carolyn's baby carriage in the shade of a tree. "It's hard to know who's more excited, me or Davey. I've never seen a circus."

"Me either," Josie said, tightening her grip on her nephew's small hand. Spotting her other sister in the crowd, she waved. "Amanda, over here.

"Hurry, Aun' 'Manda," Davey shouted, jumping up and down.

Acknowledging them with a smile, Amanda threaded her way through the thong of people and squeezed between Josie and Meg, her infant son, Jerrod, cradled in her arms.

Businesses were closed for the day in honor of the occasion, and Josie searched the spectators for Haley. She'd searched for the girl at the Fourth of July picnic and later, during the fireworks display, but didn't see her. Come to think of it, she hadn't seen Haley for a while and missed her.

Spotting her now across the street, Josie waved. It seemed that they'd made eye contact, but maybe not. For Haley abruptly turned and vanished from sight.

Hoping to pick the girl out again in the crowd, Josie craned her neck. Instead, she spotted Brandon Wade, and her breath caught in her lungs. Even with all the colorful circus pageantry, he stood out and commanded the eye. It was downright annoying.

Their gazes met, and he tipped his hat.

Cheeks flaring, she returned his greeting with a slight nod. Last week's editorials had been received with great enthusiasm. It hadn't taken long for word to spread that the feud had resumed. It was all everyone had talked about at the picnic. People left early to purchase both papers, leaving the mayor's annual Independence speech poorly attended.

The sudden *oohs* and *aahs* rising from the crowd drew Josie's attention away from Wade. All eyes were riveted upon a crimson-and-gold boxcar sitting on the track with the words "Jumbo's Palace Car" painted on the side in big, bold print. The double doors of the private railroad car slid open to loud trumpeting sounds. A moment later the star attraction, an elephant named Jumbo, appeared in the opening. The pachyderm's seven-foot trunk swung from side to side as he was led out of the car and up a ramp.

The crowd went wild. The animal was huge. Standing at twelve feet tall, he was said to weigh more than six tons.

Davey squealed with delight and tugged at Josie's hand. "Me pet. Me pet."

"No, Davey," Meg said. "We can't pet the elephant."

Amanda jostled little Jerrod in her arms and pointed at the enormous animal.

Josie had seen pictures of elephants, of course, but never had she seen one up close. It was truly a spectacular sight.

The moment the last of the circus boxcars was emptied, the brass band struck up a lively tune, and a parade wound its way along Main Street. The colorful procession offered an exciting preview of what would later be found under the big top. A crew of what seemed like hundreds of roustabouts had already set up the enormous tent outside of town.

Main Street was closed to traffic, allowing entertainers and animals to pass freely. Cheers rose from spectators stationed along the parade route. Children ran alongside the colored wagons, squealing with delight at the antics of the clowns. Dogs barked. Chickens flew out of the way, leaving a flutter of feathers behind. Never had the town seen anything so spectacular.

Davey dragged Josie along the boardwalk, shouting, "Come on, Aun' Cozy. Hurry!"

Holding up the hem of her skirt with her free hand, Josie laughed. It was all she could do to keep up with him. "I'm hurrying, I'm hurrying."

Bareback riders in dazzling costumes rode by on prancing horses, waving to the crowd. Tumblers, jugglers, and clowns, including one who stood barely three feet tall, followed. Their greased white faces sported bulbous red noses, including one that squeaked when pressed.

Robinson's celebrated twenty-piece military band marched down Main to the sound of blaring trumpets and *rat-a-tat* of drums. The musicians were followed by a calliope in a bright-red circus wagon, the bell chimes and steam organ filling the air with musical sounds.

Finally, Jumbo the elephant marched down the street. Lifting his trunk upward, he let out a bellow to the crowd's loud cheers.

Davey's eyes grew wide as saucers as the animal passed. He insisted they follow him up Main. "Hurry, hurry."

While Josie struggled to keep up with him, Meg and Amanda followed behind, Meg pushing the carriage. Davey laughed at the camels walking a distance behind the elephant.

"Horses funny," he said.

"Those aren't horses. They're camels," Josie explained.

The parade marched past the *Gazette* tent. Surprised to see Hank still fighting with the old printer, as he had been when she left him earlier, Josie waved to him.

"Take a break," she called gaily. "It's circus day."

"Give me a minute." He picked up a hammer and whacked the printer with all his might.

A loud metal clang rang out, startling one of the camels. With an earsplitting squeal, the animal reared back, straining against its harness. Cries of alarm rose from onlookers, and parents frantically reached for their young children. Josie jerked Davey away from the street, and his mother lifted him into her arms.

The trainer fought to control the panicked camel. Another trainer, running to help, cracked his whip. This only made matters worse. The camel clamped his mouth around the newcomer's head and tossed him aside like no more than a sack of potatoes. The man hit the ground hard.

Pandemonium erupted. Amid screams of terror, spectators scrambled out of the way. Josie whirled about looking for her sisters, but they were lost in the frenzied crowd. She turned around just in time to see the animal jerk back with a high-pitched growl and break free from its nose line.

Staring with horror-filled eyes, Josie's mouth opened in a silent scream. Young Haley stood motionless in the camel's path.

Chapter 16

Circus animal trainer Mr. Adams was testing his newly purchased pistol with terrible effect. He hopes to regain full use of his left leg in due time.
—The Two-Time Gazette

Josie ran toward the terrified girl. "Haley!" she screamed, her voice shrill. "Someone help!"

Brandon Wade reached Haley first, seeming to appear out of nowhere. He scooped her in his arms and moved her out of the camel's path in the nick of time. Josie followed, but lost them in the pandemonium that ensued. The circus people quickly led the rest of the animals away, leaving only a small, stunned crowd and a somewhat dazed animal trainer behind.

She finally spotted Wade on his knees, rocking Haley in his arms. With a face drained of color, he looked shaken. The sobbing girl clung to him as if to never let go, her face buried against his broad chest.

Josie dropped down beside them and ran her hand along Haley's back. "It's okay, dear heart. You're safe now."

Instead of comforting the child, her touch only seemed to upset Haley more. Her young body tensed, and a look of horror or maybe even fear crossed her pale face.

"It's only me," Josie said. "I'm not going to hurt you." When her soothing words failed to console the child, she pulled her hand away. Poor thing. Who could blame her for being scared out of her wits?

"I thought that camel was gonna hurt me," Haley sobbed. Her tears spilled onto Wade's shirt in a widening wet circle.

"It's all right, muffin," Wade said, running his hand up and down her back. "The camel's gone now and I won't let anything hurt you."

"I- I-" Haley could hardly get the words out between her sobs. "W-want to go home, Papa."

Startled, Josie met Wade's gaze. "You're . . . her father?" She'd heard something about his wife dying and leaving him with a child, but she'd discounted it along with all the other rumors, including his being an offspring of British royalty.

He answered her question with a nod. "Why so surprised?"

"I just never thought of you as a family man."

He arched an eyebrow. "Does that change your opinion of me?"

Yes, yes, it did change her opinion of him, but in which way she couldn't say.

Haley stirred in Wade's arms. He blew a strand of his daughter's hair away from his face. "Come on," he said. Lifting her off the ground, he tenderly cradled her in his arms. "Let's get you home."

***

The following morning, Josie found Hank slumped over his desk. He was beside himself, and nothing Josie said or did could console him.

"Someone could have keen billed," he lamented. "And all because of me." He said more, but his words became so scrambled it was as if he were talking a foreign language.

"Listen to me, Hank." She made him raise his head off the desk and look at her. "No one was killed or seriously injured. The doctor said that the animal trainer was just a bit shaken up and has no broken bones."

"But that gittle . . . little girl was scared out of her wits." Hank shuddered.

"Haley is fine." Josie still couldn't believe the child was Brandon Wade's daughter. Though now that she thought about it, there was a slight family resemblance, especially around the eyes. "Hank, it was an accident. You had no way of knowing how that camel would react. No one blames you."

She had just about managed to get Hank to calm down, or at least stop thinking what could have happened had the camel not been restrained, when Becky-Sue rushed into the tent, all pink cheeked and breathless.

"That was so exciting," she squealed, waving her notepad over her head. "I wrote everything down. I even interviewed the man who almost got his head bitten off. He said if he ever got his hands on the son of a—"

"That's wonderful, Becky-Sue," Josie said quickly with an anxious glance at Hank. She had forgotten that she had assigned the girl to report on the circus. Grabbing the notebook from Becky-Sue's flailing hands, she tossed a meaningful nod in Hank's direction.

Becky-Sue's eyes widened, and her mouth formed a perfect O. In her excitement, she'd evidently failed to notice Hank's presence.

"I-I-I'm sorry," she stammered.

Feeling sorry for her, Josie walked her outside. "Thank you. Your article will run in next week's edition."

Becky-Sue looked like she was about to cry. "I didn't see Hank," she whispered.

Josie sighed. "I know."

Becky Sue's forehead creased. "If you don't run the article, I won't feel bad."

"It's news, Becky-Sue. I have to run it. When newspapers start choosing the news it reports, we'll all be in trouble."

***

Brandon sat on the edge of Haley's bed, rocking her in his arms. This was the third consecutive night she'd woken from a deep sleep, sobbing her little heart out, her trembling body soaked with sweat.

How he hated seeing her so unhappy. She'd refused to have anything to do with the Fourth of July celebration and had complained of a stomachache. It was only because he'd put his foot down that the two of them had gone to see the arrival of the circus. He hadn't wanted her to miss out on that. Big mistake.

The camel episode had turned her completely against Two-Time, and all she'd talked about since was wanting to leave. Nothing he said or did could make her change her mind.

Not that he blamed her. The mere memory of seeing Haley cower in the path of that crazed animal made his blood run cold. The thought of losing his daughter was like a knife slicing through him. Mingled with the horror was the memory of Mrs. Johnson's surprised expression upon learning he was Haley's pa. If she had that much trouble believing he was a father, she mustn't have a very good opinion of him.

Before he could decide how he felt about that, Haley stirred in his arms, pulling him away from his thoughts. Staring up at him with tear-filled orbs, she asked, "Why can't we go back to San Antone?"

He brushed a strand of blond hair away from her damp cheek. "I told you, Haley. This is our home now."

"But I hate it here!"

Brandon inhaled. Reasoning with a nine-year-old was challenging enough, but at two in the morning it was downright impossible.

"Tell you what," he said. "We'll go to San Antone for a visit." Encouraged by the hopeful look on his daughter's face, he continued, "You'd like that, right? We'll see your friends and have a picnic by the river. Just like we used to. What do you say?"

Haley knuckled the tears away from her eyes. "Can we stay there forever? Please, Papa, please!"

He envied his daughter for thinking there was such a thing as forever. "We'll talk about this again in the morning. Right now, we both need to get some sleep."

Much to his relief, that seemed to satisfy her, but he knew the reprieve was only temporary. Tomorrow she'd be at him again. Once Haley got something in her head, she was like a dog with a bone.

Her eyelids closed the moment she laid her head back on her pillow. Dark lashes fanned her tear-stained cheeks. He watched her sleep, his heart filled with gratitude. What would he have done had he lost her?

He dropped a tender kiss on her forehead.

At times, it seemed like she was growing up too quickly. Tonight, however, she looked small and vulnerable, and his heart swelled with a need to protect her from the harshness of the world. If only he could. Saving her from the camel had been pure luck. They had gotten separated in the crowd. It was only by chance that he'd happened to spot her in time. But what if he hadn't? The thought sent cold chills racing down his spine.

Pulling the covers over her, he waited to make sure she didn't stir before dousing the flame in the oil lamp. He stood in the dark listening to his daughter's soft breaths and felt very much alone.

***

"Got a filler?" Hank called from his desk early that Monday morning. "I have two inches left."

Josie reached for a file where she kept interesting tidbits collected from other newspapers to use where needed. Fillers included little oddities about animals, the weather, and people. "Borrowing" from other newspapers was common practice, and most editors didn't bother giving credit. Josie always did.

One short article told about art thief Peter Osborne, who'd tried claiming the reward on his own wanted poster. Another news bit was about a stagecoach robber who turned himself in after imagining he saw his own initials in a cloud.

The article reminded her of the conversation with Scooter. "What do you think it will take for someone to come forward with information on Miss Ruby?"

Hank plucked a lead letter out of the type case before answering. "If a thousand-dollar reward doesn't do it, I sure in tarnation don't think anything will."

Josie sighed. He could be right. "Do you think running Miss Bubbles' advertisement in the paper had anything to do with the fire?"

Hank swung his chair around to face her. "What makes you think that?"

"I don't know. The timing, maybe."

He shrugged and turned back to his desk. "Maybe it was one of the ladies I turned down."

She laughed. "Now why didn't I think of that?"

She stopped to read a small clipping about the great camel experiment in Texas. The project had been a failure because of the disagreeable nature of the beasts. She tossed the clipping back into the file. A filler about camels was probably not a good idea right now.

She was still rummaging through the clippings when a shadow fell across her desk. She looked up to find Pepper staring down at her.

His glance bounced off the canvas walls and ceiling. "I see that things have taken, shall we say, a turn for the worse since we last spoke."

Sitting back in her chair, she folded her arms across her chest. "What do you want, Pepper?"

"I thought perhaps you might wish to reconsider my offer."

It took a moment for the meaning of his words to sink in. The fire and all that had happened since had commanded her attention. So much so that she had forgotten all about the riverside property. She now realized the deed had gone up in smoke along with everything else.

Pepper tapped his foot, waiting for her response, and when none came asked, "Well?"

She narrowed her eyes. "My answer still stands."

Pepper's eyebrows rose in surprise. Evidently, he had expected her to change her mind. "That seems rather foolish. This isn't exactly what you would call home sweet home."

"To me it is," she said.

'If you change your mind—"

"I won't."

"If you do, you know where to find me." He spun around and ducked out of the tent.

"What was that all about?" Hank asked, pushing his glasses up his nose.

"I don't really know," Josie said. Pepper sure did want that lot. Not that she blamed him. It was a beautiful piece of land. Still, his persistence suggested his interest went beyond the normal desire for riverfront property.

The thought led to a most disconcerting question. Her office had burned down shortly after he'd made his first offer. Was it possible that Pepper had set her office on fire to force her to sell?

Her body stiffened as the thought took hold. Oh, dear heaven . . .

Chapter 17

*The train arrived late Monday after several of its cars had been
temporarily pulled from service. A group of hoboes reportedly stole the
rubber airbrake hoses to make soles for their shoes.*

—Two-Time Gazette

The thought that Pepper had something to do with the fire sent Josie
scurrying along the boardwalk, heels pounding the wooden sidewalk
planks like two frenzied woodpeckers. By the time she swooped into the
sheriff's office she had convinced herself she was right about Pepper.

The manner by which she burst through the door seemed to startle
Scooter, and he half rose from his desk. "Josie. I was just about to pay you
a visit."

"I think I know who started the fire," she blurted out.

Eyebrows raised, he lowered himself into his chair. Giving him no
chance to speak, she paced back and forth in front of his desk and outlined
the case against Pepper. When she finished, she stopped and faced him.
"What do you think?"

Scooter tapped the edge of his desk with the end of a pencil. "Just
because he wants that property don't mean nothin'. Lots of people have an
eye on that lot."

"But not everyone tried to buy it from me." Still not convinced
Pepper hadn't purposely run her off the road during the race, she gave her
head an indignant shake. "At half of what it's worth, I might add. And I
can tell you, he wasn't happy when I turned his offer down."

Scooter shrugged. "That don't make him guilty of arson."

"No, but it does suggest a motive, and that makes him the closest
thing to a suspect we've got."

Scooter shook his head. "We might have ourselves another
suspect."

She stared at him, heart thumping. "Who?"

For answer, he pulled a sheet of parchment paper from a drawer
and slid it across the desk.

Frowning, she leaned over for a closer look. It was an old wanted
poster. An award of five hundred dollars had been offered for the capture
and conviction of a man named Jack Casey, wanted for arson. The poster
included a sketch of a man whose face looked vaguely familiar.

She lifted her gaze. "Who is he?"

Scooter folded his arms across his chest. "You now know him as
Hank."

"*My* Hank?" she gasped.

Scooter answered her question with a nod. Speechless, she stared at him in disbelief before turning her attention back to the poster, this time picking it up to study more closely. There was no denying that the man in the picture did resemble Hank—a much younger Hank—especially around the eyes and mouth.

"Hank is an arsonist?" she whispered through wooden lips.

"He served two years in the state pen for settin' fire to a school."

She dropped the poster on his desk as if it had suddenly burned her fingers. "I . . . I don't believe it."

"It's true." He reached for a telegram and planted it on the desk next to the poster. "That there is what they call confirmation."

Josie shook her head. She couldn't imagine gentle Hank doing something so awful. "Was . . . was anyone hurt at the school?"

"Not that I know of."

She drew in her breath and studied the wanted poster again. The sketch looked like Hank had still been in his teens at the time. "That was a long time ago. Before the war."

Scooter shrugged. "Like Grandpapa always said, 'Once a fool, always a fool.' I think the same holds true for arsonists."

"But that makes no sense. Hank loves the *Gazette* as much I do. He considers it his home. He would never do anything to jeopardize it. Why would he?"

"Won't know that till I question him."

Josie covered her face with her hands. Oh, God, no. Not Hank. There had to be a logical explanation. She gazed at Scooter over her fingertips. "Let me talk to him first."

"Can't do that, Josie. If he's guilty and knows we're on to him, he might skedaddle—"

"He didn't do it. He didn't burn down the *Gazette*. I know he didn't."

"If you're wrong—" Scooter shook his head. "—you could be puttin' yourself in harm's way."

She shook her head. She couldn't imagine the man she had come to know and love as a friend hurting her. The problem was she was having the same trouble thinking him capable of setting a school on fire.

"I'll take my chances. Scooter, please."

Scooter rubbed his chin and grimaced before pulling out his watch. "I'll give you a half hour, tops."

"Thank you." She frowned. "About Pepper—"

Scooter rubbed his forehead. "I'll talk to him."

Nodding, she turned to the door on wooden legs. Hank an arsonist? She couldn't believe it.

"Josie."

Hand on the doorknob, she glanced over her shoulder.

"I done heard that you have to the end of the month to remove the tent," he said. "Is that true?"

"'Fraid so. I'm looking for a new place. Any ideas?"

"I got a free jail cell," he said and tossed a nod at the cellblock in back.

She managed a wan smile. "I may have to take you up on that offer." Growing serious again, she bit her lip. "Hank's not the arsonist. I know he's not." With that she shot out the door.

***

Josie headed back to her office, her heart so heavy she could barely pick up her feet. How she dreaded having to confront Hank. She couldn't imagine his destroying property or putting others at harm. Could she really have been that wrong about him?

Hank was still setting type when she entered the tent, his back toward her. He spoke without turning. "She said yes."

Josie placed her purse in the bottom desk drawer. "Who said yes?"

He swung around in his chair, a silly grin on his face. "Why Miss Read, of course. She's havin' supper with me on Saturday."

"That's . . . wonderful news, Hank."

He raised an eyebrow. "You don't sound happy. You look . . ." His forehead creased. "What's going on?"

Stalling for time, she pulled out her chair and sat. "I just saw the sheriff."

"And?" His gaze sharpened. Remaining seated, he walked his chair to her desk. "Did he catch the arsonist?"

She clenched her hands. "Not exactly."

Hank gave an impatient wave. "What, then?"

"Scooter showed me an old wanted poster."

Hank studied her, eyes narrowed behind his spectacles, and then his face suddenly drained of color. "A panted woster?" Silence stretched between them before he spoke again. "Of me?"

She moistened her lips. "I'm sorry, Hank, but I have to ask."

His shoulders slumped as if all the air had suddenly left his body. "Seems to me I'm the one should be apologizin'."

She held her breath. "You didn't—"

"Gurn down the *Bazette*?" He shook his head. "No, I did not, and that's the Hod's Gonest truth." He spoke with such vehemence that she immediately believed him.

"What about the other?" She hated to ask, but she had to know.

"The school?" She hoped he would deny it as well. Prayed that he would say that it was all a big mistake. Instead, his Adam's apple bobbed up and down like a cork in a stormy sea.

"As a youth . . ." He pulled a handkerchief out of his pocket and mopped his forehead. "I was . . ." His face contorted as he struggled to say the words, stopping and starting over as necessary. It took a while to figure out what he was trying to say, but her heart sank as his meaning became clear. Instead of the denial she'd hoped for, he fully confessed to the crime he'd been convicted of.

She stared at him in shock. Kind, gentle Hank was an arsonist?

She fought to control her disgust, but the hurt of betrayal was not so easily contained.

"Why?" she whispered when at last she found her voice. "Why would you do such a thing?"

"I was angry," he said simply, as if that was explanation enough.

Her temper flared. "Angry? That's your excuse?"

"It's not an excuse."

She stared at him in disbelief. "What, then? Talk to me. And why a school?"

His facial features sagged, and furrows appeared between his eyebrows. "M-my pa was headmaster." He spoke slowly in a monotone voice, as if each word had to be painfully constructed before leaving his mouth. Even so, she had to mentally decipher his mixed-up words.

Hank blew out his breath before continuing. "He walked out on the family. Then one day I stopped at the school to talk to him, and I saw him with one of his pupils. It occurred to me that he was kinder to his pupil than he ever was to me." He tipped his head back and stared at the canvas ceiling. "Guess you could say I let my anger get the best of me."

He gave her a beseeching look before adding, "It's not somethin' I'm proud of. Fortunately, no one was hurt." He paused for a moment as if to gather his thoughts. "Case you're wonderin', I'm a different person today than I was back then. The war messed up my head, but it straightened out my heart."

"How do you mean?" she asked.

"Saw a lot of good people die during that war, including the man whose name I now use, Hank Chambers. He was a good man. The only real friend I ever had. I thought by using his name, it would help me be a good man too."

"Oh, Hank. I'm so sorry," she whispered. Papa had a similar look of desolation on his face whenever he spoke of that awful War between the States. His "war look," she called it. As a child, that look had scared her. It scared her now, but not for the same reason.

"I kept askin' myself why Chambers died and not me? That's when I decided to leave my wild ways behind me. Guess you could say it was my way of honorin' the good people who didn't deserve to die." He looked her straight in the face. "Jack Casey might have burned down your office, but Hank Chambers never would."

His voice, his eyes, told her he spoke the truth, and relief washed over her like spring rain. "I'm sorry I had to ask," she said. "But when I saw that wanted poster—"

"I know." He gave a bitter laugh. "I wasn't very good at hiding my tracks. Someone had spotted me with a can of gasoline and went to the sheriff. I was standing in a post office when I first saw my picture on the wall. You know what I thought at the time? I thought, 'Coly how. Someone wants me.' For the first time in my life someone really, really wants me. That's when I turned myself in."

"Oh, Hank. I want you. I couldn't run this paper without you. Your friendship means the world to me. Miss Read wants you too."

"The jury's still out on Miss Read." Hank let out a long sigh. "She's a former schoolteacher. If she finds out I once tried burning down a school, I don't know that she'll want anything to do with me."

"Everyone makes mistakes," Josie said. "And Miss Read has had enough experience working with troubled youths to know that people change."

"We'll see," he said, the hope in his eyes contradicting the doubt in his voice. "Do I still jave my hob?" he asked.

"Of course you still have your job," she said. "What do I call you? Jack or Hank?"

"Jack is dead," he said. "Let's keep it that way."

She nodded. "I'm really glad we had this talk."

With a sigh of relief, he swung his chair around and walked it back to his desk. "Me too," he said. "Me too."

"Make that three of us," the sheriff said.

Josie spun around. She had been so intent on Hank she was unaware of Scooter's presence until he spoke. "Did you hear?" she asked.

"I heard," Scooter said.

"Does that hake me off the took?" Hank asked.

Since Scooter looked puzzled, Josie interpreted.

"Yeah, you're off the hook," Scooter said. "Least for now."

Chapter 18

If the news seems a bit on the slim side this week, please bear in mind that the telegraph office was closed, the mail from the east held up and no one was accommodating enough to get married, die, or have a baby. —Two-Time Gazette

Almost three weeks had passed since the mayor gave his ultimatum, and still Josie had made no progress in finding office space. The recent success of her paper made the problem even more dire.

She still ran the "Love Links" column, but with a difference: the *Gazette* now had a strict advertisement policy. Those wishing to describe themselves as rich, beautiful, thin, or handsome were charged double. A woman asserting to be younger than her years, or a man professing to own a suspiciously large spread, were referred to the nearest notary for claim validation.

The policy didn't do away entirely with exaggerations and downright lies, but there were fewer reader complaints.

Though the "Love Links" column was popular, the real attraction was the rekindled feud that now raged between Josie and Wade. Bets were placed as to which publisher would win the next round.

Even though Hank had doubled and nearly tripled the *Gazette*'s print run, they still had trouble keeping up with demand. The way papers were flying out the door that Friday morning, it looked like it would be another great week.

Wade had been right about her selling more newspapers than she ever thought possible. But even with her sudden success, she couldn't afford to pay rent—not while she was still paying on the mortgage. The prospects of rebuilding anytime soon didn't look all that promising either.

That's why Josie had arranged to meet with the bank president, Mr. Mooney, that morning.

"What can I do for you, Mrs. Johnson?" he asked as she entered his office. Standing politely until she sat, he then lowered his bulky form onto his chair and folded his hands on an oak desk the size of a boxcar.

Everything in the office was large, including Mr. Mooney, and Josie felt uncommonly small and insignificant seated in front of him. No doubt that was the banker's intention.

In an effort to compensate, she sat tall, chin held high, and lowered her voice an octave to sound more businesslike. "As you know, I've had a recent setback."

His gray eyes met hers. "Ah, yes, the fire. Any news of who might have started it?"

"Not yet." She cleared her voice and lowered her voice yet another notch. "I wish to renegotiate the terms of my mortgage."

His eyebrows shot up. "Renegotiate?" Somehow, he managed to make it sound like she had asked him to turn over the contents of the safe.

Relying on her carefully rehearsed words, she plowed on. "My intention is to rebuild, but that would be difficult under the current terms of the loan."

"Your father agreed to those terms."

Actually, she was the one who had agreed, but since the bank required a male signature, her father had signed the contract.

"I have every intention of living up to my obligations," she assured him. "I'm just asking for more time."

He tapped the edge of his desk with a pencil. "I'm afraid changing the terms of a contract at this late date would be impossible."

"Why impossible?" she asked.

The question seemed to surprise him, and the pencil stilled in his hand. "Why, it's simply not done," he said. He made it sound like no other explanation was needed. When she demanded clarification, he simply shrugged. "The bank has a strict policy against changing the terms of a contract."

"I'm only asking for an extension," she said.

He tossed the pencil aside. "I'm afraid that's out of the question. As you must know, I stuck my neck out in the first place by approving the original loan."

She narrowed her eyes. "Because I'm a woman?"

"I was just following bank policy."

"The bank makes concessions to farmers whose crops fail," she said. "*Male* farmers."

With a sigh of impatience, he reached for his pocket watch. "A woman in business does not command the same, shall we say, confidence as a man. Nevertheless, I approved the loan as a favor to your father. As for changing the original terms, I'm afraid my hands are tied. It's nothing personal." He rose, signaling the meeting was over. "Hope you understand."

She stood as well, almost trembling with anger. "And I hope you understand why I find it necessary to write an editorial regarding the bank's unfair practices toward women." Her sister Amanda would be so proud. Stalking across the room, she reached for the doorknob before leveling one last glance at the bank president. "That's Mooney with an *e*, right?"

Josie left the bank feeling worse than when she'd arrived. She hadn't really expected the bank to comply with her wishes, but she had to try.

Now what?

She stepped off the boardwalk and dodged around the wagons and buggies that had come to a standstill. Curses were directed at the hapless man who had accidentally dumped a pushcart of bricks in the middle of Main.

As she made her way across the street, a red-white-and-blue banner announcing the opening of a new photography studio caught her eye. Josie brightened. If she could convince the new photographer to advertise in her newspaper, the morning wouldn't be a complete waste.

Josie stopped to look at the photographs displayed in the window before stepping inside. She was greeted by a large portrait of Mrs. Gilbert arranged on an easel. The bank clerk's wife was dressed in the same fancy gown worn at the May dance, with the same cameo and earbobs. The black-and-white portrait failed to do the dress justice, but the camera had captured the woman's delicate features and large expressive eyes. She looked even younger in the photograph than in real life.

A voice from the back room called out. "May I help you?"

Drawing her gaze away from the portrait, Josie turned toward the speaker. Through the open doorway, she could see the shop owner fiddling with a large boxy camera saddled upon a tripod. A tall, thin man with long sideburns, he looked like he was preparing to take someone's picture, but his client was not visible from where she stood.

She glanced at the sign over the counter. "Are you Mr. Farthing?"

"Yes," the man answered, adjusting the camera's bellows.

"I'm Mrs. Johnson, publisher of the *Two-Time Gazette*. I'm offering an advertising special this week."

Mr. Farthing admonished his client to stand still before addressing his comments to Josie. "I'm already advertising. In the *Lone Star Press*."

Admonishing herself for not having approached the newcomer earlier, she went into her spiel. "My newspaper has more female readers. As I'm sure you're aware, it's the woman of the house who usually decides on a family portrait. Also, many single women read my newspaper, which means you'll be reaching potential brides."

It was hard to tell from Mr. Farthing's profile if anything she'd said had made an impression. There was only one way she knew to find out. "You'll find my rates lower than Mr. Wade's."

"Lower than free?" he asked, draping the black focusing cloth over the back of the camera. "Don't move," he called to his hidden client.

She sucked in her breath. Free? Wade gave away ads for free? Why that low-down, sneaky— Surprised by the fierce competitiveness that made her shake, her fingers curled around the purse clutched in her hands.

Mr. Farthing ducked beneath the black cloth. "Hold it." A flash of white light exploded from the magnesium tray.

Josie waited for the photographer's head to reappear. "Not only will I charge you nothing for trying out the *Gazette*, but I will also double the size of Mr. Wade's ad." *Just don't let it be page size.*

"I think you should take the lady up on her generous offer," came a male voice that made Josie's jaw drop. Before she could recover from her surprise, Brandon Wade stepped out of the back room, hat in hand.

Josie forced herself to breathe, but nothing could be done about her flaming cheeks. "I didn't think you'd be the kind to subject yourself to a camera," she said. He seemed much too restless to sit still for any length of time.

He smiled. "A surprise for my daughter. She's always complaining that she doesn't have a photograph of me."

At mention of Haley, Josie forgot her irritation with him. "Is she all right?" Josie hadn't seen the girl since the day of the circus, though she'd looked for her daily.

"She's . . . recovered from the camel ordeal. Thank you for asking."

Josie's senses sharpened. Had she only imagined his hesitation? "Such a lovely child. You must be very proud."

His handsome smile offered reassurance. "I've been very fortunate."

She recalled Haley asking to see a photograph of Ralph. "I'm sure your surprise will make your daughter very happy."

Mr. Farthing stepped forward and handed her a sheet of paper. "That's the information for the ad."

"Ah, yes." The *free* ad.

Brandon must have read something in her face because he said, "Don't worry, Mrs. Johnson, you only have to double a quarter of a page. That shouldn't be a problem now that the *Gazette* is doing so well."

"For which you take full credit, I'm sure."

"You have to admit, our editorial wars are turning out to be highly successful," he drawled.

Had he not looked so downright smug, she might have agreed. "Modest as always," she retaliated.

"I personally find modesty to be greatly overrated."

Before she could respond, Farthing addressed her. "Would you care to have your portrait taken, Mrs. Johnson?" His gaze dropped to her dull black dress. and she imagined him trying to think up ways to make it appear less . . . dreary. "Since you're kind enough to run a free ad, there'll be no charge."

"Perhaps another time," she said. Standing next to Mrs. Gilbert's portrait made her feel plain and unattractive. Was that how she looked to Brandon? She crossed her arms in front in a vain attempt to hide from his probing gaze.

"Very well." Mr. Farthing was saying. "Can't wait to see which ad brings in the most business—yours or Wade's."

"I'm curious to find out myself," Wade said, his eyes bright with challenge. "I hope you won't be too disappointed in the results, Mrs. Johnson."

She tucked the ad copy in her purse. "It's been my experience that the biggest disappointments come to those who get what's coming to them."

"I guess it says something that I've never been disappointed," Wade said. "But I have on occasion been surprised. Sometimes even pleasantly so." He slapped his hat on his head and adjusted the brim. "Good day, Mrs. Johnson."

"Good day, Mr. Wade," she said and watched him leave. For some reason, all that talk about disappointments and surprises made her think about lot eleven. She still hadn't turned it over to its rightful owner. Life had been hectic since the fire. She hadn't even had time to stop at the county office for a copy of the deed that had gone up in smoke. Combined with the problem of trying to relocate her business, lot eleven felt like an albatross around her neck.

✳✳✳

The following morning, Mama turned from the stove and almost dropped the pan in her hands. "Oh, my! Look at you."

Josie spun around. Yesterday, after leaving the photography shop, she'd decided to make some changes in her life. The mantle of grief hung heavy, but never as heavy as it had in that shop, standing next to Mrs. Gilbert's photograph.

Now, one hand at her waist, she struck a fashionable pose. The yellow chintz dress had always been one of her favorites. Ralph's too. The years she'd spent with him had been a joy and a pleasure, and the yellow dress reflected and honored that time more than any black dress could do.

The color also went perfectly with her dark-brown hair. Next to the dreary widow's weeds, the light fabric made her feel young and carefree again. And, more than anything, cooler. The heat in the tent was bad enough without having to bury herself in black crepe or wool like an overburdened sheep.

"What do you think, Mama?"

Mama set the pan on the counter. "I think you look pretty as a picture, but—" She wiped her hands on her apron. "It's too soon."

Josie dropped her arms to her sides. "It'll be two years after the first of the year." So much had happened in that time that in some ways it seemed like she'd been a widow forever.

Her mother studied her with questioning eyes. "Why now, Josie? Why today?"

Josie wasn't sure her mother would understand if she knew the truth. Josie planned to meet with the mayor and needed to look and feel confident and like a woman in charge. She hoped that offering him her paper's endorsement for reelection would convince him to give her more time to relocate. He wasn't the best mayor Two-Time had ever had, but neither was he the worst. Getting him on her side was her last resort.

She also needed to take care of old business, including the little matter that continued to press on her conscience: turning the deed to lot eleven over to its rightful owner. So stopping at the county office was on her list of things to do.

"Maybe I'm just tired of being the *widow* Johnson."

That part was true. She felt more like herself today than she'd felt in months, maybe even years, and was suddenly excited about the future. Readers had responded in positive ways to the clash of opinions printed weekly. As much as she hated to admit it, she kind of liked trading editorial barbs with Mr. Wade.

A newspaper could be both a weapon and a tool, and she enjoyed wielding it in both capacities. If newspaper sales continued like they had in recent weeks, she would soon be on sounder financial footing. Her dream of rebuilding and putting out a paper twice weekly, and maybe even daily, might very well come true.

Since her admission only increased her mother's disapproving frown, Josie added "I'm especially tired of having people look at me with pity."

"No one pities you, Josie."

"Some do, Mama. I see it in their eyes. And I'm tired of having to look like a dour old lady." That's certainly how the photographer Mr. Farthing had looked at her. She didn't want to speculate as to what Brandon Wade had thought. "What gives people the right to tell me how to feel and act as a widow? Ralph wouldn't recognize me, and he'd hate seeing me dressed all in black. I know he would."

Mama sighed. "You're a grown woman. I can't tell you what to do. But I do wish you'd take things more slowly."

Josie squeezed her mother's hand. Mama's deportment—her dress, her speech and impeccable manners—were perfect in every way. She had done her best through the years to make sure her daughters lived up to the same high standards, though not always with the best of results. That's why Josie had been shocked to learn that Mama had been carrying her when she walked down the aisle. Josie still couldn't believe it. Was the shame of conceiving a baby out of wedlock the reason her mother tended to go overboard in following society's rigid rules? Perhaps it was her way of trying to keep her daughters from making her same mistakes.

"Don't worry, Mama. I'm not going to do anything rash. I just want to get back to being my old self again. Is that so bad?"

With a loving smile, Mama nudged a strand of hair away from Josie's cheek. "No, dear heart. That's not bad, but I do worry about you. It's not easy running a newspaper. You're working far too hard. Why, we hardly see you anymore."

"I'm not working all that hard." The public feud with the *Lone Star Press's* editor had energized her in ways she couldn't fully understand. The rebuttals she wrote to his columns required numerous interviews and fact checking. In addition, the sudden surge of new advertisers took up much of her time. She looked forward to each new day like never before and resented anything that kept her away from work.

"Please don't worry, Mama."

"How can I not? Some of the things you write in the paper . . . Must you resort to such . . . uncivil language?"

"It's what sells papers, Mama. But that's not all it does. We're making people think about all sides of an issue before forming an opinion. That's making a huge difference in the town. People are talking about things that matter and are now making more informed choices. The school board even voted to change how textbooks are purchased. I'm helping to make a difference, and that should please you."

"I'm proud of what you're doing, Josie. I just wish you didn't have to resort to such unladylike tactics to do it."

"It's theatrics, Mama. That's all. It means nothing."

Mama shook her head and suddenly looked tired. "I know you and your sisters think I'm old-fashioned. But in my day, a woman would never draw attention to herself with a public dispute."

"That was never my intention, Mama. But journalism is a tough business, and if I don't give the public what it wants, I lose out."

Mama rolled her eyes to the ceiling. "Dear God, what is the world coming to?" To Josie, she said, "I fear that this will only ruin your reputation. After the last edition, even the ladies of the church auxiliary found it necessary to offer a special prayer for you."

Josie pressed the palm of her hand against her mother's smooth cheek. Women, and especially widows, were expected to adhere to certain rules of deportment. And though many women might secretly admire what she was doing, few would dare admit such a thing in public or rise to her defense.

"I'll be fine, Mama," Josie said.

Mama looked doubtful, but nonetheless nodded. "I do hope so, pet."

Lowering her hand, Josie backed away. She plucked a ripe peach out of the fruit bowl and walked out of the kitchen.

Only three things prevented her from enjoying the recent success of her newspaper—four if she counted that unfinished business with lot eleven. She had yet to find new office space and only a week was left before she was to vacate the premises, no one had stepped forward to claim Miss Bubbles' award, and the arsonist had yet to be caught. There was nothing she could do about the unsolved crimes, but the future of lot eleven was clearly in her hands.

Chapter 19

A wool blanket hanging on a bush to dry was mistaken by a hunter for a bear. The blanket now makes a fine strainer.—Two-Time Gazette

The door to the *Lone Star Press* office swung open, and the man Brandon recognized as Josie's father barreled inside with the force of a runaway freight train. Lockwood came to a skidding stop in front of Brandon and slapped the morning's edition onto the desk.

The slamming door brought Booker on the run. Catching his compositor's eye, Brandon gave his head a slight shake. Lockwood was obviously riled, but Brandon didn't think he would do bodily harm. At least he hoped not.

He stabbed his pen into its holder and sat back in his chair, hands folded across his middle. "What can I do for you, sir?"

"For starters, you can stop slandering my daughter!" Lockwood bellowed. A big, broad-chested man, his face was as red as a trainman's flag.

"Slander?" Brandon cringed at the thought. Defaming Josie was the last thing he ever wanted to do. "I assure you I have nothing but the greatest admiration and respect for your daughter."

Leaning over, Lockwood stabbed at the newspaper with the tip of a stubby finger. "You certainly have a fine way of showing it!"

"Our written exchanges are strictly business." Refusing to raise his voice, Brandon spoke with measured calmness. "I take issue with some of her opinions, but otherwise—"

Lockwood's fist hit the desk with the force of a sledgehammer. "I take issue with her opinions, too, but you don't see me embarrassing her in public. And I want it to stop. Do you hear me? I want it to stop now!"

Brandon sucked in his breath. He had no desire to fight with the man, but neither did he want to be told how to run his newspaper. "If you will kindly have a seat," Brandon began. Keeping his voice low, he hoped Lockwood would take the hint and do likewise. "I'm sure we can come to some sort of understanding."

"I doubt that very much!" Lockwood roared.

Over the next few minutes, Brandon tried several different tactics, at one point taking a firmer tone and at another a more conciliatory approach. But any effort to reason with Lockwood was met with hostility. Seeing the futility of discussing the matter further, Brandon rose to his feet, hoping that would encourage the man to leave. It did not.

Instead, Lockwood wagged a finger and issued an ultimatum. "Either you issue a public apology to my daughter or I'll personally sue you for slander."

Brandon rubbed the back of his neck. That's all he needed—to be dragged into court. Lockwood had a reputation of being sue-happy, so it hardly seemed like an idle threat. "Sir, I think your daughter might have something to say about that."

Lockwood opened his mouth, but before he could deliver another spew of outrage, the door flew open and in walked Josie Johnson herself.

***

"Papa?"

Surprised to see her father, Josie's gaze threaded back and forth between the two men who faced each other rigid as tin soldiers.

"What . . . what are you doing here?" she asked.

Papa swung his bulky form around to face her. "I'm here on your behalf," he said. "I will not let this man continue to besmirch your good name."

Letting the door slam shut behind her, Josie took in the scene before her. Brandon looked solemn, but so did the faces of his employees peering from the open doorway of the other room.

She drew in her breath. She could well imagine what had transpired before she walked in. Her father was not one to mince words. "You have no right, Papa."

Papa's eyebrows shot up. "No right? No right, you say? I'm your father. I have every right to look out for your welfare."

Something snapped inside her. Today, she'd needed to feel confident and in control. But here Papa was treating her like a child. In front of Brandon Wade, no less. "Not when it involves business."

"That's what you call it? This man is dragging your name through the muck, and you call it business?"

"He's not—" Never one to go against Papa in the past, she now lifted her chin and glared back in defiance. "Brandon . . . Mr. Wade and I have an agreement. A *business* agreement."

Papa reared back, eyes nearly popping out of his head. "An agreement, you say? You mean you approve of the rubbish he writes about you?"

"It's no worse than what I write about him."

"I won't have it, Josie. I won't have my daughter subjecting herself to such obnoxious—"

"And I won't have you telling me how to run my newspaper!"

Her father's face crumbled in disbelief. Amanda and Meg had fought him and his old-fashioned views, but never her. It pained her to do so now, but she couldn't help but resent the way he still treated her like a child. She had lost a husband, fought off Indians, survived a stampede, and battled a raging brush fire. The horrors she'd lived through in Arizona Territory had earned her the right to make her own decisions. Even so, knowing her father was acting out of concern for her made her soften her tone.

"Papa, please. I know you mean well, but I'm quite capable of taking care of myself."

"You're not doing a very good job of it, are you?" With that her father streaked past her.

"Papa!"

He whirled around to face her, his finger practically in her nose. "If you continue this unsavory . . . feud, you are no longer my daughter or welcome in my house."

His words sliced through her like a knife, and her temper flared. "You are a fine one to talk about feuds!" For years Papa had fought with the owner of Two-Time's other clock shop. Their feud had affected not only the family but the entire town.

Her father's eyes glittered with anger. "I have nothing more to say to you." With those chilling words, he stormed out of the office. The door slammed in his wake with a finality that made Josie's heart sink and the *Press*'s employees scramble back to their desks.

Josie stared at the closed door and gritted her teeth. "Ohh, he makes me so mad."

"Don't be too hard on him," Brandon said. "He's concerned about you. I'm afraid I'd feel the same way if I thought Haley was being mistreated."

She turned to face him. "Haley is only nine."

"Age makes no difference to a parent."

Reminded that parenting was something she knew nothing about, she clamped her mouth shut.

Now that her father had left, she took stock of her surroundings. The orderly atmosphere seemed more suited for a house of worship than a newspaper office. Reams of paper were stacked neatly on shelves, along with cardboard boxes clearly marked with the names of various metal letter types. Like her, Wade made additional income by printing handbills and pamphlets between newspaper runs, and samples were neatly arranged on a felt-lined bulletin board.

A quiet shushing sound floated from the press in the back room as it efficiently printed copies without benefit of a hammer or even curses. It was a far cry from the sound of grinding rocks her own printer made on press day.

The neatly organized office made her wish she'd taken Brandon's offer to use his printing press. Only pride had kept her from doing so. She did not want his charity.

She turned her gaze back to Brandon to find him studying her with curious intensity. A new wave of feeling came over her. This time it wasn't anger that fueled her emotions. It was a sense of uneasiness. Papa hadn't seemed to notice her change of apparel, but it appeared that Brandon had.

"Look at you," he said, confirming her suspicions. He gave her a visual sweep that extended all the way down to her polished high button boots, bringing a flush to her cheeks. His admiring gaze lingered perhaps a tad too long at her small waist for her peace of mind. Only when he'd glanced away could she breathe easy.

It had been a long time since a man had looked at her like a woman and not someone who had to be handled like fine china. She'd thought she was ready for this, ready to leave the protective cover of widow's weeds behind. Now she realized how totally unprepared she was. Maybe Mama was right; perhaps it was too soon.

"To what do I owe the pleasure of your visit?" he asked.

Josie handed him a small paper sack. "Would you give this to Haley? I have it on good authority that peppermint sticks cure just about everything."

Curiosity filled his eyes. "And you think Haley needs curing?"

"The last time we spoke, I got the impression that maybe there was a problem." When he neither denied or admitted anything was wrong, she added, "I haven't seen her since the day the circus came to town." If she didn't know better, she would think that Haley had purposely tried to avoid her.

He hesitated a moment. "Haley's . . . going through a difficult time right now." he said, his voice taut.

"Because of the camel episode?"

"It didn't help. I'm afraid she's missing her old friends back in San Antone."

"I thought she was making friends here."

"She was, but as I'm finding out, things don't always go smoothly with nine-year-old girls, and that includes friendships."

"I guess that can be a difficult age," she said. "Is there anything I can do?"

"Thank you, no. But I'll tell her you asked about her." He set the sack of candy on the desk and cocked his head to one side as if expecting her to say more.

"There is one other thing," she said. Determined to put her father's stinging words behind her, she tried to recall her carefully rehearsed speech. "It's about lot eleven." *Ralph's lot.* The sudden thought momentarily distracted her. No, she mustn't think of it as belonging to her late husband.

"Go on."

She reached for her locket as she tended to do whenever thoughts of Ralph threatened to overcome her. Finding her chest bare of any ornament surprised her. Shocked her. Had she lost it? Or simply forgotten to put it on?

The argument with her father had affected her more than she'd liked to admit. Instead of feeling strong and in control, she felt unsure of herself. Brandon's steady gaze didn't help.

"It's nothing, really." She shook her head and backed away. Better to come back when she was feeling more like herself. "I'm sorry to have taken up your time." With a sense of dismay, she turned. Before she'd taken but a few steps, he caught up to her. Hand pressed against the door, he barred her escape

She swung around to face him—big mistake. For that only shortened the distance between them. If the thin space that separated them wasn't worrisome enough, he leaned forward, placing both hands on the door on either side of her, locking her in place.

"What's going on? Why did you really come?" He was so close she could smell his bay rum hair tonic. So close she could see the golden tips of his dark eyelashes. So close she could feel the heat radiating from his body. "If you have something to say, say it."

Hands pressed against his manly chest, she tried pushing him away, but he refused to budge. Gazing up at him, she felt a flash of anger. How dare he hold her captive! Her still in widow's— Okay, maybe she should have listened to her mother and abandoned the yellow dress. Still, he had no right. No right at all!

"You'll have to let me go first," she said coldly, though she was more irritated at herself than him. She wanted to be treated like an equal, and here she was acting like a child. It was time she showed Papa— showed them all—that she was a strong, capable person.

"Very well." He dropped his hands and backed away.

Stepping away from the door, she held herself as rigid as a man in armor. Reaching into the purse dangling from her wrist for the carefully folded deed obtained from the county office, she slapped it on his desk.

Brandon stared at it with furrowed brow. "What is that?"

"The deed to lot eleven. It's yours."

He frowned in puzzlement. "I thought that matter was settled."

"It wasn't," she said. "At least not to my satisfaction." Meeting his visual hold with a boldness she didn't feel, she added, "It's yours."

"I don't understand. If you didn't want the property, what took you so long to tell me?"

She didn't want to admit the truth: that she still thought of the property as Ralph's, even though he'd never owned it. Nor did she want to think about Ralph proposing marriage by the river and carving their initials onto the trunk of a tree. The truth was too personal to share, and revealing it might make her lose her composure.

She let the silence stretch between them until, at last, he answered for her. "Ah, don't tell me. You still suspect me of setting fire to your office."

She no longer thought him guilty—hadn't for a long time. Still, he offered her a way out and she took it. "You once told me that all was fair in love and journalism."

He tilted his head. "And you took me at my word? I guess I'll have to be more careful what I say in the future." He gave her a sharp, assessing look. "You don't really believe I would resort to arson, do you?"

She hesitated. It was either play along or tell him the truth. "The fire occurred after the *Gazette* started selling again. Even you would have to admit the timing is suspect." She gave him an angled look. "You said it yourself. You're an all-or-nothing type of guy."

"I don't deny that. But if you recall, I was the one who came up with the idea of clashing editorials."

Feeling more like herself, she allowed herself to smile. "A ploy, perhaps, to throw me off the track?" she asked.

He laughed. "You give me more credit than I deserve. Sorry to disappoint you, but as I told you before, I had nothing to do with the fire."

"Then I would say our business here is complete."

She quickly left the building, and this time he made no effort to stop her. There. It was done. Ralph's dream was now in the hands of that disturbing man, where unfortunately it belonged. She'd hoped that ridding herself of widow's weeds would take the sting out of burying Ralph for what seemed like a second time.

It did not.

***

For the remainder of that day, Brandon hadn't been able to stop thinking of the unexpected visit from Josie Johnson. She sure had been a sight to behold in that bright-yellow dress of hers. He could still envision the play of emotions on her pretty, round face. The fiery depths of her eyes. The . . .

He clamped down on his thoughts.

The woman was messing with him. No question. She'd come prancing into his office, exchanged heated words with her father, and, after inexplicably handing him the deed to lot eleven, taken off like a cat with its tail on fire. Never had he professed to understand the way a woman's mind worked, but Mrs. Johnson had him buffaloed.

"When are you going to print my picture, Papa?"

With a guilty start, Brandon turned his attention back to his daughter. "Right now."

He fed Haley's drawing into the printer and turned the crank. The grippers pulled the paper through the roller carriage to the ink press and shot it out to the delivery board, where he lifted and held it up. Haley's drawing of him had been scrupulously chiseled into a wood block. "What do you think? Is that magic or what?"

The corners of Haley's mouth lifted. It was the first semblance of a smile since the circus fiasco. "Oh, Papa, that's amazing."

He handed her the paper. An imaginative child, she'd always been prone to nightmares, but they'd steadily increased in recent weeks, and the camel episode had only made them worse. He'd thought bringing her to the office would cheer her up. It did, but only slightly.

"How many copies do you want? A dozen. Five hundred? A thousand?" He was teasing, of course, and when she didn't answer, he turned to look at her. "What's the matter, muffin?"

She stared at the picture in her hand. "I want to go back to San Antone."

Brandon grimaced. Here they went again. "The circus is gone. You no longer have to worry about camels."

The eyes looking back at him swam with tears, and once again he felt remiss as a father. As if he didn't feel guilty enough for not having taken her back for a visit as promised. The paper had demanded so much of his time.

Along with the tears came a look he couldn't put his finger on. Fear? Panic? Desperation? How could one so young feel such strong emotions?

"I hate it here," she said, and this time her lower lip trembled.

Hand on her chin, he tilted her head upward, forcing her to look at him. "Since it's summer, I know it's not school that has you so upset. Did you and your friend have an argument?"

"No."

He drew his hand away from her chin. "What is it, then? Tell me."

The tears welling in her eyes spilled down her cheeks. "I just want to go home!"

"Haley, this *is* our home."

He felt a sharp twist of frustration. Surely there had to be something he could do to draw her out of this terrible melancholy.

"Tell you what," he said. "We'll ask Mrs. Greer to pack a lunch, and tomorrow I'll take you to a special place by the river for a picnic." Since he hadn't told her about lot eleven, he added, "I have a surprise for you."

"I don't want to go on a picnic. Not here!"

"Haley—"

"I hate it here," she cried with all the vehemence one so young could muster. She turned and yanked open the door.

"Haley, wait."

But already she had raced out of the office and was halfway up the street by the time Brandon followed her outside.

Brandon scratched his head. Confound it! It was the second time that day that someone of the feminine persuasion had run out of his office seemingly without rhyme or reason. Haley might only be nine, but she was turning out to be every bit as much of a puzzle as Josie Johnson.

Chapter 20

It had cost Columbus $7,600 to discover America. No doubt it would cost him just as much today to run for Congress.—Two-Time Gazette

Josie sat at her desk that Monday staring at the calendar. She couldn't believe it was almost the end of July. Only three days were left in which to find a place for her office. Sighing, she held her head in her hands.

Whatever could she do next? She'd already made a last-minute appeal to Mayor Troutman. Despite her pleas, the fool man refused to budge. Even her offer to give him her paper's endorsement for reelection in the fall wouldn't change his mind.

It wasn't just the mayor's ultimatum that weighed heavily on her. Still at odds with her father, she had moved in with her sister Meg and brother-in-law Grant. She was now without both an office and permanent home. Her life was spinning out of control, and there didn't seem to be a way of stopping it.

Voices outside the tent filtered through her troubled thoughts. Groaning, she sat back in her chair, palms on her forehead. Now what? Since she'd revamped the "Love Links" guidelines, reader complaints were down considerably, but there was always someone offended by something or other printed in the newspaper. Just last week, Mrs. Tuttle had taken her to task for a news item noting the change in the railroad schedule, as if she controlled such things.

The outside chatter grew so loud she could no longer ignore it. Leaving her desk, she lifted the tent's flap to peer outside. Much to her surprise, a large crowd was gathered in front, spilling onto the boardwalk and street.

"Looks like trouble," Hank said, looking over her shoulder.

From beneath an enormous feathered hat, Mrs. Mooney motioned for her to join the throng. Josie ducked through the tent's flap and Hank followed.

"What's going on?" she asked, shading her eyes against the sun's white glare.

Mrs. Mooney cleared her throat with an important air. "We've come to tell you—"

"Wait!" T-Bone stepped next to her and ran his hands down his blood-stained apron.
The butcher's pox-marked face looked redder than usual. "Why do you get to tell her?"

"Yeah!" shouted a voice from the crowd.

Josie's gaze shifted from Mrs. Mooney to T-Bone. "Tell me what?" she asked, but the two of them were too busy scowling at each other to pay her any heed.

Mrs. Mooney crossed her arms across her ample chest. "I get to tell her because I'm the bank president's wife, that's why."

T-Bone made a dismissive gesture. "That gives you no right—"

"It most certainly does—"

The argument might have raged on indefinitely had Mayor Troutman not stepped between them, arms spread wide as if warding off two advancing armies. "As mayor of this fine town, it's my duty to make the announcement and—"

"It was my idea!" Mrs. Mooney exclaimed.

Miss Bubbles' eyes narrowed beneath her painted blue eyelids. "It wasn't just *your* idea."

Mrs. Mooney threw up her arms. "Oh, for crying out loud." Before anyone could stop her, she turned to Josie. "We're here to tell you that we've collected enough money for you to build a new office."

Not sure she'd heard right, Josie glanced at Hank, who looked every bit as perplexed as she was. She turned back to Mrs. Mooney. "Wh-what did you say?"

Scooter stepped out of the crowd and handed her a thick envelope. He grinned. "Like Grandpappy always said, 'A purse without money is called leather.'"

Josie peered inside the envelope at the generous wad of cash, and her mouth dropped open.

"Moly hackerel," Hank said, gaping at the stack of bills.

It took Josie a moment to find her voice. "I . . . I appreciate this more than words can say, but I can't accept your charity."

"Yes, you can," Hank whispered in her ear.

Josie shook her head, but Mrs. Mooney insisted with a disapproving look at her banker husband. "This isn't charity. Nor is it a loan. This is our way of preserving a piece of our history. The town wouldn't be the same without the *Gazette*."

"Yeah," T-Bone said. "If it wasn't for the *Gazette*, our Nellie-Sue wouldn't have a beau."

"Nellie-Sue has a beau?" Josie asked. That was a surprise. The girl stood six feet tall, looked like a beanpole, and had a personality to match.

"Yep," T-Bone said proudly. "Thanks to the 'Love Lock' column."

"'Love *Links*,'" Hank said.

Farmer Haines spoke up. "And if it weren't for the *Gazette*, my Katherine wouldn't be getting married. That's one less mouth I'll have to feed."

A birdlike woman spoke up. "Because of the *Gazette*, I found me a gentleman friend from the next county who appreciates my cooking." She gave Hank a glaring look. "He also approves of the way I keep house."

More and more people stepped forward to tell how the *Gazette*, and particularly the "Love Links" column, had changed lives for the better. Josie felt a warm glow stirring inside her.

"I feel like I'm at a revival," Hank said, but he looked pleased too.

When the last of the testimonials had been given, Mrs. Mooney pressed her hands together. "So, you see, your newspaper provides a valuable service. The money in that envelope is our way of saying thank you."

Josie drew in her breath. "Well . . . I—"

Hank plucked the envelope out of her hand. "We accept."

Josie wiped a tear from the corner of her eye. "I don't know what to say."

"Well, when you figure it out," T-Bone said, scowling at Mrs. Mooney. "You can tell that Wade fella to take his gun-banning idea and stuff it in a well."

T-Bone wasn't alone in his thinking. Wade's last editorial had caused much in the way of controversy, splitting the town in two.

Mrs. Mooney glared at him. "I happen to think banning guns in town is a great idea."

"It's a terrible idea," Mr. Walker, owner of the gun shop, said with a shake of his fist.

While the argument raged around her, Josie couldn't stop gazing at the envelope in Hank's hand. The town's generosity touched her more than words could say, and her heart nearly burst with gratitude.

"What do you think, Josie?" Mr. Walker's gun-toting wife asked. "Do you or do you not think gun banning is a good idea?"

Josie smiled and, swiping away her tears, gazed at the *Lone Star Press* office across the street. The publisher was nowhere in sight. She'd already written a scathing column regarding the bank's unfairness to women. But, in light of these new developments, she decided to save that article for another day. "You'll just have to wait for Friday's paper to find out."

***

Josie stayed at her office late that night so Hank could go to press the following day. Things were moving quickly, and there was still much work to be done. Already, sun-dried adobe bricks had been delivered, and the ground preparation was scheduled to start on Thursday. That gave them two days to pack up and move the tent to the rear of the lot to make room for the new building.

She still couldn't believe how the town had rallied around her. The mayor had reluctantly agreed to allow Josie's tent to remain on site while the new office was under construction, but only because Mrs. Mooney and the others had pressured him.

A thrill of excitement rushed through her whenever she thought about a new building to call her own. She still couldn't believe it.

Forcing herself to concentrate on the task at hand, she ripped the paper out of the type-writing machine and rolled in a fresh sheet. It was getting late, and she couldn't go home until she'd finished writing that week's editorial.

Wade would no doubt take issue with her stance on making Two-Time a gun-free town. She had written that firearms were a dangerous companion for any man, especially when combined with whiskey. Other towns, including Tombstone, Deadwood, and Dodge had banned weapons, and many more planned to follow.

Wade called the idea of controlling guns unmitigated cockamamy and an assault on the second amendment. His argument was that outlaws would rather rob a bank in Tombstone or Dodge than a town like Two-Time, where almost every man and some women were armed.

Though it was true that the town hadn't had a bank robbery in at least two years, it had no shortage of shootings. Most, but not all, were harmless.

"I'll give you cockamamy, Mr. Brandon Wade," she murmured beneath her breath. Her fingers pounded the keys with such force that, had they been matches, flames would have shot from her nails.

The editor of the Lone Star Press *likes to draw his weapon when editorializing, but this time he is clearly off his mark.*

Fingers posed over the keyboard, she sat back in her chair. What was the word that meant outdated and unreasonable? Ah, yes. *Mumpsimus.*

She completed the article and pulled the paper from the rubber cylinder. With pen in hand, she read what she'd written. Crossing out the word *malarkey*, she changed it to *rubbish*. After making a spelling correction, she placed the finished article in the basket for Hank to set in type.

Satisfied, she stood and stretched her cramped muscles. Writing rebuttals to Mr. Wade's editorials was nothing short of challenging. She could hardly wait till he read her latest column. No doubt he'd fire back with a barrage of forceful wordage, though she'd noticed that her sister had been right—Wade avoided directing any disparaging language toward her. It was always the idea he objected to and railed against, never her personally.

The war of words was proving to be more popular than she'd thought possible. Subscriptions to the paper poured in faster than she could fill them. Everywhere she went, people commented on how much they enjoyed reading her rebuttals. It wasn't exactly what she'd had in mind when she took over the newspaper, but she'd gained a certain satisfaction in watching her paper fly off the stands. The success of her "Love Links" column was the icing on the cake.

Just as rewarding was the fact that people were taking an interest in community affairs like never before, and a new civic pride had emerged. No longer were Two-Time residents content to sit back and leave the mayor and town council members solely in charge. Town meetings were now packed to overflowing, and debates often raged into the wee hours of the morn.

Following Josie's strongly worded editorial regarding the need for electricity, people had stormed the town council meeting demanding to know why Two-Time was still in the Dark Ages. Instead of posing a contrary viewpoint, Wade had criticized the lack of a telephone system in the town. The resulting mayhem forced beleaguered council members to promise to consider the matters.

She only wished Papa wasn't so stubborn and could appreciate the positive ways she and Brandon were changing the town.

She and Brandon.

Just thinking about her unconventional relationship with the handsome publisher of the *Lone Star Press* made her giggle. She had to admit she enjoyed their banter, both in print and in person. His feigned indignation at what she'd written, even as he egged her on, made her laugh.

Never could she remember having so much fun.

Yawning, she stood and, after making sure that Mr. Whiskers' bowl was filled with water, turned off the gas lantern. Pulling her cape tight around her shoulders, she stepped out of the tent and into the cool night air. The street was deserted, and a thin crescent moon hung from a star-studded sky.

Before she reached her horse and wagon parked in front, she heard footsteps. Startled, she whirled about.

"You're working late, Mrs. Johnson," shot a voice out of the dimness. "Thinking of nice things to say about me, no doubt?"

Catching her breath, she waited for Brandon to move into the yellow circle cast by the gas streetlight. "You'll just have to read Friday's paper to find out," she said with a coquettish toss of her head.

He flashed a smile, his teeth gleaming like lustrous pearls. "While I'm waiting, perhaps you would favor me with an explanation as to why I'm now in possession of the deed to lot eleven."

"I told you, I have no use for it. You have a daughter, and I'm sure you'd much rather raise her in a proper home than a boarding house."

"At least let me pay for your half."

"That won't be necessary," she said. "It's rightfully yours. You won it fair and square."

"As I recall, so did you. And I'm sure you have good use for the money."

"Perhaps you haven't heard, but I now have enough money to rebuild, thanks to the generosity of the town."

"I did hear. Congratulations." he said. "I'm sure that takes a load off your mind."

"Yes, it does."

"But it still doesn't explain why you handed over a deed that is rightfully part yours."

Hesitating, she considered her answer. His journalistic instincts no doubt told him there was more to the story than she'd let on. That meant he would keep hounding her till he knew the full story. Might as well get it over with.

"That's where you're mistaken," she said at last. "About my winning the land, I mean. You see, I wasn't even in the race."

"But that's not true. I saw you."

"What you saw was me riding through town on the way to Austin. On the way, I saw a cloud of dust behind me and thought it was a cattle stampede." It sounded dumb even to her own ears. Heaven only knew how it must sound to him. "I tried to outrun it, and my hope chest landed on the property merely by chance."

An incredulous look crossed his face before he threw his head back in a hearty laugh. "That's the most ridiculous thing I've ever heard."

"I'm glad you find it so amusing," she said coolly.

He studied her, the streetlight turning his brown eyes into glints of fiery gold. "You have to admit, it *is* funny."

She hadn't thought about it in those terms before, but now that he mentioned it she did see the humor. Now she laughed too.

Suddenly aware they were staring at each other, she became flustered. "Yes, well . . . If you'll excuse me, it's late." She turned toward her wagon and reached for the grab bar.

"Let me help you." He placed a hand at her waist. Rattled by how the impact of his gentle grip affected her, she missed the step and was suddenly in his arms.

"Oh!" she gasped. She reached for her locket like she did whenever she felt insecure or apprehensive, only to find that for a second time in so many days she had failed to put it on. "I'm s-sorry."

"I'm not," he murmured, his breath hot in her ear. Steadying her on her feet, he ever so gently swung her around to face him. His gaze dropped down to the hand still at her chest before meeting her startled eyes.

"Don't look so alarmed, Josie Johnson," he said, his hands exploring the small of her back. "I'm not going to harm you. I'm simply going to grant your wish."

Locked in his embrace, her mind told her to resist, but her silent protests didn't have a chance next to the need his touch awakened. A shiver of anticipation ripped through her, followed by a warm, tingling sensation.

"My w-wish?" she stammered in a whisper.

For answer he lowered his head. His lips brushed against hers once, twice, three times before taking full possession of her mouth. Startled, she raised her hand to ward him off, but her palm never reached its intended target. Instead, she found herself melting into his manly embrace and absorbing the full pleasure of his heated lips. Oh, sweet heaven . . .

His lips were gentle at first as if testing her, but when she offered no resistance, he deepened the kiss until she could no longer hold back. Flinging her arms around his neck, she buried her fingers in the softness of his thick hair and succumbed to the sweet burning need his touch aroused.

His kiss reached into the deepest depths, filling the void in her heart and healing the holes in her soul.

"Papa?"

It took a moment for the young voice to break through the dreamlike aura of their kisses, but when it did, they both pulled away with a guilty start, like two thieves caught with their hands in a safe.

Brandon turned to his daughter, his face grim. "Haley? What are you doing here?"

In the yellow glow of the gaslight, Haley looked scared, and Josie's heart went out to her. Dressed in a thin muslin nightgown, she also had to be cold.

"I had a bad dream, Papa."

Brandon gave Josie a look of apology.

"Go," she whispered. As much as she wanted to continue where they'd left off, his daughter needed him, and that was where he belonged.

Regretting the interruption, she watched him wrap the shivering child tenderly in his coat. He then lifted Haley in his arms and carried her across the street to his tethered horse.

Josie pressed her fingers against her still-heated lips. Oh, my! What had just happened?

***

Brandon was still reeling when he settled Haley in his horse's saddle. After making sure his daughter was secure, he mounted behind her, the leather squeaking beneath his weight.

Before riding away, he glanced across the street to where Josie stood in the shadows of the night where he'd left her. He couldn't see her face, couldn't begin to know what she was thinking. Was she as stunned by what had happened as he was? Stunned by how easily they had locked embraces and given of themselves?

From the moment he'd captured her sweet, sweet lips, never once had he thought about his late wife. That was the worst part. Even now, as guilt racked his soul, he ached to go to Josie, take her in his arms, delve into the depths of her lush mouth once again, and—

No, no, no! He had no right thinking such thoughts. Josie—Mrs. Johnson— was still a fairly recent widow, no matter how much it seemed that she welcomed his advances. If anything, he should fall on his knees and apologize to her. To Colleen.

But for now, at least, his first consideration was to his distressed daughter. As if to remind himself where his loyalties lie, he pulled his gaze away from the lone figure across the street, but there was no stopping his thoughts. Nor could he ignore Josie's flowery fragrance that clung to him like perfume. He couldn't believe what had transpired moments earlier. Never again had he thought to feel the things he'd felt when Josie's sweet, passionate mouth met his.

With a sigh, he tugged on the reins and guided his horse down the dark alley toward the boarding house.

"Papa?"

Keeping one hand on the reins, he slid an arm around his daughter's small waist. "What is it, muffin?"

"Are you angry?"

"No, I'm not angry." Okay, maybe a little. At himself. For giving into his impulses. The editorial feud had provided a financial boom to both newspapers. Word about the heated exchanges had spread far and wide. Subscriptions had poured in from all parts of the county and beyond. Burying the editorial hatchet could be costly for them both. But how could he pretend to carry on the conflict knowing what he now knew lay hidden behind Josie's brilliant smile.

"I'm not angry at you, but I don't want you wandering around by yourself after dark. Is that clear?"

She started to cry. "I want to go home, Papa."

"We are going home."

Sobs shook her slight body. Fearing she would fall, he tightened his hold.

"I want to go back to San Antone," she cried in a muffled voice.

He rested his chin on her head. It broke his heart to see his daughter so unhappy. She used to be such a joyful child, and this glum and miserable side of her completely baffled him. He had the feeling he was missing something, but what?

He couldn't remember the last time he'd heard her laugh. He'd thought she'd get over the camel scare, but her fears only seemed to grow worse with each passing day.

"We've talked about this, Haley," he said. This is our home now. I'm going to build us a house by the river. You'd like that, right? You can roll out of bed and go swimming and fishing." It wasn't that long ago that those had been his daughter's favorite activities. "Think about what fun we'll have."

His consoling words failed to produce the hoped for results. The more he tried to cheer her, the more distraught she became and the harder she cried.

Chapter 21

According to a recent dispatch, people are lining up to ride on Coney Island's new switchback railway (or roller coaster, as it's called). It's hard to believe that anyone would willingly pay a nickel for a one-minute ride that goes nowhere.—Two-Time Gazette

Josie jabbed her pen into the penholder. All effort to think of a way to make the photographer's new ad more appealing had so far failed.

Mr. Farthing had been so pleased with the increase in business resulting from the free ads he'd purchased advertising space in both newspapers. Each ad was to run on alternative weeks.

"Okay." Elbow on her desk, she closed her eyes and held her head. "The power behind the picture." She shook her head and tried again. "Shutter up." She groaned. "Let Farthing Photography help you put your best face forward." She opened her eyes and jotted those exact words on a piece of paper. "What about this?" she called to Hank and read aloud the latest copy she'd come up with.

"Better," he said. "Beats the one about framing your loved ones so you can hang them."

Satisfied that at last she had something to work with, she stared down at the unfinished ad on her desk. But her mind refused to cooperate as once again her thoughts drifted back to the previous night.

She still couldn't believe the pleasure derived from Brandon's kiss. But how was that possible? After Ralph had died, she'd never thought to be with another man. Had never wanted to. True love came only once in a lifetime. Or so she'd believed. But being in Brandon's arms had opened up the possibility that lightning really did strike twice—a thought that was as scary as it was intriguing.

The intriguing part sent shivers rushing through her, reaching all the way to her toes, followed by a feeling of such utter guilt she could barely breathe. Guilt had been a constant companion since Ralph had died. Like an ever-present chaperone, it had reared its ugly head with every laugh and grief-free moment. Ralph was dead, and she had no right to happiness, no right to feel pleasure in another man's arms. Such were the dictates of the heart.

In her mind she knew that wasn't true. Life was for the living. But the heart always spoke the loudest and required the most attention.

Today, when she reached for her locket, it was on her chest where it belonged. She'd made certain of that.

She could never have romantic feelings for Brandon. Or for anyone else, for that matter. Ralph was the only man she'd loved, the only man she could ever love. Last night was a fluke. A mistake. It would not happen again.

Forcing her attention back to the ad, she quickly finished it and tossed it into the basket to be typeset.

Earlier, Hank had asked for a filler. Maybe that would help clear her mind. She thumbed through her files and came across the article about the man who saw his initials in the clouds.

"I have an idea about how we might be able to catch Miss Ruby's killer." She read the article out loud.

Hank pushed away from his desk and swung his chair around. "Far as I know, no cloud ever spelled out a word."

"Which only proves that guilt does funny things to people." Since Ralph's death, she could write an entire book on guilt. "It was guilt that made this man think he saw his name in the sky. What if we can get the killer to think he sees his name in the paper?"

"How we gonna do that?"

She thought a moment and reached for her pen. "How's this," she read as she wrote. "'A mysterious letter arrived at the *Gazette* yesterday. It contains information regarding the death of Miss Ruby.'"

He shook his head. "No one's gonna write an anonymous letter when there's a reward to be claimed."

She tossed down her pen and pushed a strand of hair behind her ear. "Guess you're right."

"'Course I'm right. The killer would have to be a fool to fall for that trick."

She sighed. Why did Miss Ruby's death continue to gnaw at her? She hadn't even known the woman. Hadn't even been living in Two-Time when it happened.

"Have you got a better idea?" she asked.

He turned back to his desk "Nope. Can't say that I do."

***

That afternoon the fire alarm rang. The persistent bell clawed the air with great urgency.

Josie grabbed her notebook and ducked out of the tent.

Hank looked up from where he was fighting with the printing press. His limp prevented him from joining the volunteers, and today, as always when the fire bell rang, he watched with a look of yearning.

"Do you suppose it's another hotel fire?" she called.

For answer Hank shrugged and turned to give the printing press another resounding bang with his hammer.

Josie took off with a wave of the hand. Moments later she joined the growing crowd that spilled from the boardwalk and onto the street like a bunch of worker ants. Horses and wagons were forced to stop, their drivers joining the thong on foot.

Running along the boardwalk, Josie couldn't see any smoke or flames. Instead she spotted people gathered in front of the sheriff's office. Scooter stood on the boardwalk, waving his arms for quiet. Puzzled, Josie moved closer. If not a fire, then what?

"Okay, folks. Listen up," Scooter yelled into a speaking horn. "We got ourselves a missing child." A hushed silence followed his announcement, and he continued. "Haley Wade hasn't been seen since morning."

Josie covered her mouth with her hand. Oh, no!

Scanning the crowd, she spotted Brandon and shouldered her way toward him.

After giving a description of Haley, Scooter continued. "If anyone knows her whereabouts, now's the time to step forward. Otherwise, I want every square inch of this burg searched. Like my grandpapa liked to say, 'That which is hidden under a rock is best found in daylight.'" Ignoring the groans of the crowd, he yelled, "Let's get to work!"

Murmuring among themselves, search volunteers disbanded, taking off in all directions. Josie hiked up her skirts and ran.

"Brandon!"

He stopped and spun around, his face a wooden mask as he waited for her to catch up.

"Oh, Brandon, I'm so sorry," she said, stopping in front of him. "We'll find her. We will." *And when we do, God, please let her be safe.*

"Mr. Wade, Mr. Wade!"

A boy ran up to them. Josie immediately recognized him as Charlie Hatcher, a newsboy who had worked for her before jumping ship and taking a job at the *Lone Star Press.* A flat cap with a stiff peak and buttoned crown flew off his head and he stooped to retrieve it before addressing his current boss.

Holding his cap with both hands, Charlie said, "I saw her." He puffed out his chest with a look of importance.

Brandon regarded the boy with furrowed brow. "Where? When?"

The boy brushed a lock of hair away from his eyes. "This morning. On the train."

Brandon reared back with a startled look. "Was . . . was she with anyone?"

"No, sir. She was all by herself." He went on to explain that he was selling newspapers during the train stop that morning when he saw her, but Brandon had already left with long, hurried strides.

Josie chased after him. "Wait!" She finally caught up to him at the train station in front of the ticket booth.

"Where are you going?" she asked.

"I know where Haley is. She's gone back to San Antone."

The thought of a child traveling by herself gave Josie the chills. She glanced at the station clock. The train was due to arrive in less than half an hour. "I'll go with you."

His gaze alighted on the notebook in her hand. "This is a private family matter."

His words hurt. After last night, did he really think her interest in Haley's safety was strictly business? "Haley is a friend and was once very kind to me when I was having a bad time. I'm concerned. That's the only reason I want to go with you." To prove she spoke the truth, she dumped her notebook into the nearby waste barrel.

He studied her for moment as if to weigh the truth of her words before turning back to the ticket booth. "Make that two tickets to San Antone."

***

Less than forty minutes later they had boarded the train and now sat across from one another, their feet mere inches apart. The train was relatively empty at that time of day, and for that Josie was grateful.

Before leaving the station, Brandon had sent a telegram to the San Antonio city marshal asking for his help. Now he stared out the smoke-smeared window at the big yellow sun slowly working its way across a pale azure sky. Josie could only guess what was going through his mind.

She tried thinking of something to say to ease his mind. "Haley's a smart girl." That had been evident on their first meeting during Haley's encounter with the grocer. "Any nine-year-old brave enough to travel by herself is smart enough to take care of herself," she added with more conviction than she felt. She didn't want to think about the possible dangers found in a city the size of San Antonio.

Brandon pulled his gaze away from the window. "How did you come to know my daughter?"

Josie thought back to that first meeting. "I don't know if I should tell you this, but she'd let Mr. Gardner's chickens out of their cages, and he was fit to be tied. She said the cages were dirty and smelled."

He chuckled ruefully. "Sounds like my girl."

Josie's mouth curved upward in a half smile. "She reminds me of my sister Amanda. She was always trying to save the world and everything in it. Still is."

"I guess that's not such a bad thing." His gaze dropped to her lips before he quickly looked away.

An awkward silence stretched between them, broken only by the clickety-clack of steel wheels against track. Sighing, Josie followed his gaze out the window. It must have been a shock for Haley to find her father in a woman's arms. Did he blame their kiss for his daughter's disappearance? Was that why she had run away?

Casting her gazed downward to her clenched hands, she moistened her lips and reached for her locket. "Do you think Haley left because we . . . because of what happened last night?"

She heard his intake of breath. "Haley's been going through a bad time lately. She's pretty much had me all to herself since her mother died. It probably didn't help."

She lifted her gaze to his tortured eyes. "I'm so sorry—"

"It wasn't your fault." His gaze fell on the hand on her locket before he turned back to the window. "It won't happen again."

The gold heart beneath her palm offered no comfort. Nor had Brandon's promise. Instead of feeling relieved by his vow she felt . . . what? Not saddened or disappointed. For that would imply the kiss meant something. And it hadn't. Couldn't.

After a long silence, he said, "Tell me about your husband."

The question, coming as it did from seemingly nowhere, surprised her. No one had allowed her to talk about Ralph. Just the mere mention of his name never failed to create an awkward pause in conversation, followed by a hasty change of subject. Her friends and family didn't mean to be unkind or thoughtless; they honestly believed that loss and grief was best served by silence.

What they didn't know—couldn't know without firsthand experience—is that after death came the dying, and it was a long, painful ordeal that no amount of suppression could prevent.

.   She dropped her hand to her lap and began. "Ralph owned the leather shop in town." Pausing, she waited for the pain that inevitably followed the mention of his name. The gut-wrenching grief. The burning sensation in her chest. The clenched stomach and sudden tears. Surprisingly, she felt none of those things. Instead, she felt only the sadness that continued to dog her. This was followed by an overwhelming need to talk to someone who had walked the same dark valley.

And so she continued, slowly at first, as if to weigh his reaction before spilling the contents of her heart. "As a child, he had consumption that left him with weak lungs." She went on to explain how they had met at a barn dance. "He was in Two-Time visiting his cousin and liked it so much he'd decided to stay."

"I'm sure you had something to do with that decision," Brandon said.

Feeling heat rushed to her face, she didn't know she'd unconsciously reached for her locket again until she saw Brandon's lowered gaze.

This time when she dropped her hand to her lap, she held it there with the other. "We moved to Arizona hoping the dry climate would help his lungs." She went on to describe all that had happened there. Talking about Ralph felt surprisingly satisfying. Cleansing.

It was only afterwards, when she fell silent, that she felt Brandon's magnetic pull. By opening up emotionally, she had somehow created a dangerous undertow that threatened to overtake her.

"Tell me about your wife," she said, hoping to break the tension between them.

He took so long to answer that she began to think he wouldn't. "I'm sorry, Brandon. If you'd rather not talk about her, I understand. It helped talking about Ralph, and I thought it would help you to talk about your wife."

He inhaled as people tended to do when faced with a difficult task. "Her name was Colleen. We met at church." After the initial hesitation, the words began to flow. He described his wife so vividly, Josie could almost picture her in her mind. She'd died of Bright's disease after contacting malaria. "Haley was only four and has no clear memory of her."

"It must be difficult. Raising a child by yourself."

A muscle quivered at his jaw. "As you can see, I'm not doing a very good job."

"Don't say that, Brandon. Haley is a delightful child. You've done a terrific job."

"I should have paid more attention when she told me she wanted to go back to San Antone. I thought it was a passing phase and she'd get over it. I was wrong."

"It's hard adjusting to a new town, even for an adult. But for a child . . ." She still remembered the difficulty of settling in Tucson. It had been like a foreign country. But then, even Two-Time had seemed strange and new when she'd returned. She still couldn't believe the changes that had occurred in the two years she was gone.

He gazed out the window. "What made you take over the *Gazette*?" he asked. "The newspaper business is tough even for a man."

"I like to write," she said. "And I strongly believe that newspapers keep people connected and can do a lot of good." She also needed something to do to help fill in the void left by Ralph. "I heard you once wrote for *Democratic Statesman?* Is that true?" The *Democratic Statesman* was Austin's largest and most prestigious newspapers.

"It's true."

"Most people would give a right arm to work for that paper."

His gaze returned to her. "Even you?"

"I'm not particularly fond of politics," she admitted.

"I had no problem with politics. That is, until the editor contracted small pox and called me to his quarantined house. I stood outside the fence some twenty feet away while he yelled that week's editorial from the window. I had to write down word for word the fool man's glowing appraisal of a candidate I was totally against."

"And did you?" she asked with a wry smile. "Write it word for word."

"Yes," he said, rubbing his upper lip. "Okay, maybe I changed a word or two or three. Naturally, I blamed it on the typesetter not being able to read my poor handwriting."

"Naturally," she said. "So, did you get fired."

"Let's just say it was a mutual parting of the ways. He said 'You're fired' and I said 'I quit.'"

She laughed. "That's about as mutual as you can get."

A young girl walked past their seats, a reminder of the reason for their journey. The rapport that had sprung up between them suddenly faded into silence.

It was late afternoon by the time the train rolled into the San Antonio station. The sun now looked like a golden disc slowly falling to earth. Outside the ash-covered window Josie spotted beggars and pickpockets. A city this size was no place for an unaccompanied child, and she shuddered at the thought.

Chapter 22

Dave Woodridge has flown the coop. Mrs. Woodridge is offering a five-dollar award to anyone who finds him and brings him back—and a ten-dollar award to the person who keeps him away.

—Two-Time Gazette

The San Antonio city marshal greeted Brandon as they stepped off the train, and the two men shook hands. The marshal was a solidly built man with a crooked nose and what appeared to be a perpetual frown.

"Sorry," he said. "Nothing yet, but my men have been alerted."

After a brief conversation, Brandon thanked him and the marshal rode away on a black gelding.

Josie stared at the milling crowd around them. "Now what?"

"We'll check the old neighborhood." Brandon tossed a nod at the street where a mule-driven streetcar waited to take travelers to one of the many hotels in town.

Boarding, they sat side by side on a stiff horsehair seat. The narrow streets could hardly accommodate all the traffic, and the going was slow. Next to her, Brandon tapped his foot, his impatience growing more evident each time the driver was forced to stop to let a wagon, mule team, or carriage pass. She thought the traffic in Two-Time was bad, but it was nothing compared to here.

Josie scanned one side of the street and Brandon the other on the outside chance they might spot Haley among the throngs streaming along the wooden sidewalks. It had been years since Josie had stepped foot in San Antonio, and she hardly recognized it.

"It's grown so much since I was last here," she said, and her heart sank. Finding anyone in a city this size was like finding a needle in a haystack.

"It helped that the city council passed an ordinance exempting new businesses from municipal taxes," Brandon said. "Nothing brings commerce to town faster than the lack of taxes."

He indicated the number of carriage factories, tanneries, breweries, and bookbinders that lined the streets and had sprung up like mushrooms following a spring rain. Gone were the caravans of Mexican carts of the past. The train had nearly put the teamsters out of work, but not the burros. Roan-gray donkeys lumbered ahead of their drovers, their backs piled high with mesquite firewood. Indians and former slaves worked together unloading wagons filled with adobe brick and other building materials.

The streetcar crossed over a bridge, the iron wheels rumbling over wooden slats. Josie sat forward to scan the grassy shores of the San

Antonio River. The river was a good sixty feet wide. Weeping willows dangled long, graceful branches into the river as if testing the temperature of the murky green water.

"This was Haley's favorite place to picnic," Brandon said. "We used to come here all the time."

Josie's heart went out to him. Never had she seen him look so dejected. "We'll find her." Sounding more positive than she felt, she covered his hand with her own.

He studied her, his eyes dark with emotion. "Thank you for coming with me. It means a lot."

"Isn't that what friends are for?" she asked. Referring to him as a friend seemed like an odd thing to say given their history together, but the word slipped out without conscious thought.

The corner of his lips curved upward. "Don't let our subscribers hear you say that. It'll spoil their fun."

The streetcar stopped with a jerk, and she pulled her hand away from his to brace herself against the seat in front. The driver yelled out something in German.

"Let's get off here," Brandon said, rising to his feet.

They walked the short distance to Brandon's old house, an adobe with a flat roof and blue trim. The current owner was an older gray-haired man. Both he and his wife were hard of hearing, and it took several exchanges and much in the way of hand signs and head shakes to determine they had not seen Haley. The news was the same at Haley's former school and church.

The sun dipped lower, and shadows grew long. Josie felt fingers of icy fear wrap around her heart. It would soon be dark. She glanced at Brandon's grim face and could well guess what was going through his mind.

By the time they worked their way back to the center of town, the velvet covers of dusk had fallen. All at once the recently installed electric lights burst into brightness. Josie gasped. Never had she seen such an amazing sight.

"It's like a hundred little suns," she whispered in awe.

"In the future, there won't be any such thing as darkness," Brandon said.

Gazing around in awed wonder, she nodded. Man had effectively conquered the dark of night. What would be next, she wondered? What else would man conquer? The light of day? The moon and stars? The secret longings of the heart?

Brandon pulled his watch from his vest and thumbed the gold case open. "Let's get something to eat, and I'll check you into a hotel." He slipped his watch back into his pocket.

She shook her head. "Forget the hotel. I'm not sleeping till I know Haley is safe."

He looked about to argue, but instead took her arm as they crossed the road, his touch playing havoc with her senses. "Come on," he said. "I see a restaurant."

It was a German restaurant, and the waiter seated them at a corner table overlooking the sidewalk. Red-and-white checkered tablecloths matched the curtains and added warmth to the wood-paneled walls. High shelves held a collection of beer steins with hinged pewter lids.

Though neither of them felt much like eating, the bratwurst and braised cabbage was delicious.

Brandon talked about Haley and the challenges of raising a motherless daughter. She told him about how she and Ralph had wanted a family. Surprised to find herself talking about something so painful and personal, she dropped her gaze to her plate.

"I'm sorry," he said. "You'd make a terrific mother."

She swallowed the lump that rose to her throat and pushed her plate away.

As if sensing her reluctance to continue the discussion, he rubbed his forehead and reached for the bill of fare "Soon as I get you settled into a hotel, I'll mosey on over the marshal's office and see if there's any news."

"Forget the hotel," she said. "I told you I'm—"

"I know, I know. You won't sleep until we find Haley." His eyebrow quirked. "Are you always this stubborn?"

"Only some of the time," she said.

While Brandon paid for their meals, Josie's gaze fell upon an oversized pewter stein decorated with an iron cross, and something occurred to her. She turned to Brandon.

"Does Haley know where her mother is buried?"

"Yes, why?" His gaze sharpened. "You think there's where—"

"I don't know, but when I was feeling alone and scared in Arizona I found comfort in sitting by Ralph's grave."

His worried expression turned to a look of hope. "I should have thought of that. Let's go."

***

The San Antonio cemetery was located a mile and a half from downtown. It was actually a grid made up of dozens of individual cemeteries spanning several city blocks. Each house of worship had its own cemetery within the network, as did the Masons, Oddfellows, and Confederate veterans.

Brandon lifted a lit lantern from a hook on the surrounding wall and held it aloft. They followed a series of streets and paths that wound around fences and statues of saints and angels. It was like a maze. At last, they reached a small grave beneath a sprawling oak.

"How'd you do that?" she asked.

He raised an eyebrow. "Do what?"

"Find this." That particular grave wouldn't be easy to find even during the day.

"Practice," he said. He dropped down on one knee and brushed the leaves off the gravestone with his one free hand. The inscription read "Colleen Haley Wade, beloved wife, mother and daughter."

Rising he swung the lantern from side to side, but there was no sign of Haley or even that she'd been anywhere near the grave.

"In the past, whenever we came here, Haley always left a drawing for her mother," he said.

Josie cast an anxious glance around them. Outside the circle of lantern light, it was pitch black. Any light from the moon and stars was blocked by the trees.

"Could Haley find this by herself?"

"I don't know."

"What if she tried and couldn't find the grave?"

He handed her the lantern. "Hold that." Cupping his hand around his mouth, he called Haley's name. Neither moved as they listened for an answer that failed to come.

Walking the length and width of the grid, they circled around fences and monuments. They roused a couple of sleeping hoboes, but both were two sheets to the wind and offered no help.

Brandon continued calling, his voice like a siren in the dead of night. They had just about given up when Josie's ears perked up. "Wait," she whispered. "I think I heard something." She pointed to the far wall. "It came from over there."

They stood motionless for a moment, and the silence was almost deafening. "Maybe it was just an animal," he said. "A stray cat."

"Call again," she said softly.

"Haley! Haley! Is that you?"

More silence. They were just about to continue on their way when a small, wavering voice made them both freeze. "Papa?"

Josie heard the air rush out of Brandon's lungs with a whoosh. He shot from her side and ran in the direction of the thin voice. Holding the lantern in front of her, Josie followed him to the far wall. Haley was huddled beneath a large tree, her face as pale as the moon. She looked like she'd been sleeping.

Brandon lifted his daughter into his arms and held her close. "Thank God you're all right," he said, his voice breaking.

Holding back tears, Josie dropped to her knees with a prayer of thanksgiving.

***

Brandon checked them into a hotel, and Haley fell asleep the moment her head hit the pillow. He stood by the bed gazing at her, his heart filled with gratitude. Had anything happened to her . . . He closed his eyes and blocked out the thought. It was just too painful to bear.

Haley was safe. That's all that mattered.

A sound made him turn. Josie stood at the doorway. "If you don't need me, I'll go to my room."

He blew out his breath. The problem was he needed her more than words could say. The uncertainty of not knowing Haley's whereabouts would have been unbearable had it not been for Josie.

"Wait," he said and pulled out his watch. It was only a little after eight p.m. "I have an errand to run. I won't be long."

She rested a questioning gaze on him. "You want me to stay with Haley?"

He hated asking it of her. She looked exhausted. But what he had to do was as much for her as it was for him. "If you don't mind."

"I don't mind," she said.

"I won't be long," he repeated and dashed out the door, not sure what he was running to or escaping from. Less than twenty minutes later he arrived at Colleen's graveside out of breath.

He had so much to say to her, his wife, but his mind suddenly went blank. How did you tell the woman who had been so much a part of your life—who had taught you to love and be loved and was the mother of your child—that another woman was now tugging at your heart? What did you say after you'd said good-bye?

He sank to his knees. Around him, the cemetery was as dark and silent as an empty tomb. As dark and silent as the love he'd thought would never die.

The day he'd married Colleen was the day the words "For as long as we both shall live" had become a promise and a vow. He'd seen firsthand what his father's many mistresses had done to his mother. His earliest memory was of lying in bed and hearing her cry on the nights his father didn't come home.

Brandon let out his breath. Even now the memory pained him. Though death had released him legally from his own vow of fidelity, it hadn't relieved him of the guilt he felt for having feelings for another woman.

He laid a hand on his wife's headstone. "Forgive me."

Oddly enough, he felt his wife's forgiveness. Felt it in the sudden stir of the trees. In the slight whisper of air touching his heated brow. Now if he could only find a way to forgive himself.

***

The following morning Josie sat at a corner table in the hotel dining room looking at her watch. The restaurant was brimming with activity, and the buzz of the other diners mingled with the clatter of dishes and silverware

Brandon had told her he'd meet her there at eight. It was now past eight-thirty. If he and Haley didn't arrive soon, they would miss the morning train back to Two-Time.

Maybe they'd overslept. She considered going upstairs and knocking on the door to Brandon's room, but decided to wait another five minutes.

Finding Haley had been a miracle. She had been scared to death and absolutely exhausted. Unable to find her mother's grave, she had huddled next to the wall to wait for morning.

Josie's heart went out to the her. Poor child. Maybe Brandon had decided to let her sleep and take a later train. He was so good with his daughter; so kind and gentle. Even after she'd put him through hell. Haley was lucky to have him as a father.

Josie finished her coffee and was just about to pay for it when she spotted Brandon and Haley coming down the stairs. Haley looked like she'd been crying and Brandon appeared grim-faced.

Walking side by side, Haley and her father entered the dining room. Since neither showed any indication of seeing her, Josie waved. Haley stopped and her father said something to her. Neither looked happy.

They walked through the hotel dining room toward her table like two wooden soldiers, reluctance written all over Haley's face.

"Good morning," Josie said, cheerfully. Neither father or daughter returned the hoped for smiles.

"'Morning," Brandon muttered. Dark stubble shadowed his lower face, emphasizing his strong-cut jaw. His eyes looked dark and bleak. He pulled a chair away from the table.

Josie took a deep breath. Something was definitely wrong.

Haley gazed at the floor as if she wanted it to open and swallow her. Only at her father's urging did she sit on the chair he held for her. He followed suit.

Josie looked from one to the other. She was more convinced than ever that something awful had happened. A dozen possibilities flitted through her head. Had someone hurt Haley while she'd wandered the streets alone? The thought sent chills racing through her.

A waiter started toward their table, but Brandon waved him away.

Josie's gaze shot back and forth between father and daughter. "Is everything all right?" Fearing the answer, she twisted the linen napkin on her lap.

Brandon's mouth was tight and eyes remote, his expression a mask of stone. "Haley has something to tell you."

Josie felt something like a rock settle in her stomach as she turned to Haley. The girl's face was drained of color, and her lower lip quivered as if she was trying not to give in to more tears. Josie ached to take the child in her arms and tell her everything would be all right.

"Maybe it should wait," she said. A public restaurant was hardly the place to divulge bad news.

"This has waited long enough," Brandon said, his dark eyes on his daughter. "Tell her."

Josie stared across the table aghast. What was wrong with him? This was so unlike him. Could he not see how upset Haley was? How absolutely devastated?

As if to guess Josie's thoughts, Brandon softened his voice, but his grim expression remained the same. "Tell her."

"I-I . . ." Haley let out a sob."

Josie pulled a handkerchief from her purse and brushed it lightly against Haley's damp cheek. "It's okay, dear heart. Take your time." She shot a reproachful gaze at Brandon, but the eyes looking back remained unfathomable. Swallowing hard, she turned back to Haley. "What do you want to tell me?"

"I . . . I . . ." Haley's body shuddered, and fresh tears rolled down her cheeks. She then pulled away from Josie and clutched her hands to her chest. "I-I . . ." She sobbed. "Burned down your office."

Chapter 23

Fire poses a constant threat for the Two-Time Hotel. Due to smoke damage, guest rooms have to be repainted and refurnished with such regularity, the hotel owner claims to have little use for maid service.—Two-Time Gazette

For several moments, it seemed as if time had stood still. No one spoke. Even the muted voices of the other diners and the clanking sound of china and silverware had faded away. Nothing penetrated the thick tension that held the three of them in its grip.

Haley covered her face with her hands as her body shook with soundless sobs.

When at last the shock of Haley's confession wore off, Josie's mouth dropped open and she fell back in her chair.

"You? You did that?" she said, struggling to find her voice. She shot a puzzled glance at Brandon's stoic face. "But . . . but why?"

"Tell her how it happened," Brandon said, his low voice failing to mute the sharp edge.

Haley lifted her head, rivers of tears spilling down her pale cheeks. "You were so sad because of your h-husband," she stammered. "I-I . . . I just wanted to make you happy."

Josie pressed her hand to her forehead. This couldn't be happening. She drew in her breath and dropped her hand to her lap. "You wanted to make me happy?" None of this made any sense. "By . . . by burning down my office?"

"It w-was . . ." Haley looked like she was having trouble breathing. "It was an accident, honest. I-I drew a picture of your husband. A large picture that you could hang on the wall. I wanted to surprise you by leaving it on your desk so you'd find it in the morning." Haley's voice trembled as she struggled to get the words out. "When I opened the window, t-the . . . the cat jumped up and scared me. I dropped my lantern and . . ." A look of horror crossed her pale face, as if she was reliving the scene even as she spoke. "I-I . . . didn't know what to do. The fire . . ."

Josie stared at her, but her disbelief soon gave way to sympathy. The poor child must have been terrified. "Oh, dear heart." Rising from her chair, she dropped to her knees by Haley's side. "Don't cry," she whispered. "Don't cry." Wrapping her arms around Haley's trembling body, Josie pulled her close

"I was so scared." Haley murmured, her head pressed against Josie's chest. "I knew you would hate me."

Josie stroked the child's head. "Oh, no. I could never hate you. I'm just so glad you weren't hurt." She glanced over Haley's head at Brandon. "Don't be angry with her," she mouthed, shaking her head lightly.

Brandon's gaze met hers. His expression was still tight, but some emotion flickered in the depth of his eyes. After a moment he left his chair and dropped down on one knee next to Josie's side.

Haley lifted her head. "Papa?"

Without a word he wrapped Haley in his arms, holding her close. But his tender expression was for Josie, as were his whispered words. "Thank you."

***

No one felt much like talking on the train ride back to Two-Time. Haley was pale with exhaustion and slept all the way, her head against her father's shoulder. Even in sleep her lower lip trembled as if she was reliving the horror of the fire in her dreams.

"I'll pay for the damages," Brandon said after a while, his voice low.

Jolted out of her thoughts, Josie shook her head. "That won't be necessary. It was an accident."

His jaw tensed. "Accident or not, Haley has to learn that actions lead to consequences."

Josie lowered her gaze to the sleeping child. Haley looked so small and vulnerable next to her father's broad chest. Poor thing. What a terrible burden of guilt she must have carried on her young shoulders. *No wonder she ran away.* With the thought came an overwhelming, almost maternal, need to protect her.

"My new office building is almost complete. People have been most generous and—"

"I'll pay back everyone who contributed." His voice forbade further argument.

She gazed out the window, and the scenery flew by in a blur just like the thoughts racing through her head. "If word gets out that Haley started the fire—"

"*If* word gets out?" He arched a brow. "Are you saying you're not running this in the *Gazette*?"

The question surprised her, and she drew in her breath. For the first time since taking over the newspaper, she'd failed to think as a journalist. Previously, any thought of holding back the news would have been out of the question.

She moistened her lips as she considered her answer. "Something like this could follow her the rest of her life."

He pierced her with a narrow-eyed gaze. "Would you feel the same if it were someone else? Another child?"

She thought about her nieces and nephews. About other children she knew. The little Matthews boy. The Spencer twins.

"Yes," she said. It wasn't an answer she was especially proud of. She owed her readers a clear, honest, and unbiased rendition of the news.

"Suppressing a story is serious business," he said, his voice showing neither approval or disapproval.

"I know. But I prefer to call it protecting a child." Newspapers routinely printed the name of children accused of crimes or mischief. Until now she hadn't given the matter much consideration, mainly because child criminals were a rarity in Two-Time. But now that she thought about it, the practice of treating young offenders in newspapers the same as adults struck her as all wrong.

She leaned forward, beseeching Brandon with an outstretched hand. "We can say the mystery of the fire has been solved and it was an accident. End of story." If that qualified as suppressing the news, she was guilty as charged.

He glanced down at his sleeping daughter. "I appreciate what you're trying to do, Josie." He lifted his troubled gaze. "But she caused you a great deal of trouble. I can't let her off the hook that easy."

"I'm not saying you should. I'm just saying there has to be another way for her to make amends. Just not in public."

His thoughts crossed his forehead in fleeting shadows, and they rode the rest of the way home to Two-Time in silence.

***

Following the trip to San Antonio, Josie and Haley started spending a lot of time together. Haley stopped by the newspaper shop every day. The two of them often walked the short distance to the hotel for ice cream or to the general store for penny candy.

Sometimes they'd go shopping together. Haley enjoyed trying on all the "grown-up" hats at Amanda's hat emporium. She even liked pretending she was a newspaper reporter and walked around with a notebook.

On other occasions, Haley would help Hank set type or run errands for Josie. It was as if, in her own small way, she tried making up for the fire.

In return, Josie felt a fierce need to protect the child and had made Hank swear not to tell anyone how the fire had started.

"You two sure are spending a lot of time together," he said one afternoon after Haley had left.

"She's a delightful child," Josie said. Come to think of it, Haley's father wasn't that bad either. "If ever I had a daughter, I would want her to be exactly like Haley."

"Hmm."

Josie looked up from her desk. "What?"

"I just don't want to see you getting hurt," he said.

"How could I possible get hurt?" she asked. "We're just friends."

"And are you still gonna keep up the editorial wars feeling the way you do about Wade's daughter?"

Josie chewed on her lower lip. Hank had raised a good question and one she wasn't ready to tackle. When she didn't respond, he turned to his desk.

"I guess I got my answer."

She studied the back of his head. Not wanting to argue with him, she changed the subject. "Speaking of spending time together. What's going on with you and Miss Read?" There had to be a reason why Hank had been spending so much time at the barbershop lately. The whole tent reeked of bay rum hair tonic.

For answer, Hank started humming Mendelssohn's *Wedding March*. His gravelly rendition brought a smile to Josie's face.

***

Two weeks later, Brandon sat in front of his type-writing machine late at night staring at a blank piece of paper. His efforts so far to produce that week's editorial were scattered on the desk and floor in a barrage of white paper balls.

That week's topic was the mayor's idea to turn Main Street into a plank road. Troutman had insisted that a better road through town would solve the traffic problem, as it would allow for a smoother flow and prevent wheels from being caught in ruts.

In last week's editorial, Josie had agreed with the mayor's solution, though she did raise the issue of costs and upkeep. Brandon found no argument with those concerns, but that would never do. Their readers expected the *Lone Star Press* to take the opposite view to the *Gazette*. He'd never had trouble seeing both sides of an issue and taking whichever side was called for. But that was then and this was now.

Never would he forget Josie's kindness to Haley. She'd handled the fire so expertly in her newspaper that no one questioned her contention that Mr. Whiskers was the culprit behind the fire. As far as everyone was concerned, arson was not involved.

Since the trip to San Antonio, any effort to rebut Josie's editorials or in any way discredit her paper had ended in failure. He no longer viewed Josie as a rival, but rather a joint force working toward a single goal: to inform, entertain, and educate the public.

But it wasn't just what Josie had done for Haley that had him wound tighter than a banjo string. It was the way she'd seemed to take over his every thought. He couldn't even close his eyes without thinking of her and how she'd felt in his arms. If only he hadn't kissed her. If only he hadn't felt the graceful curves of her body molding against his own. If only he hadn't stroked the softness of her skin or tasted her honey-sweet breath.

Grimacing, he rubbed his hands over his face. Blast it all! No wonder *his* writing now sounded like Sunday-school fodder.

Haley was spending the night with a friend, and he'd hoped to complete Friday's paper while she was gone and he had this extra time. It did his heart good to see his daughter happy again and acting more like herself. The outcome could have been so much worse if not for Josie's forgiving heart.

He groaned. Josie again. Every waking thought led to Josie.

He stood and stretched. Maybe a short walk would clear his head.

Outside, he was greeted by the squeaky sound of a fiddle wafting from one of the saloons. It was dark, and a sliver of the moon hung against a velvet-black sky. The soft glowing stars reminded him of the way Josie's eyes had shimmered the night he'd kissed her. Gritting his teeth, he shook the thought away, only to find his gaze lighting upon the horse and wagon parked across the street.

Josie was still working? Was she having the same trouble with her editorial as he was having with his?

The *Gazette*'s new adobe building was halfway built, but the uppermost tip of the tent was still visible from the boardwalk. The light shining from beneath the canvas roof confirmed her presence, and his breath caught in his chest.

The urge to go to her was so strong he practically had to hold on to the post to keep from doing so. The success of both newspapers depended on keeping up the editorial wars. Business aside, there was a much more personal reason why the two of them couldn't be together. She was still mourning her husband and he was still . . . what? Grieving for his wife? Yes, that was true, but not in the same way as before. Sadness still washed over him whenever he thought of Colleen, but no longer did grief hit him like a punch in the stomach. God forgive him, but a lot of that had to do with Josie.

Heaving a sigh, he was just about to go inside when he noticed the tent had suddenly turned dark. A moment later Josie stepped out of the shadows and the last of his self-control deserted him.

"Josie!"

They met in the middle of the deserted street. Even in the dim streetlight she looked radiant, beautiful, her lips dewy soft. The sweet scent of lavender erased the smell of damp muck. It was necessary to remind himself that she was still a fairly recent widow, whether she dressed the part or not. He'd also promised that what had happened between them wouldn't happen again. Such reminders didn't lessen the desire to take her in his arms, but they kept him from acting on his impulse to do so.

"You're working late," he said.

"Yes, I . . ." She sounded breathless, as if she'd been running. "Trying to put Friday's paper to bed."

"Trying?"

She sighed. "I'm afraid I've hit a brick wall. The words won't come."

"They won't come for me either," he said.

"I can't bring myself to say anything against you or your paper," she admitted.

"I'm having the same problem."

They both started talking at the same time.

"I'm sorry," he said. "You were saying?"

"Just that this is a fine predicament. You and me agreeing on something. Now what are we going to do?"

"I think you and I agree on a lot," he said, his voice heavy with meaning. As he drew in his breath, he absorbed the sudden tension between them. It was as if their kiss still stretched between them like an invisible bridge waiting to be crossed.

He swallowed hard. She looked so distressed he felt it necessary to relieve her mind. "The night I kissed you," he said, his voice low, "was a weak moment on my part. It meant nothing." Lies had never come easy for him, but this lie felt like acid on his tongue. "I meant what I said on the train. It was a mistake and it won't happen again."

He'd hoped, he'd prayed that she would voice an objection. *Say something. Oh, God, say something. Say that you feel some of the same things I feel. Say that the night we'd kissed was no mistake. Say that the man whose image you carry on your chest has finally been put to rest.*

Instead, her lips parted and her hand flew to the locket on her chest. It was as if her husband had suddenly materialized, ready to push him away should he give into the impulse to take her in his arms.

Silence stretched between them, and his heart sank. Was that relief he saw on her face? In her eyes? He took a step forward, but she warded him off with her hand.

"Have a good night," she said and walked away.

He called to her, but only because he didn't want to let her go. She stopped but didn't turn, her back rigid.

Desperate to break down the barrier between them, he blurted out the first thing that came to mind. "What do you say you write my column and I write yours?" It wasn't what he wanted to say, but it did the job, or at least made her turn to face him.

"What?" She angled her head in the way that always made him think of a sunflower tilting toward the sun.

Encouraged, he forced himself to expand on the thought. "We trade columns. I know how you stand on most issues, and I daresay you know my stance. I have no trouble writing disparaging remarks about myself. So, what do you say?"

"I-I don't know." She hesitated. "I don't want to cheat our readers."

"We won't. Not as long as we stay true to each other's opinions. Think of it as ghostwriting. If I write something you don't agree with, tell me. I'll do likewise."

"I guess it could work," she said slowly, though her voice held an edge of doubt.

"Just think," he said. "You won't have to struggle to think of something unflattering to say about me. I'll do it myself. I have no problem pointing out the error of my ways. I know I can be pigheaded and shortsighted at times."

His self-depreciating remark brought a smile to her face. A beautiful, beautiful smile that made his heart skip a beat.

"I can be stubborn and emotional," she admitted.

"I've been known to be over-confident."

"Ralph said that once I get an idea in my head I play it to the hilt."

Brandon clamped down on his jaw. Ralph again. He dropped his gaze to the ground. "What do you say?" he asked, his voice thick. "Deal?"

She held out her hand. He took it in his own, and it was all he could do not to pull the rest of her along with it.

"Deal," she said, jerking her hand away as if it had suddenly caught fire. "Meet you back here in thirty minutes."

Chapter 24

Notice: Due to the overwhelming success of the "Love Links" column, Reverend Wellmaker has announced that the church is booked solid. Couples wishing to wed will either have to pray for a cancelation or wait till next year.—Two-Time Gazette

Meg walked into Josie's new office and, after a quick glance around, clasped her hands to her chest and squealed, "It's beautiful!"

Amanda, who had arrived moments earlier, nodded. "And you have so much more room."

Becky-Sue was even more exuberant. Clapping her hands, she whirled around. "And there are no holes in the roof!"

"Yeah," Hank said, following her gaze upward. "Kinda takes all the fun out of life, don't it?"

Josie couldn't stop beaming. It seemed impossible to believe that it had taken less than a month for the completion of her new building, but that was only because so many volunteers had turned out to help.

Architecturally, the adobe building was plain as a breadbox. It had a rough-hewn floor and flat roof with no trim. Instead of a fireplace she now had a pot-bellied stove on which to make coffee or tea. Already the new printing press had arrived and now took up most of the space in the second room.

The building wasn't fancy by any means, but to her it felt like a castle.

From outside came the sound of hammering as a workman stood on a ladder, nailing the *Gazette*'s new sign in place.

Inside, the walls were bare, and Josie could hardly wait to add some personal touches. But a lot of work had to be done before she could start decorating.

"It'll be so much cooler working here," Josie said. The tent was stiflingly hot, but then so was the old wood building.

"Yeah," Hank said with a grin. "And the best part is that adobe's bulletproof."

Meg laughed and gave Josie a playful punch in the arm. "The way you and Mr. Wade have been slinging shots at each other, bulletproof is good."

Josie turned her back to hide the sudden flush of her cheeks. It irritated her that the mere mention of Brandon's name made her heart beat faster. It made no sense. He'd made it perfectly clear that theirs was a business arrangement, nothing more. It could never be anything more, and that was fine with her. More than fine.

Desperate to regain control of her traitorous heart, she reached for her locket, only to discover she'd forgotten to put it on that morning. Again.

"I think it's a disgrace what that despicable man writes about you," Amanda said with a sniff as she picked up a box of supplies. To show her disapproval, she slammed the box back down onto the desk.

"He's not despicable," Josie said, surprising herself with the emphatic response. She turned, hoping her sisters and Hank hadn't noticed, but their surprised expressions immediately relieved her of that notion.

Fortunately, the door opened and in walked Miss Read carrying a potted plant. "Just a little something for your new office." She handed the plant to Josie, but her gaze remained on Hank, who was suddenly consumed with straightening his bow tie and slicking his hair away from his forehead. Meg and Amanda exchanged knowing glances.

With everyone standing around, Josie spoke into the sudden lull in conversation. "Come on, we have work to do." Mama had agreed to take care of her grandchildren, and Josie welcomed her sisters' help.

Amanda pulled a bottle of mucilage glue out of a crate. "Where do you want this?"

"In the top drawer," Josie said, pointing to her desk.

Amanda made a face. "When's your new desk coming?"

"New?" Josie ran her hand along the purple desktop. Admittedly, it did look out of place, but it represented the town's kindness, and for that she didn't want to let it go. It also served as a reminder of the still unfinished business regarding Miss Ruby's killer.

"This one suits me just fine," Josie said, tracing a finger over the splintered wood surface that resembled a relief map. Reaching into a box for a leather-bound blotter, she centered it on top of the desk.

Amanda set to work arranging a paperweight, pen holder, letter opener, and bottle of ink in place. The box of brass paper fasteners she stuck in the top drawer next to the mucilage. "I don't understand why you're keeping this old thing. It really is an eyesore."

Becky-Sue looked up from a box she was going through. "Actually, I like the desk. It adds a lot of color. It's all the rage in Paris, you know."

Meg looked up from where she was unpacking a box. "Purple desks?"

"No, silly," Becky-Sue said with a giggle. "Purple gowns."

They all set to work in earnest, soon setting everything to rights. When the last ream of paper had been stacked on the shelves and all the

Farber #2s placed in a papier-mâché pencil holder, Hank clapped his hand to gain everyone's attention.

"I have an announcement to make," he said, motioning Miss Read to his side. He waited until all eyes were on them. "This lovely lady here has agreed to be my wife."

Josie shouldn't have been surprised, but she was. It wasn't like Hank to move so quickly. Even more surprising, he had managed to make the announcement without confusing his words.

Meg, Amanda, and Becky-Sue were quick to offer congratulations. Becky-Sue lifted her skirts and did a little jig. "I can't wait to write about your wedding gown."

Miss Read blushed. "Oh, my. I never thought I'd be getting married at my age."

Hank sidled up to Josie. Well? Aren't you gonna congratulate me?"

"Congratulations," Josie said, embarrassed at being found remiss.

"Okay, now say it like you mean it."

"I do mean it, Hank. It's just so . . . sudden."

Hank turned to Miss Read and took both of her hands in his. "When you've waited as long as I have for the right person to come along, you don't want to wait a minute longer."

The couple beamed at each other so lovingly that Josie's reservations melted away. "Congratulations, Hank," she said, and this time she really did mean it.

***

The church was packed on Hank's wedding day in late August, and Josie had a hard time finding a place to park. Due to the success of the "Love Links" column, the church was booked solid. Hank and Miss Read would have had to wait a full year to wed had it not been for a last-minute cancelation.

Just as Josie stepped down from her wagon, Haley ran up to her, flushed with excitement.

"Mrs. Johnson, Mrs. Johnson!" She whirled around. "What do you think?"

Josie folded her hands to her chest. "Oh, I think you look beautiful." Haley had worried that she had nothing to wear to the wedding, and Josie had offered to make her a new dress. Her sewing skills were nowhere near as good as her mother's, but she was pleased with the results. The ruffled hem and flared, lace-trimmed sleeves suited Haley to a T.

"Is my hair right?" Haley asked. "Papa has a terrible time with the curling iron."

Josie laughed. It was hard to imagine Brandon fussing with such a thing, but he'd done a decent job. Haley's hair was brushed back from her forehead and tied with a blue ribbon. Lush curls hung loosely down her back.

Josie straightened the bow and shaped one wayward curl around her fingers. "It's perfect," she said, stepping back.

"I made a present for the bride and groom." Haley held up a picture done in watercolors.

Josie leaned over for a closer look. Haley had painted lot eleven. She had done an amazing job of capturing the river, rolling hills, and thick grove of trees. So much so that Josie felt a squeezing pain inside and her breath caught in her throat.

A frown touched Haley's forehead. "Don't you think they'll like it?"

Josie gave her a reassuring smile. "They'll love it." Haley's artistic talent never failed to amaze her, and today was no different. "Just as I love the drawings you did for my new office."

Seemingly pleased with Josie's response, Haley skipped away to join her father waiting at the church entrance. Brandon gave Josie a lingering look before turning to his daughter.

Since his promise never to kiss her again, a barrier had fallen firmly in place. As if by some mutual agreement, glances were now guarded and verbal exchanges monitored. Nothing could be left to chance. Even the physical space between them had to be carefully measured to avoid the slightest touch. But despite their best efforts, the blockade sometimes fell, the gates opened, and, for a moment, a second, a brief dot of time, their hearts beat as one.

Josie reached for her locket and drew it to her trembling lips. Oh, dear heaven. How was it possible to have such thoughts about one man while grieving another?

With a guilty start, she let her locket fall into place and quickly walked around the church to the back door. It was Hank's wedding day, and that's what she needed to think about.

She found the groom in the anteroom pacing the floor and mopping his damp forehead with his handkerchief. Josie met his gaze in the mirror. "You aren't having second thoughts, are you?" She still couldn't believe how quickly he and Miss Read had decided to wed. Did love really bloom that fast?

"No second thoughts," he said and grinned. "I just hope I can be a good husband and do right by my beautiful bride."

Josie smiled as she reached up to straighten his bow tie. Dressed in a dark suit, he looked especially handsome today, and she suspected his ear-to-ear smile had something to do with it.

"Do you realize that you hardly mix your words up anymore?"

He grinned. "It's amazing what love can do for you."

Josie felt a pang inside. She was happy for Hank, but she wished a little of his happiness could rub off on her. "How did you know she was the right woman for you?"

"That's easy," Hank said. "When she said yes. Yes, she would marry me."

Josie hesitated. "Did you . . ."

Hank's eyebrows dipped and drew together. "Tell her what I'd done?" He nodded.

"And she still agreed to marry you? Even knowing that you . . . ?"

"Burned down a school?" He checked himself in the mirror and slicked back his hair. "Crazy, uh?"

* * *

The bride wore a simple white wedding gown with leg-of-mutton sleeves and a layered lace overskirt that ended in a slight bustle in back, topped with a big bow. Amanda had designed the floral headpiece. The white silk flowers and satin ribbons softened Miss Read's sharp features and made her look younger than her years.

Josie couldn't remember ever seeing her former teacher look more beautiful or happy.

After Hank and Miss Read promised to love and cherish each other, Reverend Wellmaker pronounced them husband and wife. "You may kiss the bride."

Hank's face turned scarlet before he shyly pecked his new wife on the cheek to thunderous applause. The newlyweds then led the way out of the church and down the street to the old Wilson barn. The structure had been decorated with white flowers, potted plants, and colored paper streamers. Since a spot had opened up on the church calendar at the last minute, friends had pitched in to make sure the wedding went off without a hitch. The ladies of the church auxiliary had provided the refreshments and decorated the barn.

As soon as the bride and groom arrived, Harry Watson tucked his fiddle beneath his chin and sawed out a foot-stomping tune. Somehow Hank's new bride persuaded him to lead off the dance. Despite his limp, the two made an endearing couple who couldn't take their eyes off each other.

It didn't take long, however, for Josie to realize that she and Brandon were the real attraction.

Gossip circulated from whispered lips. Expectant gazes bounced back and forth between her and Brandon as if waiting for one or the other to pull out a gun and start shooting. Josie couldn't help but wonder what people would think if the truth behind the faux feud became common knowledge.

She hadn't seen Brandon much during the last couple of weeks. They still exchanged editorials, but the encounters were kept short for fear of being discovered. Or at least that was the excuse she used for keeping each contact short and businesslike. In actuality she didn't trust herself to linger in his company one moment longer than necessary.

Such precautions didn't hide the fact that each brief meeting brought a new and growing awareness of him. It was now at the point of her sensing the moment he rode into town even before spotting his black horse. She even knew when he'd left by the sudden feel of emptiness in the air.

Today, as if by mutual consent, she and Brandon took great pains to stay as far away from each other as the size of the barn allowed. He stood against one wall and she on the opposite. If ever their gazes happened to meet—which occurred with alarming regularity—they quickly looked away.

Spotting Haley, Josie started toward her, but then stopped. The girl was with her friends and looked like she was having fun. It did Josie's heart good to see Haley looking like her old self again.

Female laughter drew Josie's attention back to Brandon. He was surrounded by flirtatious women who seemed to hang on to his every word.

Trying to take her mind off him, she opened her notebook and pulled a pencil out of her drawstring purse. People tended to relax at weddings. Confidences slipped out; secrets were spilled. With this many people, she was bound to find something newsworthy. Work always provided a diversion, and if ever she needed one it was now.

Becky-Sue wandered over to her side, her eyes sparkling with excitement. "Oh, look at that gorgeous dress."

Josie followed the young woman's gaze to Mrs. Gilbert, whose lavish blue ensemble outshone every other gown in the room, including the bride's.

Becky-Sue sighed audibly and held her reporter's notebook to her chest. "Oh, to have a dress like that. I really must find out who her dressmaker is."

Becky-Sue moved away, and Mrs. Tremble took her place. Though her husband had passed away more than five years ago, she still dressed in full widow's weeds. "I don't know how you can stand being in the same room with the man."

"Whomever do you mean?" Josie asked.

"Why, Mr. Wade, of course." Mrs. Tremble tutted and wagged her head. "The things he says about you."

"He says no more than what I say about him," Josie said and quickly changed the subject. "Have you any news for me?"

Mrs. Tremble gave a long, audible sigh. "I'm at that in-between age. Too old to be news and too young to be history."

Next to her Mrs. Brighten gave a haughty shake of the head. "In my day, a woman's name was in the paper only three times. When she was born, when she married, and when she passed through the pearly gates."

"You don't think a woman's accomplishments are worthy of mention?" Josie asked.

"Getting married *is* an accomplishment," Mrs. Brighten assured her.

The women drifted off, and Josie worked her way over to the refreshment table and filled a glass with punch. It was too sweet for her taste, however, and she set the half-empty glass on a tray.

The music grew louder. Watching the couples two-step the length and width of the barn, Josie couldn't help but feel envious. How she longed to kick up her heels. But even though she was no longer in widow's attire, everyone still treated her like one, and no men asked her to dance.

Her gaze traveled to the opposite side of the barn where Brandon stood. As if sensing her eyes on him, he glanced her way.

Something tugged at her insides like a ship trying to escape its moorings. She ached to go to him, ached to feel his arms around her. She wanted so much to inhale his manly fragrance and hear the rumble of his laughter in her ear. But giving into the temptation could lead to financial ruin. The success of her newspaper—of both their newspapers—depended on them keeping up the charade.

She turned her back to the dancing couples and looked for someone to talk to. Steering clear of the row of matronly chaperones, she circled the refreshment table.

And then Brandon suddenly appeared by her side. Without a word he took hold of her hand and pulled her onto the dance floor.

Alarmed, she leaned toward him. "What are you doing?" she whispered.

"What you want me to do," he murmured back. Facing her, he placed his hand at her waist. "Admit it. You want to dance with me. I saw it in your face."

"You saw no such thing," she said.

He chuckled softly before speaking, his voice loud enough to be heard over the music. "Why Mrs. Johnson, you wouldn't deny me the pleasure of this dance, would you?"

A collective gasp filled the room, and all eyes turned to them. Even the fiddler stopped playing.

Wishing that the floor would swallow her, Josie forced herself to look Brandon square in the face. The challenge in his eyes clearly laid out her options: she could either play along or walk away. Weighing one choice against the other, she quickly made up her mind.

"I'll dance with you, Mr. Wade," she said loud enough for everyone to hear, "but only because it would be rude not to. But don't expect me to enjoy it."

"I wouldn't think of it, Mrs. Johnson," Brandon said, giving his part full hilt. With a nod to the fiddler, he stepped forward.

The music started up again, and this time the fiddler surprised her by playing a slow waltz. With a slight bow, Brandon gathered her in his arms, tucking her hand in his. Resting a trembling palm on his shoulder, she forced herself to breathe as he slowly twirled her around the dance floor.

One by one, other couples joined in, casting curious stares their way.

Aware that all eyes were on them, she felt self-conscious. Her cheeks blazed, but that lasted only as long as it took to circle the barn twice. Brandon was a commanding presence and demanded her full attention. Whether from the music or the way they fell effortlessly into step, she didn't know, but the tension soon left her body and a serene sense of well-being took its place.

His dark eyes reflected glimmers of golden light as he gazed down at her. "Why, Mrs. Johnson, I can't believe you'd think such despicable things of me," he said in a loud voice for the benefit of the nearby dancers.

Playing along, she lifted her voice to be heard above the fiddle. "I'm surprised to hear you say that, Mr. Wade. I thought I made it perfectly clear what I thought about you and your sorry excuse of a newspaper."

Brandon lowered his voice for her ears only. "You don't have to look like you enjoy insulting me so much."

"You're the one who started it," she whispered back. The curious faces turned their way made her want to laugh out loud. It had been a long time since she'd had this much fun.

She felt his hand tighten at her waist as he continued to whirl her about. For such a tall man, he was surprisingly light on his feet. Warm humor blazed in his eyes as they traded loud jabs for the benefit of the other guests, followed by whispered exchanges meant only for each other.

"It seems like you're spending a lot of time away from the office lately," she said softly. At times, he was gone nearly all day.

"Ah, so you've noticed," he said, his husky voice close to her ear. Aloud he said, "Why Mrs. Johnson, I'm shocked that you would accuse me of such a thing."

His guarded look made her even more curious, but aware they were being watched, she waited before quietly asking, "Are you working on some big scoop?"

"Do you think I would tell you if I were?" he asked, his hot breath circling her head. "Would you tell me?"

"Absolutely not!" she said, forgetting to lower her voice.

All too soon the music stopped, and Josie felt her spirits drop. The look on his face, the formal way he bowed, told her that nothing had changed between them. It would be business as usual.

"A pleasure, Mrs. Johnson," he said loud and clear with no hint of a secret meaning.

She slanted her head slightly, but it was a struggle to maintain her stiff demeanor. "The pleasure was all yours." No one could guess from her voice how false those words were or how much she regretted the end of the dance.

Since she was in terrible danger of bursting into tears, she quickly turned and walked away. Like two obedient children they took their rightful places on opposite sides of the room to the collective sigh of the other guests.

* * *

The following afternoon Josie sat at her desk reading Becky-Sue's article about Hank's wedding. The girl showed real writing ability. She'd described every detail of the bride's attire down to the little bows on the white satin slippers.

"You're so good with fashion," Josie said. "Maybe you should forget about writing for newspapers and write instead for *Harper's Bazar*." The woman's periodical advertised itself as a repository of fashion, pleasure, and instruction.

The complement brought a blush to Becky-Sue's face. "I did have a little help," she admitted, digging into her portfolio. She pulled out a drawing that Josie immediately recognized as Haley's work.

"This is Mrs. Gilbert, but the one she drew of the bride was even more detailed," Becky-Sue said.

Josie studied the drawing up close. Haley had done a fine job of capturing Mrs. Gilbert's image. Her nose was a bit long, the eyes perhaps a bit too almond shaped, but the bow-shaped mouth was just right. The neck, however, was too thick, and the shield-like ornament at the throat looked more like a belt buckle than a cameo. But Haley had expertly reproduced the gown with its rows of ruffles that almost overshadowed the woman's delicate form.

Josie's gaze returned to the cameo at the neck. Something like a forgotten dream tiptoed around the edges of her consciousness. The more she tried to recall the memory, the more elusive it became.

Becky-Sue slid the drawing into an envelope. "Maybe you should hire Haley to sketch pictures for the newspaper," she said.

"Not a bad idea," Josie said, her mind still on the cameo.

Becky-Sue started to leave, but stopped at the door, her forehead rippled with concern. "Is everything all right?"

Josie's nod hardly did her distracted thoughts justice. "Yes, everything's fine." After a beat she added, "Would you mind leaving Haley's drawing here? I'll see that Haley gets it back."

If Becky-Sue thought the request was an odd one, she showed no sign. "No, of course not." She pulled the drawing out of the envelope and left it on the desk.

Chapter 25

Iron worker Matthew Kimble was arrested for disorderly conduct and locked in a jail cell he built himself. He said if he had it to do over again, he would have made the cell less secure.

—Two-Time Gazette

Mr. Farthing was nowhere in sight when Josie walked into the photography shop that Tuesday morning. She expected to see Mrs. Gilbert's photograph on display. Instead, it was Brandon's image that greeted her, and it looked so lifelike it near took her breath away.

Mr. Farthing called from the backroom. "I'll be right with you."

Shaken by the impact the photograph had on her, Josie cleared her throat. "Take your time," she finally managed.

Farthing hadn't just captured Brandon's likeness. With a clever combination of shadow and light, his camera had revealed both Brandon's inherent strength of character and zest for life. Most people tended to look serious in their photographs, but not Brandon. The corners of his mouth lifted in a half smile as if he was enjoying a private joke. His deep-set eyes reflected intelligence and wit. She raised her hand to the intriguing curve of his mouth, her body trembling from the memory of his lips on hers.

"Come to have your portrait taken?"

Startled by Mr. Farthing's sudden appearance, Josie dropped her hand. Embarrassed to be caught staring at Brandon's photograph, she answered quickly. "Not today. Perhaps another time."

"I liked what you did with the advertisement. It has already brought loads of wedding business my way, thanks to the "Love Links" column. I'm so busy I don't need to run any more ads. Least for a while."

"That's wonderful," she said, trying to sound happy for him. The baker Mr. Hobson had pulled his advertisements for the same reason, as had the dressmaker. Her "Love Links" column was turning out to be a tad *too* successful.

She glanced around. "The last time I was here I noticed a photograph of Mrs. Gilbert. We're doing a story on her for the newspaper, and I wanted to have another look at the dress she was wearing in her portrait."

"'Fraid I can't help you there. Mr. Gilbert has already picked up his wife's photograph."

"Oh."

"Sorry. Anything else I can help you with?"

Josie shook her head. "No, thank you."

After leaving the shop, Josie started along the boardwalk toward Madison and First. There had to be a way to get another look at Mrs. Gilbert's photograph, but how? She was so deep in her thoughts she failed to notice Brandon on horseback until he called to her.

"Ah, Mrs. Johnson, you look like you're in a hurry." They still called each other by their formal names in public. "You must have gotten wind of a big story."

She slowed down to match his pace. One hand on the reins of his horse, he sat tall in the saddle, the brim of his Stetson shading his face. He looked as at ease riding as he'd appeared on the dance floor or behind his desk.

"Perhaps," she said.

"Care to share?"

"I don't see you sharing the story you're working on," she said. There had to be a reason he kept riding out of town and staying away for hours at a time. Not that she was keeping track of his coming and goings, but it was hard not to notice.

"Still miffed about that, are we?"

"Just curious."

"Don't worry, Mrs. Johnson," he said with a mysterious air. "You'll find out soon enough what I'm working on." With that he rode off.

Josie watched him until he was out of sight. Now she really *was* curious. What in heavens name could he be up to? Shaking the thought away, she picked up her pace. She turned on Madison and, dodging traffic, crossed over to the two-story brick building with the green trim.

The house looked surprisingly respectable in the glare of the morning sun. It was only at night when the red light glowed from the parlor window that the bordello lost its cloak of respectability.

Her reporter notebook in hand, she waited for what seemed like forever for the door to swing open.

"May I help you?" asked a young woman dressed in a pink satin gown that was far too fancy for daytime wear.

"I came to see Miss Bubbles."

The woman looked her up and down before inviting her in and telling her to wait in the entry.

A man's laughter wafted from the parlor, and Josie immediately recognized it as belonging to Pepper. His presence gave her pause. She had been wrong to think Pepper had anything to do with the fire. Was she also wrong to think that he might have known Miss Ruby?

Before she could follow that thought any further, Miss Bubbles greeted her from the top of the stairs, dressed in a cloud of blue satin.

"Do you have news for me?" she asked before reaching the bottom.

"Is there somewhere we can talk?" Josie asked with a meaningful glance toward the parlor.

"Oh, yes, of course." Miss Bubbles led the way down the hall and into a small office. Closing the door, she pointed to a chair. "Have a seat."

Josie sat and waited for the madam to take her place behind the desk. Her businesslike demeanor seemed incongruous given her shiny gown and brightly painted face.

"So, tell me, did my reward bring the desired results?"

"I'm afraid not," Josie said. Miss Bubbles' disappointed look made her quickly add, "But I do have a question that might help. It's about the photograph you showed me of Miss Ruby. I believe she was wearing a cameo." Josie hadn't paid much attention to it at the time and only vaguely remembered it. "Would you mind if I have another look at it?"

"Not at all." Miss Bubbles opened a drawer. "Here it is." She pulled out the photograph and slid it across the desk. "That cameo was her most treasured possession. I believe she inherited it from her Italian grandmother."

"It has the most unusual shape," Josie said. Most cameos were oval or round, but Miss Ruby's was shaped like a shield. "Would you happen to know where it is?"

Miss Bubbles blinked. "I'm sorry?"

"What happened to the cameo Miss Ruby is wearing in this photograph?"

The madam sat back in her chair. "Why . . . I have no idea," she replied. "I mean, I never thought about it. I know it wasn't among her things. I went through them myself."

"Do you think any of the other girls might know where the cameo is?"

"I don't know, but I can certainly ask."

"Do you mind if I keep the photograph for a short while?"

"No, I don't mind."

Josie tucked the photograph into her purse. "Did Pepper—Mr. Kerrigan—know Miss Ruby?"

"Yes, he did. And he was quite upset about her demise, as were all her clients. Why do you ask?"

"No reason," Josie said, standing. Knowing Scooter, he'd probably checked everyone on Ruby's client list.

Miss Bubbles' eyes narrowed. "About the cameo. Is it important? Do you think the killer might have taken it?"

"I don't know." She didn't want to get the madam's hopes up, but neither did she want to dash them altogether. "I suppose anything is possible."

***

Two days later Miss Bubbles informed Josie that none of her girls knew anything about the cameo's whereabouts.

Still, Josie was reluctant to jump to conclusions. She didn't know the Gilberts that well. At most, they were nodding acquaintances seen at church and various social affairs. They'd moved to Two-Time while she was still in Arizona. Neither struck her as killers. What motive could either one of them possibly have for killing a prostitute?

She placed Miss Ruby's photograph next to Haley's drawing of Mrs. Gilbert. The fact that Anna-May Gilbert and Miss Ruby had what looked like similar or maybe even identical cameos could be a coincidence—nothing more. Yet Josie's journalistic mind kept gnawing away at her. She decided to do a little investigation. Her notebook tucked beneath her arm, she paid Anna-May a visit.

The Gilberts lived in a small adobe brick house surrounded by farm animals a couple of miles out of town. Anna-May seemed pleased to see her. So much so, Josie wondered if visitors were a rarity. "Do come in!" she gushed in her soft southern drawl

Josie stepped into the relatively cool entry hall. "I hope you don't mind my dropping in like this."

"Oh, no. I love company. It gets kind of lonely out here." Anna-May led Josie into the parlor. "Make yourself comfortable. Would you care for refreshment? Some lemonade, perhaps?"

"No, thank you." Josie seated herself upon the mauve velvet settee and leaned against its button-tufted back. The room, with its floral flocked wallpaper, tapestry carpet, and delicate lace curtains, looked like it belonged more in Boston or Europe than in Texas.

"We're doing a fashion story for the newspaper," Josie explained. "Of course, it wouldn't be complete without you."

Anna-May's hand flew to her chest. "Oh, my," she said in a breathless drawl. "How exciting!" She straightened the lace antimacassar on the back of the upholstered chair before daintily seating herself, the whisper of silk emulating from her every move. "What do you want me to do?"

"Nothing, I just have a few questions. I want to make sure we have the details of your dress right. The one you wore to the wedding."

Anna-May looked pleased. "That's my favorite dress." She fluffed out the lace of her sleeves.

Since it was the same dress Anna-May had worn in her photograph, Josie gathered as much. "Could you tell me a little about it?" Josie chose her words carefully. Asking about the cameo too soon could rouse suspicion.

"Nothing much to tell. I ordered it from a store in Boston that specializes in French fashions." She reached for a catalogue on the end table. "Here." She handed it to Josie. "Don't you just love the dress on page four?"

Josie turned to the specified page. "I do," she said, though she could never imagine herself wearing a dress so elegant. But it wasn't the multilayered skirts or even the low neckline that raised her eyebrows. It was the cost. She doubted if anyone in Two-Time made that amount of money in a year's time. Certainly Anna-May's husband didn't.

Josie flipped through the rest of the catalogue. Some gowns cost less, but all were expensive. "I'm afraid that the prices are too high for my blood," Josie said, returning the catalogue.

Anna-May shrugged as if cost was of little or no consequence. "Beauty doesn't come cheap."

Josie picked an imaginary piece of lint off her brown calico skirt. "The cameo you wore to the wedding . . . It's exquisite. Is it a family heirloom?"

A smile curving her mouth, Anna-May patted the twisted rope of hair at the nape of her neck. "My husband gave it to me last year for our first anniversary."

Josie pretended to check her notes. "I don't know if you've heard, but there's a new photographer in town. You should think about having your portrait taken."

Anna-May's face lit up. "But I did already. Would you like to see it?"

"I would love to," Josie said.

Anna-May rose from her chair in one graceful move. "Give me just a minute." She left the room with a sense of purpose, her dainty satin slippers quiet as a kitten on the wooden floor.

Josie sighed in relief. That had been easier than she thought it would be.

A young Mexican girl entered the room carrying a feather duster. "Oh, I'm sorry, *señora*." Without waiting for Josie to reply, she backed out of the room and vanished.

Less than five minutes later, Anna-May returned with the photograph. With loving care, she centered it on the mantle and stepped back. "What do you think?"

Josie rose and moved closer to the fireplace. Her gaze zeroed in on the cameo, and her breath caught in her lungs. There was no question. The cameo was identical to the one worn by Miss Ruby.

"What do you think?" Anna-May asked again.

"You look beautiful." Josie commented on the photograph's composition and lighting, but her gaze remained on the cameo. Fortunately, Anna-May was too enamored with her own likeness to notice the strain in Josie's voice.

The gold-mounted cameo was even more exquisite close up; The piece had been expertly carved from a shell, a woman's head raised in relief.

"I've never seen a cameo shaped like a shield," Josie said when she thought enough time had passed.

Anna-May nodded. "It is different, isn't it? My husband said the shield is to protect our love."

Josie couldn't help but wonder why her husband felt their love needed protection, but she kept her thoughts to herself. "It's exquisite," she said instead. "Your husband has excellent taste." He also had some explaining to do.

Anna-May nodded. "Yes, doesn't he?"

"How did you two meet?" Josie asked. Craig Gilbert didn't seem like Anna-May's type and probably didn't even travel in the same social circles.

"We actually met on a train. A thief stole my purse and I was without a ticket or money. Craig came to my rescue. He was such a sweet man. After that, he kept sending me gifts. So many gifts. At first I couldn't figure out how he could afford it. But then he told me he'd inherited money from some rich uncle. I told him he should use the money to start a business or something, but he said he would much rather spend it on me." She shrugged. "So, what's a girl to do?"

Josie stared at the cameo. "What indeed?"

***

When Josie shared her suspicions with Scooter later that same day, he looked dubious.

"I don't know, Josie," he said, swiveling his desk chair from side to side. "Like Grandpappy always said, 'One sprinkles the most sugar where the toast is burnt.'"

Hands at her waist, Josie frowned. "And what's that supposed to mean?"

"It means that's it's easy to sweeten the facts to prove a theory."

Sighing, she dropped her hands to her side. "Is that what you think I'm doing?"

Scooter stilled his chair and rested his folded hands upon his desk. "All we have are two identical cameos. We could probably think up a dozen different explanations for that—all pointing to Gilbert's guilt."

"We don't know that there're two cameos," Josie said, stubbornly. "It could be one and the same."

"Or it could be one of hundreds. I just ordered me a ring from a catalogue. Do you think I'm the only one who chose that ring?"

Her eyes widened. "What? You bought a ring? Does that mean what I think it means?"

Scooter's face turned a vivid red. "I took your advice and hired a deputy. He starts work next week."

Josie grinned. "And?"

"And I plan to ask Becky-Sue to marry me."

Josie could hardly suppress her delight. "Oh, Scooter. That's the best news ever!"

He looked pleased. "Don't go sayin' anythin'. I want to surprise her."

"Don't worry, your secret's safe."

Scooter blew out his breath. "Who-wee!" He fanned his face with his hand. "It's a big step. Askin' a woman to marry you."

"You're doing the right thing." She was convinced Scooter and Becky-Sue were the perfect match. "Does this mean I lose my reporter?" she asked.

"I reckon that's up to Becky-Sue," Scooter said.

Josie smiled. "I'm so happy for you both."

His grin vanished. "About Gilbert—I'll keep an eye on him. If I see anything suspicious, I'll haul him in for questionin'." He tilted his head. "Anything else."

Josie thought a moment. "Did you know that Pepper was Miss Ruby's client?"

"Yep, I did know that. 'Case you're wonderin', he was out of town the night she was killed." He rubbed his temple. "What is it with you and Pepper, anyhow? First you accuse him of arson and now this."

"I don't know." Josie shrugged. "He always seems like he's up to something."

She left the office feeling unsettled. Scooter would do what he said he would do, but she didn't have much hope of it leading anywhere. On the surface, Gilbert looked like a hard-working man with an extravagant young wife. Maybe he really did have a rich uncle. But if that were true, why the need to work at such a dull job? For that matter, why work at all?

Chapter 26

The grass is so scarce from lack of rain that it now takes four cattle to cast a single shadow.

—Two-Time Gazette

A week later, Josie sat at her desk staring at Haley's drawing of Mrs. Gilbert when a former newsboy walked in and handed her a note.

"From Mr. Wade," he said, peering through a curtain of straw-like hair.

The mere mention of Brandon's name was enough to send warm quivers surging through her veins. "Thank you, Mikey."

Reaching into her purse for a coin, she placed it in the boy's grimy hand and waited for him to leave before quickly unfolding the paper.

Meet me at Baker's windmill at three.

— Brandon

Josie stared at the bold handwriting, not knowing what to make of it. They'd exchanged no more than a few brief words since Hank's wedding. Now this. What could he possibly want to see her about?

Perhaps it had something to do with what had kept him out of town so much of the time in recent weeks.

She read the note twice before folding the paper and slipping it into her pocket. He hadn't even asked if she would meet him. It was more of a command. She was tempted to ignore it, but the same curiosity that had led her into journalism soon got the best of her.

She glanced at her watch. Sighing, she grabbed her purse and called into the other room where Hank was printing off Friday's edition.

"I'm leaving."

"Coming back?"

That depended on why Brandon wanted to see her. "I'm not sure," she said, feeling as nervous as a schoolgirl. "If not, would you lock up for me?"

"Sure thing."

Tucking a loose strand of hair into her bun, she donned her bonnet. She then pinched her cheeks for color and grabbed her purse from the desk drawer.

Less than a half hour later she spotted Brandon and Haley in the shade of Baker's windmill. Brandon sat astride his black gelding and Haley rode a brown-and-white pony, probably rented from the stables.

Josie pulled her horse and wagon alongside them. "What's going on?" she called, shading her eyes with her hand.

"It's a surprise," Haley called back and giggled.

"Follow us," Brandon said with a wave of his hand. He rode off with Haley by his side, their horses kicking up clouds of dust.

"What in the world?" Shaking her head, Josie flipped the reins and took off after them.

Some twenty minutes later they reached the river. Josie's heart sank upon seeing the large structure on lot eleven. *So, this is what Brandon has been up to these past several weeks.*

A sharp pain ripped through her and she gripped the reins tighter. She wasn't ready for this. Brandon had every right to build on the property, and it was foolish of her to feel the way she did, but she couldn't help it. Swallowing hard, she blinked back tears. She should be happy for him. Would pretend to be happy, even if it killed her.

It was an impressive building, no question. The house wasn't finished. The windows lacked glass, and the roof still had to be tiled. The walls were built from adobe bricks with large windows overlooking the river. Brick chimneys anchored the house on either side like a pair of bookends.

"What do you think," he asked as she pulled up next to him and set the brake.

"It's . . . amazing," she said for want of a better word. "So, this explains why you've been spending so much time out of town." It surprised her that Haley hadn't said anything. Not a word about the house.

Overseeing such a building project couldn't have been easy. Up close, the house was even larger than it looked from a distance. Even the multiroomed home she and Ralph had envisioned all those years ago couldn't compare. Why anyone would need so much space she couldn't imagine. It appeared to have at least a dozen rooms and maybe a whole lot more. Keeping up such a house would be a full-time job.

"It's enormous," she said. "I hope you're prepared to hire a slew of servants."

Laughing, he dismounted and tethered his horse. "The inside is even less finished than the outside. I wasn't going to show it to you until it was completed, but Haley couldn't wait, and I was afraid you'd hear about it from someone in town. Come on, I'll show you around."

She swallowed hard and forced a smile. Why, oh, why, had he brought her here? Had he stuck a knife into her heart, it couldn't have hurt more.

"That would be . . . g-great," she stammered.

He hurried to help her from the wagon. Strong hands at her waist, he lifted her gently to the ground. Their gazes met and held for a moment before they quickly drew apart. Feeling her cheeks flare, she looked away.

In the distance, workmen were cutting down trees and tossing logs into a wagon. It nearly killed her to think that the initials Ralph had carved in the trunk of the old cottonwood would soon be turned into firewood.

Brandon must have seen something in her expression, because he offered an explanation. "We're making room for the stables."

She moistened her lower lip, but said nothing.

He cleared his throat. "Before we go inside, Haley has something she wants to show you."

Since Haley could hardly seem to contain her excitement, Josie asked, "What's going on?"

Still giggling, Haley took Josie by the hand and drew her a short distance away to a sign attached to a wooden post. The sign read "Two-Time Old Folks' Home."

Josie blinked and read the sign again. She swung around to face Brandon. "I don't understand. Home . . . ?"

Brandon's crooked grin made him look like a mischievous schoolboy. "You said there should be a better way to handle people like Mr. Pendergrass, and soon there will be."

"Now he can live here," Haley added, her eyes shining brightly.

"Here?" Josie said in disbelief. "In this house?"

Brandon answered her question with a nod. "He and others like him will be properly cared for. Dr. Stybeck and his wife have agreed to live on the premises free of charge. In exchange he'll provide medical services. We'll also hire a housekeeper and caretaker."

"Don't forget a cook," Haley added.

Josie stared at them, shock waves working their way down her spine. "Why would you do such a thing?"

"It's cuz I burned down your building," Haley said.

Josie pressed her palm against Haley's smooth, round cheek. "You mean *accidentally* burned down my building."

Brandon laid a hand on Haley's shoulder. "Since you refused to let me pay for your new office, Haley and I decided this would be the next best thing."

"I've been helping out," Haley exclaimed.

"And she's been working hard," Brandon added. "She's worked her fanny off."

Haley kicked a small rock away with her foot. "Now that's school's started, I can only work here on Saturdays."

Tears sprang to Josie's eyes. "I . . . I don't know what to say." If Ralph were there, he would wholeheartedly approve. The thought made her cry even more.

Brandon handed her a clean handkerchief. "I didn't mean to upset you."

"I'm just so happy," she said, dabbing her wet cheeks.

The tenderness of his gaze warmed her like the brilliant rays of the sun. Like a flower, her heart opened to a possibility that both intrigued and frightened her. Could this—this strange combination of euphoria and confusion—be the beginning of something more than just friendship or even gratitude?

"You can kiss Papa if you want," Haley said. "I won't mind."

Josie gasped softly, heat rising to her face. "I-I . . ."

"Right now, I think Mrs. Johnson would rather have a tour of the house," Brandon said, looking and sounding every bit as uncomfortable as she felt.

Josie jumped on the lifeline he offered. "Yes, yes, I would," she said, starting up the path as if her life depended on it.

Falling in step by Josie's side, Haley reached for her hand. This time there was no question as to what to call the warm, fuzzy feeling inside that was soft as a kitten's fur. She couldn't love Haley more if she were her own flesh and blood. With this happy thought in mind, she held on tightly to Haley's hand as they followed the winding path to the home.

***

Two days later, Josie stopped at the family house with Haley in tow. They found Mama in the garden picking the last of the blooming marigolds. It was a beautiful, warm day in September. The sky was clear and the air filled with a riotous twitter of birds.

Leading the way along the garden path, Josie joined her mother and introduced her to Haley. "This is Haley Wade."

Mama straightened. "Pleased to meet you."

Haley grinned up at her. "Mrs. Johnson and I went shopping. We purchased sheets and pillows."

Mama's eyebrows shot up and disappeared beneath the brim of her brown calico sunbonnet "Really?"

Before Josie could explain, Haley grabbed her arm and pointed. "Oh, look, a rabbit."

"It's a cottontail," Mama said, "and he's eating my lettuce."

Haley took off after the rabbit while Josie watched her with fond regard. "Isn't she the most delightful child? And she's a very talented artist. You should see some of her drawings."

"'Sheets and pillows'?" Mama asked.

Josie pulled her gaze away from Haley. "What? Oh, it's not what you think. Brandon built an old folks' home on lot eleven. Oh, Mama, you should see it. It's beautiful. Brandon is doing a fantastic job."

Her mother clipped a stem and laid the blossom in the wicker basket. "Brandon?"

"Mr. Wade."

Her mother's mouth formed a perfect *O*. "But wasn't that the lot you won?"

"Not exactly," Josie said and explained how she'd happened to end up with the property. "It was a mistake. I wasn't even in the race."

Lips pursed, Mama resumed clipping flowers. "I see," she said.

"Brandon asked Haley and me to purchase bedding and pick out wallpaper." When Mama failed to respond, Josie added, "Just think, Mama. Now poor Mr. Pendergrass and other people like him will be taken care of. I only wish Grandfather . . ."

"I know," Mama said, her voice strained. Mama still blamed herself for her father's death, even though it hadn't been her fault. The state-run old folks' home had come highly recommended. "I must say, I'm surprised. That's a very generous thing Mr. Wade has done."

Josie smiled. "Yes, it is, Mama. *Very* generous."

Mama gave her a funny look. "You and Mr. Wade aren't—"

"What? Oh, no, Mama. Of course not." Josie moistened her lips as she studied her mother's profile. "I don't know that I could ever truly love another man." There was no question that she was attracted to Brandon, but that was hardly enough on which to build a future. "Could you?"

Mama's back grew rigid. "My word, Josie. What a question!"

"I don't mean now." Josie ran the back of her hand across her damp forehead. It was hot and getting hotter. "I mean—God forbid— should something happen to Papa."

Mama's eyes softened as they always did whenever she talked about her husband. "No one could ever fill your father's shoes."

"But if something happened." Josie persisted. "You are still relatively young." Her mother was also attractive, her figure as slim as a young girl's. Her hair was the color of hay, except for a few silver strands at the temples.

Mama's sweet smile seemed to shave even more years off her age. "Thank you for saying that, but your father and I have been together for a very long time. I can't imagine another man taking his place." She tilted her head. "Only we're not talking about Papa and me, are we?"

Josie frowned. She reached for her locket. Just having this conversation filled her with such feelings of guilt and betrayal she could hardly breathe. "Ralph meant everything to me."

"Yes, but he wouldn't want you to spend the rest of your life alone. You know that, don't you?"

Right now, Josie didn't know what she knew. "I always believed that true love comes but once in a lifetime."

Mama's steady gaze bored into her. "What I believe is that true love comes as many times as you want or need it to come. For some people, it may be only once. For others, it's more. There's really no right or wrong answer."

"I hope you're right, Mama."

"Of course I'm right." Mama tossed a nod at Haley. "I think your little friend wants to show you something."

Nodding, Josie, picked up her skirt and hastened along the garden path to Haley's side.

***

Josie was still thinking about the conversation with her mother that night as she sat at her desk pasting the last of the ads in place.

"What I believe is that true love comes as many times as you want or need it to come."

She reached behind her neck to unfasten the gold chain. Holding the open locket in the palm of her hand, she stared down at the miniature photograph. A heavy feeling washed over her like a wave and settled in her chest. This time it wasn't grief that weighed her down but regret. No matter how hard she tried holding on to Ralph, he kept slipping farther and farther away.

Stuffing the locket into her pocket, she sat back and yawned. Time to call it a night.

Just as she reached into the desk drawer for her purse, the door flew open, startling her. In walked Craig Gilbert.

Her stomach knotted as a taste of metallic fear filled her mouth. What was he doing there? All she knew was that she didn't want to be alone with him. Neither did she want him to know she was afraid.

"I was just leaving," she said. "It's late."

He looked like he was having trouble focusing. Had he been drinking? "Anna-May said you paid her a visit," he slurred. "Why?"

"I'm sure she told you that we're including her dress in our fashion column."

His face darkened, and his eyes looked like two black pools. Funny, he didn't look so mousey now. He looked dark and menacing, and Josie's finger tightened around the edge of her desk.

"Anna-May said you asked about the cameo."

So, the cameo worried him, did it? Gulping, she dropped her hands to her lap and fought to remain calm. He was only one man, and she'd once stopped a small group of Indians from stealing her livestock. The thought gave her a measure of comfort—until she recalled that at the time she was brandishing a shotgun.

"It's a beautiful piece," she hastened to say, hoping her calm voice and manner would have a similar effect on his demeanor.

Visually inspecting her desk for weapons, she mentally measured the distance to a bronze paperweight. That's when she noticed Ruby's photograph laying face up . . . next to Haley's drawing. Her mouth went dry. *Oh, dear heaven.*

"You have marvelous taste," she added. If she'd ever needed flattery to work, it was now. "Anna-May is very fortunate."

The compliment failed to soften his dark expression. "I don't want any mention of the cameo in the paper."

Steady, steady. If she agreed to his wishes too quickly, he might grow suspicious. "I think the readers will enjoy reading about the beautiful gift you gave your wife."

His smile failed to reach his eyes. "That's just it. It was a gift. A personal one."

What he said made sense. Maybe he felt as protective of the cameo as she was of her locket.

She was just about to give him the benefit of the doubt when he leaned forward, palms on her desk, his fingers mere inches from Ruby's photograph. "I said I don't want it in the paper!" This time each word sounded like cracking ice.

His menacing voice made Josie flinch. More than that, it made her even more nervous. "As you w-wish," she stammered. "I-I'll delete any references to the cameo."

He lowered his gaze and she abruptly stood, hoping to distract his attention away from Ruby's image. "Now, if you'll excuse me."

Instead of backing away and leaving as she'd hoped, he stayed rooted in place, his gaze riveted upon the photograph on her desk. Seconds stretched into what seemed like hours. The only sound was the pounding of her heart.

Finally, he raised his head, his eyes dark with accusations. "You know, don't you?" he said, his voice strangely calm. Lethally calm. "You know." This time it wasn't a question, but a statement.

Willing her knees not to cave beneath her, she fought to find her voice. "I don't know what you're talking about." She tried for a lightness that she didn't feel. "W-what do I know?"

"You know that Anna-May's cameo once belonged to Ruby. I didn't think anyone would recognize it as the same one owned by my sis—" He stopped, but not soon enough.

Josie's mouth dropped. "Ruby was your sister?" When he failed to respond, a cold chill shot through her. She couldn't help the next question that fell from her lips.

"You killed your own sister?" she asked, the calmness of her voice belying the horror she felt inside.

She expected him to deny it—prayed that he would. Instead, his eyes glittered with a look that turned her stomach.

"I didn't want to hurt her," he said, his voice cold. "But when she threatened to tell Anna-May the truth, I snapped."

"Truth?" Her hands curled by her sides. "What truth?"

"About my family. We were poorer than church mice."

At first she was confused. What he said made no sense. Many people grew up poor. That wasn't a crime. But then she remembered something his wife had said, and the full implication of his words became clear.

"There was no rich uncle, was there?"

He scoffed. "My only uncle is serving time for killing a US marshal."

She stared at him. "Then how . . ." The image of him leaving the bank after hours came to mind, and the pieces suddenly fell into place. "Your sister knew you were embezzling from the bank, didn't she?" She was guessing, but it was the only thing that made sense. When he failed to deny it, she continued, "What did she do? Threaten to turn you in?"

His eyes flashed with hatred. "She had a nerve judging me after the life she led. I came to Two-Time to escape my family. Escape their crooked ways. Can you imagine my shock when I discovered her living here? She threatened to tell the sheriff what I was doing if I didn't give her a cut of the money I'd stolen from the bank. Of all the towns she could have settled in, why did it have to be this one?"

Josie was thinking like a reporter now, and a dozen questions came to mind. "Does Anna-May know that Ruby was your sister?"

"No, and I mean to keep it that way." He then reached into his coat pocket and pulled out a revolver. "How about you and me taking a little walk?"

No sooner were the words out of his mouth than Josie spotted a black bundle of movement. Suddenly appearing out of nowhere, Mr. Whiskers took a flying leap at the shiny weapon.

Gilbert fell back with a startled look and his gun fired with a puff of smoke. A chunk of plaster the size of a quarter fell from the ceiling.

With a cry of alarm, Josie reached for the paperweight. But before she could put it to good use, the door flew open and in ran Brandon.

Chapter 27

Renowned mountain climber Joseph Kinder, who successfully scaled some of the tallest mountains in the world, including the Matterhorn, is dead. He fell off a kitchen stool.

—Two-Time Gazette

Brandon stood motionless in the doorway, his gaze swinging from Gilbert's pointed weapon to Josie and back again. "What's going on?"

"Your lady friend here got too nosey," Gilbert said.

"He k-killed Miss Ruby," Josie stammered.

Brandon stared at Gilbert with narrowed eyes, and a muscle twitched at his jaw. "In that case, I guess you could say we have a problem," he drawled.

Gilbert's eyes glittered, and he drew attention back to his gun with a slight movement of his arm. "Looks like you have a bigger problem than I do."

"I wouldn't be so sure of that," Brandon said as calmly as if talking about the weather. "You see, I'm a big believer in keeping guns away from killers."

No sooner were the words out of Brandon's mouth than he kicked the pistol clear out of Gilbert's hand. The Colt flew up before landing with a thud next to the desk. Mr. Whiskers let out a wail and took off in a screeching black streak.

Gilbert barreled into Brandon head first. The two men fell to the floor and proceeded to punch each other in deadly earnest.

Josie dived for the gun and lifted it with shaking hands. Pointing the weapon at the two battling men, she didn't dare pull the trigger for fear of hitting Brandon. A shiver of panic rushed through her. Dear God, where was Scooter, and why hadn't he heard the shot?

Panting in terror, she whirled about and slid the window open with her one free hand. Leaning over the sill, she pointed the gun upward and shot bullets into the sky—one, two, three—spacing them a few seconds apart so Scooter wouldn't think it was just some cowboy letting off steam. She pulled the trigger a fourth time, but a hollow clicking sound signaled an empty chamber.

A sudden silence made her spin around. She almost fainted with relief. Brandon was standing over Gilbert's prone body

Breath escaping in a whoosh, she dropped the empty gun on the floor. "Is he . . . is he dead?"

Brandon wiped his mouth with the back of his hand, ignoring a thin stream of blood trickling from his forehead. "No, but when he wakens, he'll wish he was."

"You're hurt," she said in alarm.

Brandon pulled out a handkerchief and gently dabbed his brow. "Not as much as he is."

The door flew open, and Scooter burst inside like a tornado. Tripping over Gilbert's body, the sheriff fell flat on the floor, sprawled out like a discarded ragdoll.

Brandon stared down at him with a wry smile. "Now that's what I call laying down the law."

***

When the worse was over and Gilbert had been hauled off to jail, Josie insisted upon attending to Brandon's wounds. He had a black eye and red chin, but it was the cut on his forehead that worried her.

"You should have Doc Stybeck look at this."

"Maybe later." Brandon flinched when she dabbed at the wound. "I still can't believe Gilbert killed that woman. But why did he come to you? How did he know you were on to him?"

Josie tossed the wet sponge into the basin of water. She was still trembling, but whether from the near brush with death or from the nearness of Brandon, she couldn't say.

Reaching for her scissors, she snipped a square of gauze and applied it to Brandon's forehead. The gentle pressure of her fingers made him grimace in pain, and she quickly drew her hand away.

"I didn't mean to hurt you," she said in alarm.

"I'm okay," he said.

She reapplied the soft fabric ever so gently and reached for the tape. As she worked, she explained how Haley's drawing had helped the pieces of the puzzle fall into place. "Haley didn't fill in the details of the cameo, but she got the shape right, and that got me to thinking about the portrait in the photographer's shop."

"I can't believe that all this happened because of something Haley drew."

Josie smiled at mention of his daughter's name. "Thanks to Haley and her God-given talent, we caught a killer, I have a new office, and Mr. Pendergrass will soon have a new home."

Brandon shook his head. "Incredible. I can't imagine what she'll do next."

"Neither can I." Josie said with a laugh and then grew serious. "It's kind of ironic in a way. Gilbert tried distancing himself from a family he loathed. Instead, he ended up becoming as lawless as they were. Maybe even worse."

She opened a desk drawer to replace her medical supplies, but Brandon stopped her with a hand to her wrist. A moment ago his eyes had glazed over with pain. Now the deep-brown depths were filled with concern and something else. Something that took her breath away.

"You could have been his next victim," he said, his voice husky.

The full impact of what happened hit her like a slap in the face. "You could have been shot," she whispered back.

Their gazes held, each second seeming to fill them with each other.

Brandon was the first to break the silence. "After my wife died . . ." His voice was thick with emotion. "I didn't think there could be anyone else."

Something intense flared inside her, matching the smoldering flames in his eyes. She felt like she had toed a line and either had to cross it or move back. "I felt the same way after losing Ralph," she said, her voice choked.

He studied her, a hopeful glint in his eyes. "But after what happened tonight . . ." His expression clouded for a moment before he continued. "The thought of what could have happened. That I might have lost you like I lost—" He stood and took hold of her hand. "Do you think . . . ? Josie, be honest with me. Is it too soon for us?"

She lifted her free hand to his cheek, careful not to hurt him. His rough, manly skin felt oddly comforting next to her palm. "Too soon?"

"I want us to be together. To build a life." He drew in his breath as if trying to absorb her. "I want to marry you."

Her breath caught in her lungs, and her heart practically leaped out of her chest. She flung her arms around his neck before guilt or anything else could spoil the moment. "Oh, yes, yes, yes!"

Hands at her waist, he pulled her closer. "That wasn't a proposal," he murmured in her ear. "I simply said I *want* to marry you. You deserve a proper courting and you're only now coming out of your mourning period." One hand explored the soft lines of her back as he spoke. "There's also the problem of our newspapers. If word gets out that we've made peace, our readership will take a perilous dive and—"

Gazing up at him, she touched a finger to his lips. "The stubborn, maddening editor of the so-called newspaper known as the *Lone Star Press* talks way too much."

He arched an eyebrow. "Is that so? Well, what do you think about this?" And with that he crushed her to him, covering her mouth hungrily with his own.

Word of Mr. Gilbert's arrest traveled through Two-Time with the speed of lightning. It was all anyone could talk about. If traffic through town wasn't bad enough before, it was nothing compared to that morning as knots of people gathered up and down the street to discuss the latest news or purchase the one-page extras that Brandon and Josie had each independently published.

Josie arrived at the office later than usual and found Miss Bubbles waiting for her outside.

"Oh, Josie!" She took both of Josie's hands in her own. "I can't tell you how relieved I am." Dropping Josie's hands, she dabbed at her eyes with a lace handkerchief. "But . . . but you could have been killed."

"Let's not think about that. The main thing is that justice will finally be served."

Miss Bubbles stared at her with tear-filled eyes. "I don't know how to thank you."

Josie placed her hand on the woman's shoulder. "No need to," she said.

Miss Bubbles thanked her again and left. Josie waited until her garish wagon was out of sight before entering the office, where she found her father waiting for her.

"Papa?"

His eyes held a suspicious gleam as he looked her up and down. "I had to see for myself that you were all right."

"Oh, Papa." She fell into his arms. "I'm fine."

After hugging her close, he held her at arm's length. "I want you to move back home where I can keep my eye on you."

She studied his dear, craggy face. He drove her crazy at times with his old-fashioned ideas, but she loved him without measure. The thought was not without worry. What would he say if he knew she had fallen in love with the editor of the *Lone Star Press*? Would he be so willing to take her back into the house if he knew?

"Papa—"

"I know, I know." He rolled his eyes. "You're perfectly capable of taking care of yourself. But can't you just this once humor me? Hmm?"

She heaved a sigh. Papa had a way of disarming her, and this was one of those times. "I missed you, Papa."

He nodded. "I know. I missed you too. So, what do you say?"

"I say I'm coming home."

Josie arrived at her office early the following Friday morning and found her two sisters waiting on the doorstep. Surprised, she greeted them with a smile, but neither smiled back. Amanda stood with folded arms, and Meg looked fit to be tied.

"It's about time you got here," Meg snapped.

Josie studied their serious faces with alarm. "What's wrong? The children—"

"They're fine," Meg and Amanda answered in tandem.

Josie's gaze slid back and forth between them. "Then . . . what?"

Meg shook a previously unnoticed newspaper in Josie's face. "I take it you haven't read your competitor's newspaper."

"Oh, for goodness' sake. Is that all?" She placed a hand on her chest with a sigh of relief. "You two had me worried there for a minute." Josie unlocked her office door and held it open to allow her sisters to stomp inside. Inside, she tossed her key on the desk. "What's got you both so riled?"

For answer Meg stabbed the newspaper with her finger and began reading aloud as if she was auditioning for a part in a Shakespeare play. "'Could two people unable to see eye to eye on politics, civic matters, and the renaming of this fine town live happily ever after under the same roof?'" She glanced at Josie with a look of horror before reading the rest. "'Could this poor, love-starved editor find happiness with the stubborn, albeit beautiful, owner of the *Gazette*?'"

Josie's mouth dropped open. "Let me see that!" She reached for the paper, but Meg pulled it away and kept reading.

"'Could matrimony squelch the fires of journalism, giving opinion the same bland consistency as overcooked porridge?'" Meg rolled her eyes and kept reading. "'To keep peace in the family, would this tortured editor find himself agreeing with the *Gazette*'s laboriously wrong stance on—'"

Josie laughed out loud. She couldn't help it. Brandon had boldly laid out his intentions to marry her for all the world to see. Apparently, he was counting on readers voting in his favor. The plan could easily backfire, of course. She'd given up trying to guess how readers would react to any given topic or opinion. Editorials she'd thought would earn nodding approval often received stinging criticism. Still, if readers could be convinced that it would be business as usual between the two rivals, the idea of marriage might not be so far-fetched.

The feather on Amanda's tall hat swayed like a woman about to faint. "I don't see what's so funny," she said tersely. "The nerve of the man suggesting that you would consider marriage to the likes of him."

"Yes," Meg agreed. "And you being a new widow and all."

"I'm not a new widow," Josie said.

Aware suddenly that both sisters were staring at her like she'd lost her mind, Josie tried to look contrite. "It's been nearly two years," she said.

"Not quite," Amanda said, much to Josie's irritation. Since when did her suffragist sister concern herself with society's dictates?

"And what do you think Papa will say when he reads this?" Meg asked.

Josie winced at the thought. What a pity that their recent truce was already doomed to failure.

"It's outrageous," Meg agreed. "You should ask Grant about the possibility of filing a suit for libel."

"Oh, I think I'm quite capable of handling Brandon Wade without legal intervention," Josie said with a mysterious air. After all the trouble and worry her sisters had caused her through the years, she enjoyed turning the tables on them for a change.

"What are you going to do?" Meg asked, eyes rounded.

Josie kept them hanging a moment in suspense before responding. "You'll have to wait for next Friday's *Gazette* to find out."

"You better put him in his place," Meg said. "That's all I've got to say."

Josie managed to hide her smile behind a well-placed hand, but could do nothing about her reddening cheeks. "I fully intend to," she said. Oh, yes, indeed, she did.

No sooner had her sisters left than Becky-Sue burst into the office, all smiles and wiggling fingers. It was hard to miss the sparkling diamond flashing from her ring finger.

"Oh, my," Josie said, rising to take hold of her friend's hand. "It's beautiful." The solitaire diamond was centered on a gold band and accented with delicate engravings.

"When's the big day?"

"Not until after the first of the year," Becky-Sue said and giggled.

Josie released her hand. "Does this mean I lose my star reporter?"

Becky-Sue blushed. "I was hoping I could still write an occasional article for you even after I'm married. Scooter said he won't mind if I do."

"I'd like that," Josie said. She opened a drawer and pulled out an envelope. "Here," she said, handing it over the desk.

"What is this?" Becky-Sue asked.

"It's called pay," Josie said and laughed at Becky-Sue's astonished expression.

Becky-Sue stared at the bills in the envelope. "But you said you couldn't afford to pay me."

"That was before. But things have taken a turn for the better. And now I can."

Becky-Sue's face lit up. "Oh, thank you. I'm now a professional reporter!" She practically danced out of the office.

Josie was still smiling when she took pen in hand. Surprised to find herself envying Becky-Sue, she thought for a long moment before starting to write.

The editor of the Lone Star Tribune, *a misguided and sorry excuse for a newspaper, posed an interesting question. Could two people with opposite viewpoints find happiness under the same roof? The answer, of course, is no. How could anyone, let alone a wife, ignore Mr. Wade's woefully outdated views on guns? Or his ridiculous insistence upon renaming the town after its unsavory founder. Then there's Mr. Wade's ponderous . . .*

She smiled at the words flowed from her pen. Inspiration had never been so sweet.

***

"'Ponderous'?" Brandon said aloud as he read Josie's latest column. He couldn't believe his eyes. Whenever he'd asked her what she'd thought about his editorial laying out his marriage plans, she'd smiled and said he would just have to wait for Friday's paper to find out. For seven long days she'd kept him in suspense, and for what? To be rejected in the worse possible way!

Not only had she turned down his proposal, she'd laid out in excruciating details every opposing viewpoint and conflicting opinion they'd shared.

Pacing back and forth in his office like a hungry lion, he slapped the rolled newspaper against his hand.

She was messing with him. No question. She had privately told him in no uncertain terms that she wanted to marry him and then publicly—*very* publicly—changed her mind. She'd kissed him silly and then turned around and stuck a knife in his back. What kind of woman would do such a thing? Certainly not the woman he'd fallen in love with.

What was going on here? What was she thinking?

The door swung open, and in walked his typesetter, Booker, his broad ebony face sporting a silly grin. "Good morning."

Brandon flung the newspaper into the wastepaper basket. "Nothing good about it."

Booker's face crinkled into a frown. "Thought you'd be happy."

"Happy? Happy! Have you read this morning's *Gazette*?"

"'Course I read it. Everyone in town's read it."

Brandon rolled his eyes to the ceiling. "Don't remind me."

"What's wrong with you, Chief? I thought you'd be hopping with joy about now."

Brandon stared at him. "Do you understand what's going on here? Josie Johnson turned down my proposal of marriage. But she couldn't do it to my face. Oh, no! She had to do it in the most underhanded way possible. In print. Furthermore—"

Booker's laughter stopped him. "You didn't read what she had to say, did you?"

"I read it. Well, half of it. I got so disgusted I didn't even finish."

"That's what I thought."

Brandon frowned. "What's that supposed to mean?"

Booker reached into the wastepaper basket for the newspaper and tossed it to him. "It means you better read to the end. "Cuz if you don't, you'll be sorry."

Chapter 28

For sale: A used tombstone. It would be ideal for a man named Jacob Frederick Alderman.

—Two-Time Gazette

As predicted, Papa hit the roof and showed every sign of aiming for a celestial body or two. "In my day, a man asked the father's permission before he blasted a proposal from a newspaper for all the world to see," he bellowed. "And you, young lady! What could you possibly be thinking to play along with him?"

Josie sat on the sofa in the parlor, feet together, eyes cast downward. Trying to reason with Papa when he was in this frame of mind was a waste of time. Better to wait till he wound down or the world ended—whichever came first.

Papa streaked back and forth in front of her, arms beating the air with his every word. "And another thing—" He launched into another tirade.

Mama sat silently knitting in her chair, her face pinched. It wasn't until Papa stormed upstairs that she set her yarn aside and laid her hands on her lap.

"Do you love this man?" she asked quietly.

Josie lifted her gaze to her mother's. "You never asked that question of me when I became engaged to Ralph."

"That was a different time. You were different."

Mama was right. When she'd married Ralph, she had been young and innocent. More than that, she'd believed in fairy-tale endings and love everlasting. Now she knew that the only thing she could count on was the present, and she meant to make the most of it.

"Why would I marry Brandon if I didn't love him?"

Mama pursed her lips before answering. "Perhaps because . . . he can give you the one thing that Ralph never could."

Josie's forehead creased. "What, Mama? What can Brandon give me that Ralph couldn't?"

"He can give you a child."

Josie stiffened. "You think that's why I want to marry him?" she asked, her voice incredulous. "Because of Haley?"

"I know how much you want children. Have always wanted children. I see it in your eyes whenever you look at your niece and nephews. Hear it in your voice each time you mention Haley's name."

Josie couldn't argue with her mother on that account. "I love Haley. I do." The thought of being a part of her life and watching her grow into young womanhood would be a dream come true. "But that's not why I want to marry Brandon. I want to marry him because he's kind and funny and smart and . . ." She could go on and on. "He makes me feel alive again. Oh, Mama, you have no idea."

No one could possibly know how it felt to lose a husband without going through it firsthand. There was no way to describe the pain, the loneliness, the utter desolation she'd felt in those first early weeks and months. To feel this hopeful for the future following such a loss was nothing short of a miracle.

"After Ralph died, it was all I could do to get through each day. I was just going through the motions. Brandon changed all that. He made life worth living again."

"That's good, Josie," Mama said. "I just wish . . ."

"What, Mama? What do you wish?"

"I just wish the two of you were more alike in your thinking. He's so different than Ralph."

Josie frowned. "Is that such a bad thing, Mama?"

"Not bad, but marriage is hard under the best of circumstances. When two people have no common ground, it can't possibly work out well."

"Brandon and I are newspaper people. That's common ground. We've also both lost someone we loved."

Mama sighed. "That's what I'm worried about. Loss and loneliness can sometimes make people jump into situations they're not ready for"

Josie knew her mother was concerned for her welfare, but why couldn't she at least pretend to be happy for her? "I know what I'm doing, Mama."

Her mother studied her. "In matters of the heart, I don't know that any of us know what we're doing."

"I'm not some silly schoolgirl infatuated with love," Josie said. "Both my feet are squarely on the ground."

"I read his paper, Josie. I read what he writes. What he's written about you."

Josie drew in her breath. What would Mama say if she knew that she and Brandon had written each other's editorials? At least most of them. "That's for public show. Privately, he's a completely different person."

Mama's hands fluttered to her chest, but the stubborn look remained. "All I ask is that you take your time. Make sure that you're getting married for the right reasons."

When Josie failed to reply, Mama silently gathered up her knitting and left the room, leaving Josie to ponder the depths of her heart.

What if Mama was right? What if the real reason she wanted to marry Brandon was because of his daughter? Despite six years of marriage, she had never borne a child. She had no way of knowing if she or Ralph had been at fault, but it was entirely possible that Haley might be her very last chance at motherhood.

Once her thoughts took off in that direction, questions kept popping in her head. Questions for which she had no answers.

Would she be so eager to marry Brandon had she not felt so lonely? Or didn't miss the security and companionship of marriage. Or wasn't so desperate to experience the thrill of motherhood? They were questions for which she had no answers.

***

Josie stared in dismay at the diamond engagement ring Brandon had slipped on her finger and didn't know what to say. Her conversation with her mother had kept her twisting and turning the night before, leaving her utterly confused and unsure of her own mind. Her own heart.

Now she stood with Brandon in the middle of the street halfway between their offices at their usual meeting spot. She had expected to receive Friday's column from him. Instead, he'd surprised her with a ring.

He studied her face with knitted brow. The flickering gas streetlight cast a yellow pool around them, turning his probing eyes into gold. "I expected a little more in the way of excitement from my future bride."

"I . . ." She pulled her hand from his.

Her gesture confounded him, maybe even hurt him. She could see it in the rigid set of his jaw, hear it in his ragged breath. "If you don't like the ring, we can change it,"

"Oh, no. It's beautiful."

It was in fact the most beautiful ring she had ever laid eyes on. Even in the dim light the gold ring looked perfect in every way. A large sparkling diamond stood out like a bold headline, surrounded by two smaller stones that matched the exact color of her eyes. It was just the kind of thing she would expect from him.

"It's exquisite. It's just . . ." Mama was right; Brandon was completely different from Ralph. Ralph would never have done anything so impulsive.

"I should have waited to give it to you," he said with an apologetic shrug. "I should have taken you for a ride in the country. Planned something special. But the ring came today, and I couldn't wait to put it on your finger." He gave her a sheepish grin. "You can add impatience to my list of flaws."

She shook her head. None of this was his fault. "I kind of think of this place as ours," she said. She loved standing in the deserted street with him beneath the starlit sky, the whole town to themselves. A circle of light marking their spot. "It's just . . . I didn't expect things to move so quickly."

"If it's our readers you're worried about, you needn't be," he said. "People seem to like the idea of two battling publishers living under the same roof. I've heard no objections." When she failed to respond, a cloud of uncertainty darkened his face. He cupped her chin and tilted her head up, forcing her to meet his gaze. "I thought it was settled, Josie."

She blinked back tears. How she hated feeling so utterly confused. It wasn't like her not to know her own mind. "I'm sorry, Brandon. I really did believe I was ready to move on and start a new life. I now know I need more time."

"I'm not rushing you." He ran a knuckle from her cheek to her earlobe. "We don't have to set the wedding date right now. The church is probably booked anyway. You can take all the time you need. I just want to give you a proper courting." He tilted his head to the side. "Tell me what I can do to make this right."

She opened her mouth to say something but the voice in her head was not her own. *"He can give you the one thing that Ralph never could . . . He can give you a child."*

She drew in her breath. Dare she tell him about the doubts her mother had instilled in her? The doubts that made her wonder if she could ever truly love him as he should be loved?

"It's not just the wedding date," she said when at last she could form the words.

She pulled the ring off her finger. It near broke her heart to do so, but keeping it when she was so uncertain of her feelings would be living a lie, and he deserved so much more. Moistening her lips, she squeezed the ring gently in her palm before handing it back to him.

He stared down at the sparkler before looking up at her. "Are you saying you don't want to marry me?"

She swallowed hard. "I don't know what I'm saying, Brandon. All I know is that I can't do this. Not now." Maybe never.

His face seemed to crumble, and she heard his intake of breath. The hurt in his eyes nearly killed her. "I know you loved your husband very much. Just as I loved Haley's mother. It took me awhile to realize that loving you takes nothing away from the woman I once loved. What happened in the past is over."

She knotted her hands by her side. If it was truly over, then why did it feel like the past was still shaping her future? Still guiding her daily decisions? Still tormenting her with its unrelenting memories and unfulfilled dreams?

"Josie, I don't want you to forget Ralph or what you two shared. I would never ask that of you."

She drew in her breath. She was tempted—oh, so tempted—to put her doubts aside and melt into his arms. If only her mother's words didn't keep echoing in her head. *He can give you what Ralph never could.*

It was hard—harder than anything she'd ever done—but she managed to keep her wits about her as much for his sake as for hers. "I . . . I can't."

His eyes darkened. "What's really going on, Josie?" he asked.

She looked away, but only because she couldn't bear to see the hurt on his face. Hearing the pain in his voice was difficult enough. "I told you. I'm just not ready. Please try to understand. I'm just telling you how I feel."

He rubbed his head. "Okay, then. When . . . when do you think you'll be ready?"

Here it was. The moment of truth. "When I know without a doubt that I can give you all the love and devotion you deserve." With that she turned and fled.

✳✳✳

"Why can't we ask Mrs. Johnson to go on a picnic with us?" Haley asked.

Back turned, Brandon met his daughter's gaze in the mirror over the dry sink. Ever since she'd been knee-high to a grasshopper, she'd been asking questions. *Why is the sky blue? How come the moon doesn't fall?* Such questions were no easier to answer than the one she now posed, but at least they hadn't come with a piercing arrow aimed straight at his heart.

He swished his razor through the water in the porcelain basin. "I told you, Haley. Mrs. Johnson has other things to do."

"We can go on a picnic tomorrow instead of today," Haley said.

Brandon reached for a towel. "I'm sure she has something to do tomorrow too."

"You can ask her."

He turned and drew in his breath. Just when he thought he had a handle on fatherhood, something popped up that threw him. How did one you explain the vagaries of the human heart to a nine-year-old? How could he get her to forget the woman he himself could not forget?

"Mrs. Johnson is . . . sad."

"Because her husband is in heaven?"

He nodded. "Yes. When people are sad, they don't want to do certain things. Like go on picnics."

The look on Haley's face jolted him. Colleen used to have a similar look just before she told him something he didn't want to know about himself.

"You're sad, and you're going on a picnic," Haley said.

He raised an eyebrow. "What makes you think I'm sad?"

"You forgot to shave that side of your face," she said pointing.

"What?" He lifted his hand to his cheek. The prickly rough surface against his palm made him laugh. "That doesn't mean I'm sad," he said. "It only means I'm forgetful."

"You're always forgetful when you're sad," she said. "Remember when you promised to take me the fair? You forgot because it was Mama's birthday and you were sad because she wasn't here to celebrate."

He shook his head in wonder. That had been three years ago when she was only six.

"I made up for it the following year," he said. He didn't need yet another reminder of his failings. "Today, I just have a lot on my mind."

He hadn't been able to think of anything but Josie for days. He wasn't sure how it had happened. How he had fallen so utterly and completely in love. All he knew was that somehow Josie had burrowed her way into his resistant heart and had now left a gaping hole.

He wasn't so much sad as angry. For far too long, the past had robbed him of the joy of living. Now the past was robbing him of the woman he loved.

Chapter 29

*Dejected following the failure of his business, Miles Hinton threw himself in front of a train. He has now decided to manufacture cowcatchers. —
Two-Time Gazette*

It was overcast that Saturday in October when Josie walked the grounds of the Two-Time Old Folks' Home. Lot eleven had caused her much pain in the past, but never had she dreaded anything as much as she dreaded today.

The grand opening was meeting with great fanfare. It appeared that half the town had turned out to tour the facilities. The festivities had been preceded by a long, windy speech by the mayor, who spent more time congratulating himself than the founder of the home.

Music was provided by the Washboard Quartet, which included T-bone on the washboard and Mr. Mooney on the cowbells.

Josie had almost sent Hank in her stead, but as the publisher of the *Gazette* she could hardly skip the most important event of the year. People were sure to notice. More than that, it meant a lot to Haley to have her there.

She and Brandon hadn't talked for more than a month. Not since the night she returned his ring. Haley and her father had spent every spare minute getting the home ready for today, and Josie had purposely stayed away. Until she sorted out the knot of confused emotions inside, it wasn't fair to keep seeing Brandon. It had hurt to stay away—hurt more than she could ever have thought possible—but it was the right thing to do.

The editorial exchanges had been handled by Hank. Remarkable professionalism had been shown in keeping their private affairs out of the weekly opinion pieces. The editorial feud continued, but neither she or Brandon felt the need to address the personal rift between them in print. This led readers to believe that the previous mention of marriage had simply been a publicity stunt.

Brandon had done a wonderful service for the town, and no one suspected that the home had anything to do with the fire. Nor could anyone know from looking at Josie how much it cost her to be there that today. Or that her friendly smiles sprang from a well of hidden tears.

Mr. Pendergrass greeted visitors fully clothed in overalls and plaid shirt, thus earning everyone's gratitude. Brandon was surrounded by well-wishers and didn't seem to notice Josie's presence.

Haley was the official tour guide. The girl looked so pretty in her pleated blue dress and small-crowned, wide-brimmed hat. Upon spotting

Josie, her face lit up and she immediately ran to greet her. "I missed you, Mrs. Johnson."

"Missed you too," Josie said.

Haley tugged on Josie's hand. "Come on, I'll show you around." Haley motioned for the other guests to follow. One by one she led the group to the large parlor and through the dining room.

"This is the kitchen," she said as if the butcher-block counters, enormous ice box, and wood-burning cookstove didn't speak for themselves.

Later, while Meg and Amanda explored the facilities, Josie decided to have one last look at the property before taking her leave.

Outside she bumped into Pepper. He doffed his hat and bowed his head. "Be careful of the oil," he said, pointing to the ground.

"Oil?" She looked at the shiny puddle oozing out of the ground, and something occurred to her. "Is that why you wanted this property?" she asked. "Because of the oil?"

"As a matter of fact, it was," he said with rueful shrug of his shoulders.

She should have known Pepper was up to one of money-making schemes. What would he think if he knew she had once suspected him of arson and even murder? "Isn't lamp oil produced in Pennsylvania?"

He made a face. "Forget the lamp oil business. I'm thinking bigger. Now that the railroads are switching from coal, oil is fast becoming the new gold."

"I always thought the oil here would be too costly to extract."

"That's true of hand-dug wells. But the more successful wells are drilled with steam engines."

She hated to think of the peaceful serenity of the area being disturbed by machines. "Does that mean you intend to drill here?"

"Unfortunately, no. Most of the other lots have already sold. What's left is unsuitable for drilling."

That was music to her ears. "I guess you'll have to look elsewhere for your pot of gold."

"And I fully intended to." He tipped his hat. "Good day, Mrs. Johnson."

After she and Pepper had parted, she followed the winding path around the side of the home. Logs were stacked up in a neat pile, and a horse-drawn tractor sat parked nearby. Soon, the area would house the stables and barn.

Continuing, she saw something that surprised her. The old cottonwood still stood, surrounded by a circle of fallen trees. Even more surprising, a sign written in Brandon's bold hand and tacked to the tree read, "Do not cut down this tree."

Josie gasped. Brandon must have seen the heart with the initials. Had he guessed at their significance? Was that why he'd saved that one tree? Somehow she knew that was the reason.

The heart carved into the puckered bark was easy to find. She traced it with a finger, and something tugged at her insides. Looking at the engraving, she saw it for what it was: a grave marker of the past.

The thought curled through her like slow-moving smoke. Her husband was gone and never coming back. Their marriage belonged to a very different time and place. The woman that Ralph had left behind no longer existed. She doubted if Ralph would even recognize her as she was today.

Her gaze traveled up the length of the tree. Cottonwoods were the first to lose their leaves, but not usually this early. The drought had taken a toll. The tree that had once shaded two lovers now opened to a limitless sky.

Turning away, she was surprised by the sudden awareness that locked her into the present. It was as if she was seeing the world for the first time. As if she had just awakened from a very long sleep. The house built for the elderly loomed in front of her. With its newly papered walls, polished glass windows, and shiny tile roof, it offered a new beginning for those who had previously seemed to have so little to live for.

Beyond the house lay the river, winding its way to the sea with the swiftness and single-minded purpose of an arrow. Neither rocks nor fallen trees could stop the onward flow.

A slight breeze whispered through the dry leaves at her feet, a startling contrast to the new life around her.

Her vision blurred, but not with tears of regret or grief. This time the tears were for thanksgiving. Life really did go on. Brandon had taken her dream and turned it into reality. He had built something big and bright and beautiful. He had created a home that would give people like Mr. Pendergrass a safe place in which to spend their golden years.

And that's when it hit her: Mama was wrong. Her feelings for Brandon had nothing to do with what he could give her, but rather for the kind-hearted man that he was. She loved him for how he made her feel when she was with him. For who they were when they were together.

Joy bubbled up inside her as she started toward the house. Most everyone had left by the time she reached the wraparound porch with its white wicker chairs. That's when she got the shock of her life.

The tall wooden door that had been opened when she passed through the first time was now closed, revealing a wood carving of a sailing ship with which she was all too familiar. She rubbed her eyes and blinked, but there was no mistake. The long-lost lid of the family hope chest was now embedded in the golden oak door.

"A beautiful piece, wouldn't you say?"

Startled by Brandon's voice, she turned to find him at the bottom of the porch steps, looking up at her. He stood tall and straight as the nearby windmill, his long sturdy legs slightly apart. Broad shoulders strained beneath the fabric of his shirt as he held his powerful arms by his side.

He tossed a nod at the door. "Haley found that piece by the river. It was in bad shape but I was able to refinish it. We think it fell off a boat or something."

"It didn't fall off a boat," she whispered. "That ship was carved by my grandfather."

"Your grand—" Brandon's forehead creased, and the lines between his eyes deepened. "Are you saying it's yours?"

She nodded. "It's the lid of my family's hope chest."

He grimaced. "Of course. I should have known. The day of the race."

"I looked for it but couldn't find it."

"I'm sorry, Josie. I'll see that you get it back."

She met his gaze and felt a jolt inside. Seeing Brandon through eyes no longer veiled with the past revealed things in him previously overlooked. He was nothing like Ralph, and for that she had once thought him lacking. A mistake. Now she knew that this maddening, wonderful, opinionated, thoughtful, arrogant, kind, and loving man was perfect for the woman she had now become.

Tensing, she waited for the inevitable guilt she'd come to expect from such thoughts. Instead, she felt something shift and change inside, like a freshly transformed butterfly taking flight and suddenly able to soar to unprecedented heights. That's when she knew without a doubt that the woman she once was belonged to Ralph and always would. The woman she had since become belonged to another. And that woman was ready— more than ready—to love Brandon with her whole heart and soul for who he was, not for the dreams he could make come true.

She glanced back at the door. "That's a carving of the ship that brought my grandparents to America."

"Don't worry, Josie. I'll return it to you. The piece is embedded in the wood, so I'll have to replace the door. But it shouldn't take but a couple of days."

Her gaze locked on to his. "You'd ruin your beautiful door just for me?" she whispered.

The question seemed to puzzle him. "I would do anything for you. Don't you know that by now?"

"Even save a tree that should by all rights be cut down?"

"Like I said. I'd do anything for you."

His steady gaze stripped her of all pretenses, and she fought to hold back the tears. By all accounts he should be angry for the way she'd led him on, though that was never her intention. Instead, the tenderness of his expression was like a healing balm soothing her deepest wounds.

Fearing she was about to drown in the brown depths of his eyes, she shook her head. "I don't want the lid back," she said. "My grandfather carved the ship on the hope chest as a symbol of new beginnings. I want everyone who enters here to know it's never too late to start a new life. That's why the ship belongs on this house. On this door." Mama and her sisters were bound to agree.

His gaze bored into hers. "Are you sure?"

"Oh, yes, I'm sure. I also want you to cut down that tree. The land could be better used for something else."

"If you're sure," he said.

"I'm sure." She drew in her breath and exhaled. "Speaking of new beginnings, I'm also sure of something else."

He rested one foot on the bottom step. "What's that?" he asked.

"I'm sure that you and I belong together. That is, if you still want me."

"Oh, God, Josie. Do you know how much I've wanted to hear you say that? I never stopped hoping that you would—"

He never got to finish what he was saying. That's because she had cleared the porch and leaped into his arms with such force she'd almost knocked him over.

He steadied her with his hands to her waist, a look of astonishment on his face. "Do . . . do you mean what you said? You're not going to change your mind again."

"Not this time. I promise," she said, her voice thick with wonder and awe. "I love you, Brandon Wade." Why it had taken her so long to figure out her true feelings, she would never know. "I love you and want to spend the rest of my life proving how much!"

His face lit up and his grin practically reached his ears. Crushing her to him, he gazed at her with a tenderness that took her breath away. "I love you, Josie Johnson. I do believe I've loved you from the moment I first set eyes on you. And I intend to keep loving you for the rest of our born days."

He kissed her firmly and ever so thoroughly on the lips. And with his sweet words ringing in her ears, she ever so thoroughly kissed him back.

Epilogue

One year later

The door to the *Gazette* flew open and Brandon stepped inside, filling the office with the fresh smell of sunshine, leather, and Texas heat.

He greeted Josie with a nod before tossing a sheet of paper upon her desk. "My dear, sweet wife, this will never do."

Hank glanced over his shoulder, then quickly resumed setting type. By now he was used to their weekly disputes over wordage and article content. Their editorial feuds knew no limits, and readers kept coming back for more.

Josie raised an eyebrow. The text in question this week was not the editorial she'd written renouncing Brandon's shortsighted opinion on raising dog licensing fees. Instead, it was the announcement she'd penned about their son's birth. Since his newspaper didn't usually print such milestones, he'd asked her to write it for him.

Noting the number of circled words, she fingered her locket, which now contained a photo of her new family, and arched an eyebrow. "What could you possibly object to? Surely you don't think you could announce Tommy's arrival any better than I did."

"You gave our son only an inch."

Brandon looked so appalled she couldn't help but laugh. It was incredible to think that in little more than a year, she was now mother to both a ten-year-old daughter and newborn son. Her dearest, fondest wishes had come true in ways she could never have imagined.

"An inch is as much as any birth is given," she said. Because of the overwhelming success of the "Love Links" column, Two-Time was in the midst of a population explosion. With so many new births to report, Josie had to limit the space given to each.

"But this isn't just *any* birth," he protested. "It's the event of the year. And you said nothing about how our son took after me in charm. Nor did you mention that he has your beautiful smile and big, blue-green eyes."

"You can't print that. It wouldn't be fair to the other new parents who believe their children are just as amazing. Readers will think you're bragging."

"I don't care what readers think." He reached for the pencil on her desk and scribbled something in the margin. "How do you spell 'genius'?"

She threw back her head and laughed. "Really, Brandon. You're being ridiculous."

He grinned back, his eyes aglow with playful combat. "Readers are just going to have to get used to the fact that I'm now a father of two—who also happens to be madly in love with his wife."

His words filled her heart like a melody filled one's head. Never had she thought that love could be every bit as wonderful and powerful the second time around.

"Two inches," she said. "I'll give you two inches."

"Three."

"One and a half."

"You're messin' with me, Josie."

Her mouth curved in the widest possible smile. The good Lord willing and the creek don't rise, she hoped to be messin' with her dearest sweet husband for a very long time.

-30-

Dear Readers,

I hope you enjoyed Josie and Brandon's story.

I especially enjoyed writing about a Victorian newspaper woman. Women editors date back to colonial times, and some edited publications in the East during the first half of the nineteenth century. Still, in those early days, the newspaper business was primarily a male occupation.

This changed somewhat during the westward movement. The late eighteen-hundreds saw some three hundred females edit 250 publications in eleven western states. California led the way with 129 known female editors. No doubt there were more, but some female publishers sought credibility by listing their husbands' names on mastheads.

Newspaperwomen covered everything from national and local news to household hints. The newspaper business afforded women the opportunity to lead a crusade, promote religious and educational activities, and bring a community together. Though women still didn't have the vote, some female publishers had strong political views they were all too glad to share with readers.

Editorial disputes like the one between Brandon and Josie were common in the Old West, but not all had such a happy ending. More than one editor was known to be shot by another.

Most feuds, however, were carried out with a war of words. Rival editors prided themselves on the quality and quantity of their insults. Typesetting was a tedious job. It took less time and effort to call someone an idiot or numbskull in print than to find a gentler approach.

If editors weren't fighting each other, they were fighting readers. Any editor printing an inflammatory story could expect to be accosted at the local saloon or challenged to a duel. Things got so bad that an editor of a Kansas newspaper wrote: "What this community needs just now is a society for the prevention of cruelty to writing men, otherwise editors."

After one man was acquitted of killing the editor of the *Leavenworth Times*, the Marion County Record wrote, "That's just the way with some juries—they think it no more harm to shoot an editor than a jack-rabbit."

This completes the three-book A Match Made in Texas series. As much as I hate having to say good-bye to the town of Two-Time and the three Lockwood sisters, I'm excited about the new project I'm working on.

Until next time,
Margaret

Author note: the little newsy pieces that begin each chapter were inspired by actual clips that appeared in nineteenth-century newspapers. I do so hope you enjoyed them.

About the Author

Bestselling author Margaret Brownley has penned more than forty novels and novellas. Her books have won numerous awards, including the ACRA Heart of Excellence Readers' Choice Award. She's also two-time Romance Writers of America RITA Award finalist and has written for a TV soap opera. She is currently working on a new series. Not bad for someone who flunked eighth-grade English. Just don't ask her to diagram a sentence.

Write to Margaret via her website at www.margaret-brownley.com.

Made in the USA
Coppell, TX
02 October 2022